S0-AYP-756

"How are you feeling?"
she asked.

His grin was rueful. "Pretty awful. You okay?"

She nodded. After an uncomfortable pause, she offered a stiff little shrug. "You certainly take this whole thing with, uh, grace. Do you do it often?"

He held out his hands for her to see. They trembled as violently as hers. "I plan on getting very drunk as soon as they let me. How about you?"

For the first time since the gunman had appeared at the front desk, Abbie found herself giving a genuinely broad grin. "Oh, I don't know. I think I'll sit in a corner for a week or so."

"Well, don't sit there too long," he admonished mischievously. "We have a date."

Abbie blinked.

"Abbie, you can't have forgotten so soon. I'm the man you're going to have an affair with."

Dear Reader,

When two people fall in love, the world is suddenly new and exciting, and it's that same excitement we bring to you in Silhouette Intimate Moments. These are stories with scope, with grandeur. These characters lead the lives we all dream of, and everything they do reflects the wonder of being in love.

Longer and more sensuous than most romances, Silhouette Intimate Moments novels take you away from everyday life and let you share the magic of love. Adventure, glamour, drama, even suspense— these are the passwords that let you into a world where love has a power beyond the ordinary, where the best authors in the field today create stories of love and commitment that will stay with you always.

In coming months look for novels by your favorite authors: Maura Seger, Parris Afton Bonds, Elizabeth Lowell and Erin St. Claire, to name just a few. And whenever you buy books, look for all the Silhouette Intimate Moments, love stories *for* today's women *by* today's women.

Leslie J. Wainger
Senior Editor
Silhouette Books

IMRL-7/85

Kathleen Korbel
Worth Any Risk

Silhouette Intimate Moments

Published by Silhouette Books New York

America's Publisher of Contemporary Romance

SILHOUETTE BOOKS
300 East 42nd St., New York, N.Y. 10017

Copyright © 1987 by Eileen Dreyer

All rights reserved, including the right to reproduce
this book or portions thereof in any form whatsoever.
For information address Silhouette Books,
300 East 42nd St., New York, N.Y. 10017

ISBN: 0-373-07191-4

First Silhouette Books printing May 1987

All the characters in this book are fictitious. Any
resemblance to actual persons, living or dead, is
purely coincidental.

SILHOUETTE, SILHOUETTE INTIMATE MOMENTS and colophon
are registered trademarks of the publisher.

America's Publisher of Contemporary Romance

Printed in the U.S.A.

Books by Kathleen Korbel

Silhouette Desire

Playing the Game #286

Silhouette Intimate Moments

A Stranger's Smile #163
Worth Any Risk #191

KATHLEEN KORBEL

blames her writing on an Irish heritage that gave her the desire and a supportive husband who gave her the ultimatum, "Do something productive or knock it off." An R.N. from St. Louis, she also counts traveling and music as addictions and is working on yet another career in screen-writing.

To Rick, who made me do it.
And to Julie and Debbie, who made me do it right.

Chapter 1

Abbie Fitzgerald never thought she'd have a second chance to see her life flash before her eyes. When she did, she found herself disappointed. It was a bore. There wasn't anything to hold on to: no adventure to peruse, no great passion to sustain her in a moment of crisis. She was almost thirty, and except for a hard-earned medical degree, didn't have a lot more to show for her years than when she'd been a teen.

Foolishly, she wanted to giggle. She was staring down the slightly unsteady barrel of a .22, and all she could think of was asking the next man she saw to have an affair. Just so she could avoid wasting all this effort the next time she found herself facing a gun.

Well, it was better than thinking about the gun, or the man who held it. If she did that, she'd begin screaming and never stop.

The next man, she thought, the very next man. I swear.

"Okay, honey." The gunman smiled with dead eyes. "Let's go."

"Go?" Abbie echoed stupidly. "Where? You already have what you came for."

She'd done just what the police had always advised. If someone pulled a gun on you and demanded drugs, you gave them to him. No questions, no fuss. She'd gone even a step further, clearing the emergency halls of other people so that only she would be involved. Fear, she could handle. Guilt, she could not.

"By now somebody's called the police. I'm taking you with me for insurance. You behave, you'll be fine. You don't, you're dead."

Beside her, the outside doors slid open on electric tracks. Abbie's captor never took his eyes from her. "Get the car," he snapped. The doors swished shut again. Abbie couldn't look away from the stubble on the gunman's chin. He was sweating. His hair was slimy with it. Nothing was as unstable as a junkie in need of a fix.

"Okay," she placated, hands up, her eyes as neutral as her voice. "I'll go."

"You bet you will." His smile broadened greedily. "The cops'll be real careful with a doctor. Specially one as pretty as you are."

Abbie almost gasped. As if called by the gunman's words, a policeman materialized behind him. Silent, gun drawn, deadly. The first thing that came to Abbie's mind was that this man was the man she was going to have to ask for an affair. Then she did giggle.

The gunman grabbed her by the arm and yanked her to him. He still didn't know he was in danger. "I hope you're this amused later, cutie."

"I . . . I'm sorry," she managed, bile rising in her throat. He held her so tightly against him that her cheek dug into the wet polyester of his shirt. "Some people cry. I . . . giggle."

Absurd but true. She was beginning to sweat now. It was the policeman. He brought the memory too close, and she didn't think she could stand it. It was just all too absurd. Something like this couldn't happen twice in one person's lifetime, yet, Abbie had the most awful feeling that it was about to. She wanted to tell the policeman to run. To get away while he still could.

Suddenly the gunman's hold on Abbie tightened. The gun, that lethal little .22, was pressed against her temple.

"Back off," he yelled beyond her. "I'll shoot her now if you want."

Abbie's head was caught at his shoulder. He smelled like sour sweat and fear. His hands shook. Abbie was beginning to freeze, her breath coming in ragged little gasps. Another policeman must have arrived just out of her line of vision. This couldn't be happening. Not again. Dear God, not again!

"Let her go," a voice commanded from behind her. "You've got no place to go."

The gunman laughed against her, an abrupt explosion of sound. "Like hell."

It was then that Abbie managed to get her policeman back into focus. She saw his eyes. They were green, uncanny in his handsome face. Almost iridescent in the shadow of his cap. They spoke to her, commanded her attention when words wouldn't have. Trust me, they said, everything will be all right. I'll take care of you. Just trust me.

Abbie hung on to those eyes like a lifeline. She could still feel the bite of the revolver against her skin, still hear the exchange between her captor and the other officer. But as long as she kept those mesmerizing green eyes in focus, she remained in control.

She thought she might just be okay when she realized that she'd certainly picked a winner for her affair. He was just tall enough, just blond enough, with features that had been crafted with heartbreaking precision to complement the crisp lines of his uniform.

Keep thinking about that, about how infinitely calm his eyes are, and it would be okay. He'd be okay. Another face appeared beyond the glass doors at the periphery of her vision, just beyond the blond policeman. Abbie got a quick impression of dark features and a gun before it drifted away again.

"You're gonna give me a car and clearance," her captor was saying, trembling against her. "Or she's dead meat."

Funny. That was a phrase Abbie used. But only in jest, most often to one of her brothers. "Give that to me, Tommy, or you're dead meat..."

She didn't notice what was happening until it was too late. Didn't see how close her policeman had gotten, or that he'd holstered his gun. Her eyes flew open as the realization hit her. The gunman had actually loosened his hold on her, his attention now on his demands. It was time for her rescuer to make a try for the gun. Abbie knew the plan. She wanted to warn the policeman not to try, that it wouldn't work. She knew.

She never got her mouth open.

"Drop!" he yelled.

His hand was on the gun before her captor knew it. Abbie twisted away, down, was suddenly on her hands and knees and scrambling for safety. She heard a shout, and then a shot rang out, a sharp crack that sent her diving for the floor. Another, more powerful gun answered. Abbie kept rolling, instinct driving her. All she wanted to do was to get away.

She ignored the dull, uneven thudding near her. She ignored the silence that followed—the kind of throbbing emptiness that usually succeeds violence. Eyes squeezed tight, she huddled against a far wall.

"Michael!"

She couldn't ignore that. The agony in the older voice brought her up fast. There was a middle-aged patrolman standing behind her, the one who belonged to the voice making demands, she decided. His eyes were focused beyond her. His gun was drawn, still tight in an aiming grip.

Abbie turned. Pushed herself up. Saw the blond policeman and started to scream.

He lay next to the gunman, his eyes open, blood covering the side of his face. His hat had fallen by his feet. Abbie thought he was dead and couldn't stop screaming.

"Dr. Fitzgerald...? Abbie!"

The staff began to appear. Dr. John Williams, the medical director, reached her first. Abbie had known John since his internship. She'd sat with him through Christmas hangovers and his wife's first labor. He grasped her shoulders as if trying to hold her together.

"Get...him," she pleaded to his terrified eyes. From the sounds she'd been making, he'd been sure she'd been the one shot. The nurses appeared behind him, frightened and charged with adrenaline. They all touched Abbie's arm tentatively, as if afraid she'd shatter.

"Please," she repeated, helpless to move. "Help him."

They turned to the two injured men, quickly assessing, efficient. Abbie huddled against her wall, arms wrapped around her chest. She felt as if she were drowning. It seemed that she stopped breathing while she waited for John to check that head wound.

The policeman blinked. Mumbled an answer. Everyone moved to the gunman who had a hole in the front of his light check shirt. Instincts and training took over and the staff swarmed, carrying him to the back before he had a chance to die.

"Can you take care of him, Ab?" John asked as he went by. He meant the policeman. Abbie took great, gasping breaths to fight back the terror, and nodded.

She turned to the other policeman, a graying, stocky man with liquid eyes. "Can you help me?" she asked.

"Yeah." His nod was jerky. He'd thought his partner had been dead, too.

An hour later, Officer Michael Viviano sat on a cart in room two sporting twenty neat stitches, a large white bandage and a fierce headache. Abbie's hands still shook, but she'd kept her voice calm and friendly, her manner competent. Tim Matheson, the plastic surgery resident, had just finished giving the officer a dramatic line of stitches that ran from the corner of his left cheek to the hairline above his ear.

"Looks like a dueling scar." Tim had grinned proudly. "Very dashing."

Sergeant Viviano had had the presence of mind to grin back. "Italians don't duel. We just scream at each other."

The only other tasks left to perform on the officer were a quick recheck of his neurological status and a trip to X Ray. Abbie managed the first without too much trouble.

"Dr. Fitzgerald?" the officer quietly spoke up.

Abbie concentrated on the chart she was scribbling on, afraid to face those knowing eyes again. "Just call me Abbie," she grinned hesitantly. "Nobody's formal around here."

"My name's Michael, Abbie. You did fine back there."

Before she realized it, Abbie was snapping at him. "Why did you do that? You could have been killed! You almost—" She stopped just shy of losing control. It was getting harder. She was beginning to breathe too fast, trying to push away the terror old nightmares bred.

"But I wasn't." His voice was so calm. She couldn't understand it. Revulsion was beginning to mount until she couldn't keep her hands still or her stomach from her throat, and he sat there as if he'd just tripped over his dog.

"You have no right to take your life so lightly!" she harped.

Michael made it to his feet and took her by the shoulders. "Abbie?"

She almost faced him then, wondering if those eyes could calm her again. She was fighting so hard to regain her composure. "I think you should know before you get too familiar..." Damn it, she couldn't breathe. She felt so clammy. "I swore that if I...got out of that, I'd have an affair with the very next man I saw."

His laughter was delighted. "Me?"

Abbie got her head up. "I...I thought..." A look of fleeting surprise crossed her ashen features as she opened her mouth to finish the disjointed thought and instead fainted into the arms of the man who'd just saved her life.

Michael Viviano looked down at the woman in his arms, almost as stunned as she by the sudden turn of events. Unsure what to do, he briefly looked around for help. They were still all in with the suspect. Nobody had time yet for the victim. No news to him. As effortlessly as if he were lifting a child, Michael lifted the deceptively frail-looking doctor into his arms and carried her to the cart.

He had to give her credit. She'd handled a bad situation like a pro. He'd managed to watch a bit of what was going on before making his appearance, and he had to admit that she'd stayed ice-calm when many veterans might well have lost control.

He hadn't realized what it had been costing her until he'd seen her eyes. She had spotted him and unleashed the terror. From the minute he'd seen the distress in the depths of those elegant blue eyes, he'd wanted to reach out and hold her, protect her from what she was facing. She'd riveted onto him as if she were drowning and only he could save her. And yet, there was something more: he had the feeling that she hadn't been so much frightened for herself as she had been for him.

Michael looked down at the deathly pallor of the delicate face—the tousled, damp, chestnut hair, the sooty eyelashes that fanned out over wide, arching cheekbones, the soft, assailable mouth. He remembered the wellspring of fear in those eyes, and the courage it had taken her to do what she had. He knew that what had not happened in ten years on the force was happening now: he was becoming involved with a victim. He'd end up seeing Abbie again whether the case called for it or not. And damn it, he knew better.

Reaching down, he gently brushed an errant lock of hair back from her forehead. He wet a rag and tried his best to cool her heated face. Then he walked to the open door and called for help.

Abbie fought her way out of the blackness, furious with herself for succumbing to such weak-kneed hysterics. She felt even more angry when the first voice she heard was the man into whose arms she'd so dramatically fainted.

"Typical female reaction," he was saying, his voice wryly amused.

One eye shot open and targeted him where he stood amid the crowd that had reassembled for Abbie's benefit. She was on a stretcher. Still in room two, she guessed, feeling humiliated by the hoopla.

"I hope you're joking."

"Thought that'd get your attention." He grinned at her, his eyes brightening beneath the bandage she'd so recently bestowed on him. "I was just saying that in all my years on the force, I've become accustomed to women passing out in my arms when they get upset."

"You would have of course preferred that I just punch someone," she countered dryly without moving. "Or better yet, pull out my own gun and start shooting." She actually almost found herself grinning at the teasing light in his eyes.

Michael nodded his concession, an eyebrow arched. "Touché. Melodramatic but nonviolent. Maybe I should try fainting next time I'm challenged."

"Might save some wear and tear on your head."

"Abbie, are you okay?" someone else asked.

Abbie turned to take in the rest of the people. People who should have been in with the robber. Her stomach lurched again, even as she struggled to sit up. "I'm fine," she insisted, taking a slow, deep breath to fight back the queasiness the movement resurrected. It hadn't happened in so long. She'd almost come to believe it never would again. The brutal waves of nausea, the sweating, the shaking. All she wanted to do was get away from all the prying, anxious eyes.

She swung her feet over the side of the stretcher and smiled ruefully at everyone. "I'm sorry. I guarantee that I haven't done anything this dumb since I was fourteen."

"Well, you have every right to," John said. "I'm sure nothing like this has ever happened to you before."

He didn't notice Abbie's blank reaction.

"True E.R. doctor." Beth Helmsley grinned as she helped Abbie to her feet. "She waits till all the fun's over before passing out."

Abbie scowled at her friend. "I can assume, then, that you didn't all leave your patient just to see me inconvenience Sgt. Viviano?"

"Heck, no." Beth grinned again. "The officer here called for help at exactly the same moment John pronounced the patient dead. It was all quite dramatic."

"This whole afternoon has been," Abbie muttered as she turned for the door. John blocked her way. A great, large bear of a man with laughing eyes and steely resolve, the medical director looked down on Abbie as if she were a child.

"Just where do you think you're going?"

Abbie challenged him, knowing just how she looked and feeling every perspiry inch as bad. "Well, John, unless you guys really want more drama, I thought you'd rather the next act took place in the bathroom. Then I'm going back to work."

John shook his head. "Then you're going home. Your brother Jack's on his way in, and Sgt. Viviano promised that after initial questions by the detectives, you could finish with the police later."

"John, I'm all right," Abbie insisted, doing her best to assume a rigid posture.

John's smile was tolerant. He'd had a lot of experience with Abbie's stubborn streak. "Maybe you'd sound more convincing if you weren't on your way to the bathroom to be sick. Go on and get out of here before I have Officer Viviano force you at gunpoint."

John realized his unfortunate choice of words when Abbie paled even more and bolted from the room.

When Abbie made it back, it was to see her brother Jack breezing through the glass doors. All bluster and bad jokes, he came on as if he were going to a party. It was only when he set eyes on his little sister that his brash demeanor slipped a little.

Abbie accepted his protective hugs, grateful that John hadn't made the inadvertent mistake of calling her parents with the news of her close call. They couldn't have handled that shock. Abbie and Jack together would have to tell them with calm smiles and steady hands—although the way Abbie was feeling right now, she figured that would take about another week. The longer she faced the concerned, prying eyes of her co-workers, the thinner her composure stretched until she was afraid she might snap at them like a frayed rope.

"Do you want to take a couple of sick days?" John asked. "Might be easier to deal with the press away from this place."

Abbie stared, just shy of comprehension.

"They've already started pumping us for your name," the doctor nudged. "I told Jack I'd hold them all off till you've talked to your parents. But try to do it sometime in the next couple of hours. One TV station is already starting to make some very suspect promises."

"The press..." Abbie echoed blankly, not realizing that her eyes had widened.

"I think a couple of days would be fine," Jack intervened. Then, with an arm around her rigid shoulders, he guided Abbie toward the door.

Police already clogged the hallway—detectives to investigate the robbery, supervisors to begin clearing the shooting. The chaplain had responded to the call about a wounded officer, and other police who'd come to the aid of the "officer down" now milled about aimlessly, not quite ready to leave.

Sergeant Viviano was just being rolled back to his room from X Ray. Another young officer walked with him, and they were laughing, Viviano wincing good-naturedly with the effort. Abbie saw him and headed for the door to his room, Jack following silently on her heels.

Michael looked up as Abbie stepped in, and his eyes lightened like a spring wind. Abbie just wanted to stand where she was, bathing in their gentling light.

"How are you feeling?" she asked.

His grin became rueful. "Pretty awful. You okay?"

She nodded, unable to quite gather the words. After an uncomfortable pause, she offered a stiff little shrug. "You certainly take this whole thing with...uh, grace. Do you do it often?"

He responded by allowing the grin to return as he held out his hands for her to see. They trembled as violently as hers. "I plan on getting very drunk as soon as they let me. How 'bout you?"

For the first time since the gunman had appeared at the front desk, Abbie allowed herself a genuinely broad grin. She didn't even mind that Michael heard the definite tremor in her voice. "Oh, I don't know. I think I'll sit in a corner for a week or so and suck my thumb."

"Well, don't stay there too long," he admonished mischievously. "We have a date."

She blanked again.

Michael's eyebrows rose in mock indignation. "Abbie, you can't have forgotten so soon. I'm the man you're going to have an affair with."

When she heard the surprised noises Jack was trying not to make, Abbie knew that she was going to have a lot of explaining to do when she got home.

Chapter 2

"Abbie? Honey, I think you'd better come out and see something."

Abbie's old room was dark. She lay on the bed staring at the ceiling much as she had since she and Jack had told her parents about the robbery. Without really thinking about it, she'd decided to stay at her parents' rather than return to her empty apartment for the night. The feel of the old house around her was comforting, transporting her back to a childhood world inhabited by a close family and magical dreams.

Her father had never let bogeymen enter this room. She remembered how he'd appear in the doorway when she was a little girl—his form so big and sure, silhouetted against the hall light. And every time he did, the ghosts would flee, afraid of his substance and strength.

"Abbie?"

She turned to see that his silhouette wasn't as big to her anymore. Time and a faulty heart had eroded the substance until there was only a man there, no longer the wondrous defender who vanquished phantoms.

"I'm sorry, Dad. I was half asleep."

"I know, honey. We didn't want to bother you, but there's something you'd better see." His voice echoed with caution.

"What?"

She thought he forced a smile then. "Come on, get up and see for yourself. Your mom made you some fudge."

Abbie groaned good-naturedly and swung her feet over the side of the bed. Typical of a heredity consisting of impoverished peasant stock, her mother's attitude in life was, "When in doubt, eat." It had cost Abbie the torture of countless months of dieting and exercise, and still plagued her when she went by any sort of fast-food franchise.

Abbie followed her father in to join her mother and Jack in the living room. Her other brothers should start showing up any time now to add their support. The tension in her chest immediately increased. This was the point where she had to reassure her mother that everything was all right when it wasn't. She had to accept the smothering concern and give back bright smiles.

"Just in time for the bread and circuses," Jack greeted her without looking up. "Pull up a floor and get comfortable."

"What's up?" Abbie seated herself cross-legged on the floor in front of her mother's chair. The pan of fudge was uncomfortably within smelling distance, but Abbie knew how much her mother needed a show of strength. They'd all been through this before, and Abbie hadn't fared as well. And her mother hurt more than any of her children when they were in pain. It had made her gray and careworn in her early sixties.

"How are you, sweetie?" Her voice was tentative, afraid of the answer.

Abbie looked up at the history in those soft blue eyes and smiled. "A lot better. There's something about coming back home that makes everything okay."

"You could always stay, ya know," her father nudged. It was still a sore point with him that she'd moved away from

home at all. Not only was Abbie his only little girl, but she'd
deserted him for the streets of Chicago. As anyone from
either side of the city limits knew, the city and suburbs were
more than merely miles apart. The cultures of suburb and
city were never more dramatically different than they were
in the Chicago area, nor as enthusiastically argued. Abbie's
friends in the city called her suburban childhood neighborhood The Land Beyond O'Hare. And Abbie knew that if
they'd been the kind of parents to do it, hers would have
assured her that what had happened to her today wouldn't
have happened in the suburbs.

"Next on the news, a dramatic hostage situation at a city
hospital today..."

It took Abbie a minute to realize that the TV anchorman
was referring to *her* hostage situation. She turned toward the
television set with a look that bespoke disgust and distress
at the same time.

"You woke me for this? I can wait till the movie comes
out, thanks."

"I don't think so," Jack offered simply. "You're gonna
have to be prepared."

"Fudge, honey?"

"No thanks, Mom. Prepared for what?"

For a moment nobody answered. Then Jack stretched his
head around to take in Abbie behind him. "You've kind of
become the mystery woman of the moment."

"The what?"

"We decided to wake you up when we heard the teaser
about the story at the beginning of the news. Seems they
decided to make you famous."

The report began in the front hall by the triage desk. The
news crew had gotten there before anyone had had a good
chance to clean up the blood, and it made a very dramatic
picture. The reported looked both somber and excited at
once, recounting the events that had transpired that afternoon. In the background, police still milled about. Abbie
could feel the constriction tighten in her chest even more as
she watched.

"Mom?"

"Yes, honey."

"Can I have some fudge?"

She didn't mind so much that they made a news item out of it, or that they tried to inject whatever drama they could to make it a "real" news story. What Abbie did mind was the slant the coverage was beginning to take.

Sgt. Michael Viviano sat in a hospital bed looking dramatic as hell with his skin tone almost as white as his bandage. He sounded dramatic as hell as he downplayed his own part in the incident. But then the reporter asked the question Abbie dreaded, and Michael's answer left her open-mouthed.

"I've been in these situations before," Michael was saying, his eyes sincere, "and I have to say that I've never seen a hostage act with that much presence of mind. That young lady kept a potentially volatile situation under control by her actions until we got there."

Abbie snorted. "Remind me I'm a 'young lady' on my next birthday, will you?"

Her family shushed her.

The reporter's concerned face filled the screen. "You think that Dr. Fitzgerald may have saved lives by what she did?"

Michael nodded. "Without question. She single-handedly prevented other hostages from being taken and kept the gunman confined away from patients and staff by her quick thinking. With a gun pointed at you, that's a pretty impressive feat to accomplish."

Abbie popped another square of fudge in her mouth to keep from cursing.

"Sergeant Viviano has been commended for bravery by the police department in the past," the reporter concluded in almost hushed tones, "and is a Medal of Valor winner. Dr. Abbie Fitzgerald, an Emergency physician with the hospital for four years, could not be reached for comment."

It didn't even stop there. When the picture reverted to the anchor desk, the people there shook their heads in awe and murmured over the kind of bravery they certainly didn't think they possessed.

"Oh, for God's sake," Abbie blurted out.

"Can I be your agent?" Jack immediately demanded. "Straight ten percent and movie rights. We can get Robert Redford to play the cop, but Shirley Temple doesn't act anymore."

"Eat a snake," Abbie hissed with a surreptitious grin. She was grateful Jack had stayed to offset a little of the strain of the situation. She remembered that when he was seventeen he'd been the only one able to hold her together in those long days following the policeman's funeral. Her mother, unable to do anything but hover, had only made everything worse.

"Get used to it, kid," Jack warned. "By this time tomorrow, it'll be national, mark my words. Heroes are in."

"National what?" Abbie retorted.

"News, my love. Dan Rather and a message from the President. The only reason they haven't been here already is that we took the phone off the hook and refused to answer the door. We can't hold them off forever."

Abbie chewed slowly on another piece of fudge as she let Jack's words sink in. He was right. The reaction by the news crew had been a bit excessive. Maybe if there had been a war declared somewhere that day, or a major political figure caught in a scandal, the weight of the publicity wouldn't have fallen so hard on her. But whatever the reason, the press was enamored of the story and her. And they probably wouldn't leave it alone until they were able to serve her up for grilling.

Oh, Lord, she thought with a sinking feeling. The very last thing she needed was to have to smile and nod and wax philosophic about how it felt to almost have her head blown off. The memory still made her nauseated. She felt frustrated and lost, knowing now what the press would want from her, yet sure they wouldn't leave her alone until they got it. Sure, too, that they might somehow manage to dig up a sixteen-year-old story she really didn't want to rehash.

What was she supposed to do? How could she protect herself and her family against the press's persistent prying? And just who was she supposed to go to for advice like that?

Abbie woke the next morning without reaching any kind of satisfactory conclusions. She'd slept badly, plagued by dreams in which Sgt. Viviano refused to wake up and his wife came to blame her.

When Abbie walked into the kitchen for some coffee, her mother waited with anxious eyes. Abbie knew she'd have to get back to her own apartment today. She'd have to talk to the police and then convince the hospital administration that she could come back to work. She needed to resume her life as quickly as possible. What she didn't need was to stay here where her mother spent her time waiting for her to break.

It was as Abbie stood at the old stove that the idea about Michael Viviano first prodded her. He was a cop. He'd been awarded commendations. She bet he'd spent his share of time with the press. Maybe he'd have some insights on how to handle the whole thing. He certainly struck her as the type who could keep his cool and find the humor in any situation.

Abbie didn't realize that when she thought of the handsome blond policeman, her eyes lit with a wistful smile. Her mother noticed, though. If the doorbell hadn't rung just then, she might have asked just what it was that made her daughter suddenly look so much happier.

Abbie reacted instinctively to the soft chimes. "I'll get it, Mom," she offered, and turned into the living room.

The rooms of the little house were still in morning shadow, the curtains drawn against the summer heat. To Abbie it was like walking through an empty church. She padded across the hardwood floor, absently sipping from her cup and thinking of Michael Viviano.

When she reached the door, Abbie set her coffee on the little end table alongside. Then she took a moment to quickly run both hands though her mass of uncombed hair to force it into some kind of order. She hadn't been coherent enough yet to pull a comb through it. Having come home last night in scrubs, she now sported her brother Tommy's athletic shorts and tank top. It didn't occur to her to question her attire; she had, after all, spent most of her life in boys' hand-me-downs. Her guest wasn't to be as oblivious.

Abbie pulled open the door, prepared to be courteous. She found herself staring instead.

"I could have been a cameraman," Michael admonished after a moment's hesitation, his grin frankly flattering. His eyes raked sleek curves of the kind that made athletic clothing such big business and jogging such a spectator sport for him. It briefly occurred to him that doctors' scrub suits were sinfully unflattering. Last night Abbie's delicate features had translated into a fragile beauty in all that formless blue. Today she exuded that unconscious sensuality that made a woman dangerous. Fresh-faced, healthy, and deadly as hell. Michael couldn't take his eyes off her.

Abbie had much the same trouble. Just the sight of Michael Viviano threatened to take her breath away. He was out of uniform today, in an open-neck polo shirt that revealed curling golden hair at his chest and throat, and soft, brushed jeans that stretched tight over well-developed thighs. Abbie bet that his tush looked great in jeans and almost found herself tempted to ask him to turn around.

The knowing grin he proffered creased his face in such an inviting way. Intimate. As if they were the only two people around, suggesting that he had something very enticing he wanted to tell her. Michael's eyes assessed her, and Abbie wondered where the breeze that suddenly swept her skin had come from on this hot, still morning.

They stood across from each other for what seemed to both like hours. Neither wanted to break the tensions that stirred such surprisingly provocative currents.

"You don't recognize me," Michael finally ventured, his mouth broadening into a crooked grin that sent Abbie's heart thudding. "Maybe if I had my uniform on..."

"The uniform isn't really necessary," she said, grinning back with brightening eyes. "The bandage is a dead giveaway. I can always spot good craftsmanship."

His fingers went automatically to the gauze that still wrapped his head. "It's a bandage," he retorted dryly. "Not macramé."

Abbie flashed him an arch look. "A person should be able to take pride in her work."

He nodded, his eyes even more amused. "An admirable quality, I'm sure."

"What are you doing here? The last time I saw you, you were doing the injured hero bit on the fourth floor."

For that she got a grimace. "Can't get any rest in a hospital. You should know that."

"You're not going to get a lot more rest driving halfway to Wisconsin to interview me," she retorted more hotly than she'd intended.

Michael didn't seem to understand her objection. He deliberately shrugged it off. "I promised the doctor that if I started seeing double or talking to buses, I'd come back again."

"Damn it," she snapped, hands on hips, angry at the same disregard for one's own safety she saw every day in her E.R. She was even more irrationally angry that it was Michael who was being so cavalier. "What is it about cops that makes them act like bullheaded children?"

Michael's eyes glinted with amusement. "Just that natural urge to challenge authority, I guess."

She didn't back down at all. "I bet you displayed signs of this wonderful common sense even before you were shot in the head."

Michael shook his head with an amused grin. "Are you always so gracious to people who come to your door?"

For a moment, Abbie couldn't answer. There were just too many conflicting memories to contend with. Finally she retreated just a little, her eyes wandering away from him. "I feel responsible for what happened to you," she admitted quietly.

That seemed to surprised him. "It wasn't your fault that I bobbed when I should have weaved."

"But you were there to help me." It sounded lame even to her. She should explain the incredible coincidence that made her react so badly. But that wasn't something she thought she should do.

"I was there because I was doing my job." He smiled. "If you hadn't reacted as well as you did, it would have been a lot worse."

There was some objection Abbie should have made. She couldn't think of it. All she could think of was how very gentle and understanding Michael's eyes were. And how furious she still felt with him.

"Abbie? Do you want to invite the gentleman in?"

Abbie whirled around at the sound of her mother's voice. She'd been listening from the archway into the dining room. It was no surprise that she had sensed Abbie's distress.

Taking a deep breath to calm the irrational anger the images of Michael still spawned, Abbie turned back to him, begging appeasement. "Would you like some coffee?"

"Cream." He smiled broadly, stepping in past her. "No sugar."

Abbie was in the process of closing the door behind him when she was struck by a thought. "How do you keep doing that?"

Michael turned. "Doing what?"

She slid the door shut and reached over to pick up her coffee. "Appearing just when I'm thinking about you. That's why I was staring when I opened the door." Well, she amended to herself, not exactly the entire reason I was staring. "You did it last night. I was thinking about police...or rather, the junkie said something about police, and poof! There you were."

"You were thinking of me just now?"

They stood together by the door, oblivious again to Abbie's mother who waited patiently in the shadows. Neither took notice of the meticulously clean furniture surrounding them that bore every scar of almost forty years of child-rearing, or the soft scent of pine and roses that filled the house.

"Thinking about you in relation to the press," Abbie admitted, her concentration once again threatened by Michael's proximity. "I'm going to have to face all that today, and I was wondering who I could talk to who might give me some pointers."

"Abbie..."

The soft voice held a note of gentle reproach. Abbie turned on it. She couldn't believe she'd actually forgotten about her mother. Again.

"Oh, Mom, I'm sorry..." She didn't get any further. Michael made the mistake of turning the same moment she did, and knocked into her arm. Abbie had no trouble at all dropping the cup of coffee, splattering them both with the hot liquid. Abbie screeched. Michael cursed.

"Maybe I *shouldn't* keep showing up," he gritted, waving a scalded arm in the air. "It's probably a death wish of some kind."

It was no more than a throwaway line. A bit of black humor. Abbie heard it and went very white and still.

"Here," her mother interrupted abruptly, swooping in on them like the Red Cross. "Come into the kitchen. We'll get cold water on it."

She had Michael by the arm and on his way to the kitchen sink before either he or Abbie could manage a protest.

"You're Sergeant Viviano, aren't you?"

"Michael. Yes, ma'am." The burn was no more than irritation, but Michael submitted to the small woman's ministrations, his eyes remaining on Abbie.

"I'm Abbie's mother," Mrs. Fitzgerald went on, bathing his forearm in cold water. "I can't thank you enough for what you did for Abbie last night."

Michael felt as if he were missing something. There was a definite shell of anxiety in the room, reflected in the clipped persistence of Mrs. Fitzgerald's speech and the sudden silence in her daughter. "Oh, it was just my job."

She brushed away his humility with dispatch. "Non-sense. Ab, is your leg all right?"

Abbie nodded, the color returning to her cheeks. What a dumb stunt, she thought with some irritation. She was going to have to stop doing that, especially around her mother. And, she realized, around Michael. She didn't think she could stand solicitous pity from him.

Seeing his quizzical gaze on her, Abbie managed a smile. "You just get out of the hospital and I try and put you right back in. You okay?"

He smiled back, the flash of lost vulnerability in those soft, sapphire eyes grabbing him. "Yeah. Would you mind sticking to cold drinks when you're around me, though?"

"Only if you tell me why you came looking for me at nine in the morning."

Michael reclaimed his arm and leaned against the sink, his posture belying the import of his mission. "A little unfinished business."

For a minute Abbie thought he might actually have the gall to be referring to their "affair." He certainly looked inviting enough, leaning back with his arms across his chest. Her eyes took on a dry disdain in response to the mischief in his.

"Police business," he amended, an eyebrow arched. He'd known exactly what she'd been thinking. "Since I have an appointment with the same people who want to see you, I offered to pick you up."

"Since you were in the neighborhood anyway."

His eyes danced. "Exactly."

Abbie did take notice of her attire then. "I'm not exactly dressed for the interrogation room," she objected with a disparaging glance at short shorts and bare feet.

"Trust me." Michael grinned. "You'll be the hit of the station."

Abbie's eyes made it back up to see the frank admiration in his. There was an odd skittering in her chest that was very, very pleasant, but the smile she gave him remained dry.

"I was planning on going home to change before I dropped in on the police."

"Fine." He nodded. "I have a car."

Still Abbie refused to let the amused challenge die. Nor did she answer.

Michael's easy smile was delighted. "We can talk about the press on the way in."

Having made up her mind long before Michael had made the offer, Abbie flashed him a killer smile. "Can we turn on the lights and siren?"

Abbie's apartment was in the northwest side of the city, about a block up Fullerton. The building was old, its art deco trimmings original and the elevator an open cage straight out of an Alfred Hitchcock movie.

It hadn't been easy to find an affordable place to live this close to the lake. Most of the buildings were condos, and expensive ones at that. Hers was the only building in a two-block radius without a doorman and a garage. But she had four rooms on the fifth floor and a great view of the lake from the rooftop. She couldn't have asked for anything more.

Her parents had never understood, but Abbie thrived on the city. She cherished the vibrant, eclectic life that teemed on its streets. Within walking distance she had the lake, Lincoln Park, the hospital where she worked, seven different ethnic restaurants, any number of great little shops with everything from old clothes to movie posters, and two live theaters. She knew artists, architects, lawyers, cooks, a hooker and a violin maker. The streets were never empty and never silent. In comparison, suburbia was a landscaped mortuary.

Abbie flipped on the light and threw her bag on the couch. "Make yourself comfortable," she offered, without stopping on her way in to change.

Michael took a moment to survey the diverse tastes that made up the decor in the tiny room. Abbie called it "early garage-sale." It was in face a mélange of art deco, classical and various antiques that somehow complemented the clutter of a born pack rat. Chippendale end tables flanked a hunter-green camelback couch. The area rug was mauve and rose geometrics on a field of off-white. Erté posters graced a matching wall alongside Oriental watercolors. The bookcase along the far wall once held missals, and the tea set that shared a steamer trunk with professional magazines once belonged to a French madam.

"There's some soda in the fridge," Abbie called as she padded across her bedroom floor. "But don't trust the milk. I think I can smell it in here." The only shoes she'd had with her had been her hospital whites. Informing Michael that she even despised wearing the things at work, she'd thrown them in the back of the squad car. She now dropped them into the back of her closet and pulled out a pair of canvas flats.

"Your plants are all dead," Michael called from the kitchen.

Abbie pulled the tank top over her head and grinned. "Black thumb. My mother says they all committed suicide. Will you be with me when the press swarms?"

"They're already camped out at the station." There was a pause. "Uh, there's been another development since last night you might want to know about."

"What?"

"The guys yesterday were a couple of free-lancers who've been pulling armed robberies all over town. They've killed three people."

Coming back out of the kitchen with a soda in hand, Michael was startled to see Abbie poke her head and shoulders around the corner of her room. He wasn't sure she realized that she didn't have so much as a bra on. He certainly did. Just the sight of the smooth expanse of tanned skin across those shoulders threatened to take his breath away.

"That's gonna make us bigger heroes." She grimaced. "Isn't it?"

Michael stood very still. "Abbie."

"Uh-huh?"

"Are you planning on having that affair right now?"

"I beg your pardon?"

Then she followed his wide-eyed gaze. Lifting her eyes back to him, she flashed a bright, unapologetic grin. "Oops. Sorry."

Once she'd disappeared again, Michael sat a little abruptly on the couch. His hands were slicker than when he'd grabbed the gun the night before. Good God. He couldn't believe how quickly Abbie was getting under his skin. She wasn't the first woman he'd had to deal with. He'd sure seen them with less on. But it had sure been a hell of a long time since his body had gone amok all on its own at the sight of a lithe figure, a fragile, delicate face that could hypnotize and exhilarate, and a personality that changed faster than a sleight-of-hand routine. He took a long swig of Coke and wished it were beer—better yet, Scotch.

"You said guys," Abbie piped up from the other room.

"You saw the other one, didn't you?"

He heard a sigh. "Yeah. I saw him. He had a gun, too."

Michael wiped his hands and thought that he should have been paying more attention to the case. "You, uh, seem to be doing okay today."

"A sense of relief tends to bring out the roses on my cheeks." Abbie buckled a web belt around her hips and gave her overblouse a final tug. With the white pedal pushers, it was an attractive outfit.

"Relief how?" Michael asked.

She was running a brush through thick, nearly shoulder-length hair that fell into a disarray of loose curls. "There's just something about waking up and knowing that you're not still going to have a .22 pointed at your head that immediately makes your day brighter." She grinned at the mirror.

She didn't notice that Michael didn't have anything to say to that. She was thinking of the heat she'd surprised in his eyes when he'd spotted her leaning around the corner. Unconsciously a hand went to her throat as if she could still feel the brand of his eyes there. It was really too bad she couldn't have that affair with him. She had a feeling it would have made any more impromptu autobiographies really worthwhile.

"More acceptable?" she asked with a mischievous grin as she stepped back out into the living room.

Quickly recovering, Michael bestowed another sincere look of approval and rose. It amazed him that this bright-eyed imp could be the same woman who'd dealt with a killer with such frozen control. "Well, at least you won't have to beat them off anymore. The press is gonna love you, though."

Abbie scowled. "That's what I'm afraid of."

"You don't want to be a heroine?"

Pausing just long enough to pick up her purse, Abbie preceded Michael back out the door. He was so busy appreciating the perfume she'd applied that he missed the ghosts that briefly darkened her eyes. Abbie reached the elevator and turned to Michael with a deliberate smile.

"I guess I just don't have that talent for gracious humility."

"In that case," Michael offered, "just follow my lead. I happen to have some experience."

"I noticed." Abbie's eyes were just a bit dry. "Last night on TV you came across as a perfect cross between Jack Webb and Camille."

The elevator arrived. Pulling the steel door back, Michael held out a hand to guide Abbie in. "It's a pact I have with the department," he admitted, following her on. "Every so often I hop in the way of a bullet so the police force gets its share of good PR."

Abbie made a face. "Have you ever considered charity softball games?"

A shake of the head. "Not as dramatic."

"Have somebody hit you in the head with a softball."

"Are you kidding?" His affronted tone seemed sincere. "That hurts worse than being shot!"

It wasn't until they were back in the squad car that Abbie got up the nerve to ask what most bothered her. "Michael, about the press..."

They were headed down Lincoln Park West, the squad car getting surreptitious glances from the other drivers.

Michael turned to see frown lines appear between Abbie's eyes. "In your case—" he grinned reassuringly "—definitely noncarnivorous."

She flashed him a quick, appreciative smile. "But just as definitely curious. Right?"

"Insatiably. If I was Camille, you were Annie Oakley and Madame Curie."

She scowled again. Michael found himself wanting to touch those deepening creases, to ease their severity.

"That worries you?" he asked gently.

When Abbie looked over at him, it was with ruefully nervous eyes. "It worries me."

"Why?" He grinned back out into traffic. "Do you have a sordid past?"

For a moment there was a silence in the car broken only by the staccato of car horns and a jackhammer somewhere. The traffic light at Division turned red, and Michael pulled up behind a battered old taxi. When he looked back over at Abbie, he finally saw the ghosts.

"Yeah," she nodded slowly as if she saw something other than a taxi before her. "Something like that."

Michael didn't notice the light go green. "Do you want to talk about it?"

She looked over at the gentle concern in Michael's eyes. She thought that if anyone could be capable of understanding her old nightmare, it would be this handsome, empathetic man. But she also saw the bandage that covered a wound he'd sustained trying to save her. Her stomach wrenched with the memory of the heart-stopping fear when she'd waited for him to move, so sure he wouldn't. She knew that this was the last man in whom she should place her trust. Not because she thought he'd abuse it. She thought instead that she would find his comfort much too sweet to forfeit again.

With an effort that drew heavily on her reserves of control, she flashed him a bright smile.

"What's to talk about? I informed a total stranger that since he saved my life, he'd have to have an affair with me."

Michael wanted to challenge that smile, but the cars behind him were showing no respect for a police car. The horns were impatient and angry. "Beats a basket of fruit," he retorted instead, his eyes darting over for one more surreptitious peek as he followed the now distant taxi. Abbie was watching the passing buildings with singular interest.

"That's not what my mother would say."

Michael shrugged agreeably. "She wasn't on the fuzzy end of that particular lollipop."

"Mothers don't differentiate between lollipops," Abbie informed him with a small grin. "Especially Irish mothers."

"Even when the affair's with someone as wholesome as I am?" he demanded.

"Wholesome people don't have affairs."

Michael made a final turn and spotted the crowd of reporters that milled around the station. They recognized him and swarmed toward the curb.

"Oh, well," he sighed. "I guess I'll just have to trade in my good-conduct medal. Would you like to start with dinner?"

Abbie's eyes were also on the jostling, milling crowd that grew nearer. Her hands were starting to sweat. "Start what?"

Michael let an eyebrow raise. "Why, our affair."

He'd pulled the car neatly to the curb before Abbie turned to him with that same deliberate smile. "Michael, you don't have to keep bringing that up. I never really had any intentions of holding you to it."

His eyebrow rose a bit more. "I was hoping you would." To his surprise, he was.

Abbie's eyes grew large. "Oh, no. No, I wouldn't think of it. I don't date policemen."

"What?"

But before he could get ahold of her to demand clarification, Abbie had opened the car door and delivered herself to the press.

Chapter 3

"Miss Fitzgerald, what did you feel when Percy held the gun to your head?"

"Did he threaten to kill you?"

"Did you know he'd killed before?"

"What kind of deal did you make to keep the rest of the staff safe?"

Abbie found herself engulfed in a pushing, shoving sea of bodies, flashes blinding her, microphones bristling from twenty different hands. For a moment she had the insane urge to tell the last questioner that she'd offered to trade the staff's safety for Boardwalk and Park Place.

"How do you feel right now?"

"Grateful." She finally smiled, wondering if the whole nation would see her lose her breakfast on TV. This was scarier than facing a desperate junkie. "And a lot safer." If you didn't count having to worry about embarrassing yourself publicly.

Another face loomed before her. "How does it feel to have saved so many lives?"

"Ask Officer Viviano and his partner, Officer Mendle-sohn. They did the saving." Speaking of which, where was Viviano? He'd promised to protect her.

"But you put yourself at peril. The man was a known killer."

Abbie shrugged with a deprecating grin. "He never gave me his credentials. All I did was buy a little time."

Like hell she didn't know what to do with reporters! Michael thought to himself with a private smile as he pushed his way toward Abbie.

"Sgt. Viviano..."

"Excuse me," he interrupted, getting ahold of Abbie and steering her for the door. "We have an appointment inside."

"Aw, c'mon," they persisted. "Just a couple of shots."

"Yeah," one of the nearby photogs agreed. "How 'bout a handshake or something? One rescuer to another?"

They'd made it to the glass doors. Michael could see Lieutenant Capshaw waiting inside, a pained look of impatience darkening his heavy features. The press was still yelling for cooperation and Abbie was trying to answer a hundred questions as they backed away. Then the UP correspondent begged once more for just one picture of one hero expressing thanks to the other.

Michael turned back on the crowd. "You want a picture?" he asked with a sudden grin. He was met by a chorus of hungry agreement. "Well, charge up your flashes for this."

Even before Abbie heard his words, he whirled her into his arms. She tried to sputter a protest. Michael caught her rearing back and took her mouth with his. His arms crushed her against him, bending her back a little, her hands caught helplessly at her sides.

Abbie couldn't breathe, couldn't think for a moment to object to Michael's very public liberties. Before she realized what he was doing, she found herself held firm not by the pressure of his arms, but by the searing delight of his kiss. His touch ignited her skin like a brushfire. His mouth met hers with a tender hunger that begged communion. Abbie felt herself going limp and knew she was in danger of losing herself in that intoxicating embrace.

Michael held her only briefly, and when he lifted his head, his eyes left behind a brief message of intimacy. Then he turned to the reporters with a wicked grin. "How was that?"

The UP writer chuckled back. "Sergeant, you do know how to put on a show."

"He's also going to be sporting more bandages if he tries it again," Abbie offered dryly. Michael pulled her on inside before she had a chance to say more.

"Having fun, Viviano?" Capshaw made it a point to look long-suffering.

"Yes, sir," Michael nodded benignly, walking on past. A number of policemen working in the dark, abused old building spotted Michael and came over. It wasn't long before there was a crowd inside to vie the one outside.

"Well, if it isn't the gimp. Did you come back to ask the big boys how it's really done?"

"Yeah, Viviano, what happened? You miss the class in how to duck?"

"I *did* duck," Michael grinned, accepting handshakes and pats on the back. "He wasn't aiming for my head."

One of the men nodded sagely. "Not so dumb after all. He had the perp go for something Viviano could do without."

Abbie saw the real relief in the eyes of Michael's friends. There was such a bond there—one of trust and respect, shared experiences and an uncertain future—that brought them closer. It set them apart in a way civilians couldn't quite comprehend. She didn't think she really wanted to dwell on it right then, though. They were still too close to that dress-uniform funeral they'd almost attended.

It was as Michael guided her to the stairwell that Abbie finally found her voice again. "Why did you kiss me like that?" she demanded, wondering when her heart was going to get back to a recognizable rhythm.

"We go upstairs." Michael motioned passively, holding the door as she headed up the stairs past him. "Interrogation with Detective Swann. Diversionary tactic."

Abbie stopped climbing. "What?"

He shrugged noncommittally. "It kept them from getting to your sordid past."

Abbie responded with a decidedly unladylike expletive and continued up the steps. Michael followed with a grin.

"Why don't you date cops?" His heart rate still hadn't slowed. All that kiss had done was make him want more.

"Personal policy."

"What?"

She stopped then. Michael stopped a step below, bringing him eye-to-eye with her. She didn't tell him that the memory of his touch still crawled along her skin like lightning. Or that she wanted him to kiss her again, here where there were no prying eyes to interfere.

"It's just a policy of mine," she repeated, keeping her tone purposefully matter-of-fact. "Nothing personal."

"Saving yourself for another doctor?"

"Please." Her scowl was heartfelt. "Give me a little credit."

"Then why?"

Abbie found that she had to look away a moment. Then she shrugged again and turned back to climbing. "It just is."

For a moment Michael remained where he was, his hand on the rail, one leg up a step. Damn. He sure couldn't figure her. She blew hot and cold so fast you couldn't keep up. Yet the more she swung back and forth—the more she confused him—the more she attracted him. He really wanted to get to know Abbie Fitzgerald. Considering how much his last experience should have warned him off for good, that was something else he just couldn't figure.

When Abbie realized that Michael hadn't followed her, she stopped and looked down. He stood where she'd left him, fingers massaging the side of his head, his eyes half closed.

"Michael? Are you all right?"

She didn't wait for an answer before heading back down the steps. If he felt dizzy or sick in the middle of a flight of stairs, he could end up in a heap on the landing below.

"Michael?" She took hold of his arm, turning to him with anxious eyes. Michael looked up to see the spring-fed blue soften and felt a kick in his chest. He'd seen that expression twice in twenty-four hours and thought again how easily a man could immerse himself in the healing waters of her eyes.

"I'm fine." He grinned deliberately. "Just taking it slow."

Abbie's eyes flashed. "Then answer me, damn it! You scared me."

An eyebrow arched. "Pretty concerned for somebody who doesn't want to get involved."

"I'm a doctor. Concern is part of my job description." She still had a hand on Michael's arm, still held his eyes with the ire in hers, when suddenly her expression crumbled into timid anxiety. "Can you stay in there with me when Detective Swann talks to me?"

Michael lifted his other hand to her cheek. "I never considered leaving."

Abbie set her Styrofoam cup down on the dented, stained conference table and slowly rubbed the bridge of her nose in an instinctive expression of weariness. She was tired. After managing a total of about two uninterrupted hours of sleep the night before and a morning session of "getting to know you" with Michael Viviano, she'd used up the rest of the day reliving the events of the robbery. Minute by minute. Second by second. What did the gunman—Martin Percy, identity courtesy of the FBI—say when he first approached? When was the first time she saw the second man? What did he look like? What kind of gun did he carry? Did he say anything? Abbie had only seen him that one brief time at the doors, just before Michael had gone for Percy's gun. It hadn't been long enough to offer much of an impression.

Then she went through the mug books to try to pick the man out, all of the grainy, stark faces looking alike in their black-and-white squares. All somebody else, she thought. She'd warned them that she was bad at faces. She'd recognize him if she saw him again, but she just couldn't be sure with a two-by-two picture taken up to eight years ago.

Abbie felt as if she'd been hung out on the line like a rug and beaten with a stick. She was so dry from talking she felt as if her mouth were stuffed with old socks, and so jittery from the caffeine she could tap-dance without ever getting off the chair. She had no idea what time it was in this soundproofed little tomb. The only watch she owned was in her locker at work, and her stomach, her best timepiece, was thrown off by coffee and harsh memories. It would take at least a week to unravel.

Only Michael had made it bearable. He'd sat silently beside her as Detective Swann droned out his litany of questions. Michael gently rephrased when she'd become confused and held her hand when the retelling brought the trauma too close. He'd offered his support, his quiet understanding and empathy. Abbie had sought solace in those sweet green eyes time and again when the pressure had threatened her. When she'd had enough, he'd signaled Swann to give her some time to herself. Abbie took another sip of cold coffee, her own eyes on the scarred table surface at her fingertips, and thought of a policeman with eyes the color of soft, rolling hills.

Outside the soundproof room, Swann and Michael lounged against a graying wall, oblivious to the cacophony of the station around them.

"Sure wish she could pin Marlow down," Swann said without much enthusiasm.

Michael shrugged. "I ID'd him. That should be enough."

"Should be," Swann nodded glumly. "But something just isn't jiving."

"Maybe once we get ahold of him she can give us a more positive ID," Michael offered. "Her description fits; she just hasn't been able to make him with a snapshot."

"You sure he had on a white T-shirt?"

Michael nodded silently, taking a slow drag from his cigarette.

Swann motioned toward it. "I thought you gave those up."

"I did." He took a final drag and stubbed it out in his empty cup. "I figured that one close brush with death deserved another." Once again he found himself pressing careful fingers against the side of his head. Somebody was playing "The Stars and Stripes Forever" in his skull, and the prescription codeine he'd taken wasn't easing the percussion section any.

"You could get off the streets and join the real police up in the detectives' squad room like I ask you every time you pull special duty up there," Swann suggested dryly. "Not so many people take potshots at you when you're wearin' a suit."

Michael's answering grin was tolerant. "Pretty soon, Swann. Pretty soon."

"You wanna go on home?" The question was asked in a carefully noncommittal tone of voice. "Dixon's supposed to partner with me on this case anyway."

Michael slowly shook his head. "I started it. I might as well stay with it." He didn't notice the flash of frustration in his friend's eyes. Straightening to ease a tired back, he brought a wrist up to check the time. He'd already missed two meals. As crummy as he felt, he didn't feel like missing a third. "So what do you want to do?"

Swann shrugged again, emptying his own Styrofoam cup and flipping it into the trash can across the hall. "What I want to do is pretend that this whole mess is wrapped up like a Christmas present. What I will do is question her one more time and then throw both of you out."

"You gonna keep an eye on her?"

"Yeah." He shrugged. "At least until I have Marlow under wraps. With all the publicity you two have scared up, I'd hate to have Marlow find her before we can find him."

Michael nodded slowly. "I'll do it."

Swann grinned with lazy humor. "First time I heard you volunteer for anything. She must have great legs."

Michael grinned right back. "She doesn't date cops."

"Yeah, and your gramma eats chitlins with her pasta."

Michael found himself grinning again. "Do you really think she needs to know why we're keeping tabs on her?"

Swann shrugged. "I'm not gonna tell her you're after her."

"And I won't tell her your first name is Llewelyn."

"Not if you want to live long enough to collect pension, you won't," Swann assured him evenly. "I won't tell her there's a problem until you think there is one. Good enough?"

Michael nodded. "Good enough."

Abbie looked up with a faint smile of greeting when the door opened. Detective Swann retrieved his seat. Michael stood by the door.

"I want to ask you just a couple more questions, Dr. Fitzgerald." Swann switched the recorder back on. Abbie nodded with a pained look for Michael's benefit. It didn't escape her that the lines alongside his mouth had deepened, or that his color was getting bad again. She had to restrain the urge to go over to him.

"Now," Swann began as he set a stack of pictures before her. "I want you to look at these pictures and tell me if you recognize any of them."

Abbie took a deep breath to quell the irritation. "Do you want me to say yes?"

"I want you to tell me exactly what you remember."

She threw up her hands in acquiescence. "Okay." Rubbing again at the bridge of her nose, she sifted through the photos, all white men, all with that same air of disdain for the photographer. She wondered what attitude she'd have if she found herself posing for that camera.

It was no use. As hard as she tried, she couldn't put one of those faces at the door. A few were very close, but she just wasn't certain enough. She remembered thinking "Trick or treat" when she'd given Percy his bag of goodies, and how much he'd seemed to need them. She also remembered thinking that the man at the door didn't seem as much desperate as angry. But he was gone too fast to know for sure. Dark-skinned, with black hair and eyes, no facial hair, no discernable scars. Nothing to set him easily apart.

"No," she finally said. "I'm sorry. I just can't be sure who I saw." Lifting her head, she fixed Swann with a deliberate glare. "Now, do you want to tell me what I should have said?"

She surprised quick grins out of the two cops. Swann shot Michael a look. Michael just embellished his grin with an eloquent shrug. Swann turned back to Abbie who was doing her best to hold still. She had such an overwhelming feeling that things were about to get worse. She didn't know how right she was.

Swann absently picked up the stack of photos again and filed through them. "Viviano told you that our Mr. Percy had been involved in some other robberies."

Abbie nodded. "He mentioned murder."

Swann nodded back, his eyes still on the photos he shuffled. "Yeah, well, Percy's been pullin' these jobs with a few friends. Viviano here already spotted one of those friends in the stack here as the second man yesterday. A bad perp named Buddy Marlow."

"Perp?"

Michael spoke up from the door with a quick grin. "Perpetrator. Doctors aren't the only ones who enjoy their slang."

Abbie managed a return grin. "We pride ourselves on the fact that ours is in Latin. We like to get people really confused." Turning back to Swann, she motioned toward the photos. "Which one?"

Swann pulled out a picture and slid it over. Abbie picked it up. Another face without distinction. Without recognition. Abbie stared hard at the face, trying to will an identification. Maybe, maybe not.

She looked from Swann to Michael, trying again to remember, to pull out the memory they asked for from the jumble of emotions and sensations. If for no other reason, she wanted to be able to give it to Michael, who still stood quietly by her, even as the pain and weariness took their toll on him. But she couldn't. Nothing registered.

Michael, leaning against the door, was struck anew by that poignant vulnerability in Abbie's eyes. She wore the same look she'd leveled on him just as she'd crumpled into his arms. That heart-tugging expression that said she was trying her best and just couldn't pull anything else from within to help. Abruptly he straightened, surprised by the sudden urge to protect her, to ease the struggle that marred those delicate features.

"If you don't recognize him, it's just as well," he said, surprising Swann into turning. "That just means you don't have to put up with Swann's sunny disposition anymore. It's time for dinner. You hungry?"

Abbie flashed him a grin of relief. "Starved." Then she thought to look to Detective Swann for confirmation.

Swann waved them both away. "If we need you for anything else, I'm sure Viviano'll let you know."

Abbie grabbed her purse and stood, suddenly very anxious to get out of this dingy little cell. Michael opened the door, letting in the din of outside activity, and held out his hand to her.

"Dr. Fitzgerald," Swann spoke up from where he sat. Abbie turned. "Thanks. You did okay."

"I wish I'd been a little more help to you," she apologized.

"You want to be of more help?" Swann leveled a deadpan look at her, his sharp black eyes just shy of serious. With a cock of his head he indicated Michael. "Keep an eye on him. He's not real good at followin' orders. Especially doctor's orders."

Michael steered Abbie out before Swann had a chance to elaborate. Abbie didn't think to protest. It was too late in an already too-long day, and her nerves and sensibilities were too precariously stretched. As she walked with Michael through the crowded, noisy station, all she could seem to think of was the gentle pressure of his hand at her back, and how his support in that room had gotten her through it. She knew darn well how easy it could become to depend on the strength of that hand, the empathy in those emerald eyes. She had the feeling that Michael Viviano's arms could be the kind a woman would gladly drown in. She certainly almost had.

"Where would you like to eat?" he asked a moment later as they headed back down the stairs.

Abbie looked over to see the exhaustion that etched his features. "No place."

"What?" he demanded, forcing a smile. "After I saved you from the clutches of the infamous Detective Swann, you won't even have dinner with me?"

She smiled. "You don't need to spend the next two hours entertaining me over dinner."

"I don't? What do I need?"

"Bed."

A wicked grin appeared in Michael's widened eyes. "Come to think of it, I'm not *that* hungry..."

"Alone." Abbie got to the door first and opened it. She was having a little trouble keeping a straight face herself. Michael had such an infectious grin.

His face fell. "Swann said you were supposed to keep an eye on me."

"Sleeping isn't a team sport," Abbie informed him dryly. "And that's what you need. I know how rotten I feel after this marathon, and I wasn't shot." Knowing that he wouldn't leave it at that, she headed on down the hall ahead of him.

Michael followed, aware that Abbie had no misconceptions about the front he was putting on. Of all the times to be involved with a doctor.

"I'm still hungrier than I am tired," he objected, not relenting a bit. "And I do have to get you home."

"That's why God invented buses."

He shook his head. "Nope. It's a ride home from me or a night's lodging courtesy of the holding tank."

Abbie stopped to face him again with an enthusiastic grimace. "You certainly do have a way with an ultimatum."

"Good." He nodded, taking her by the arm and turning her back toward the door. "I'm in the mood for pizza and beer."

"Pizza—" she relented "—no beer. It's not a good chaser for codeine."

He gave her a wry grin. "You doctors take right over, don't you?"

She grinned back, the animation in his eyes washing her with a delicious little chill. It amazed her how much she wanted to stay within their reach.

"What about getting a take-out pizza?" she asked. "Then we could just eat at my place."

"Lady—" he grinned brightly "—that's the best offer I've had all day."

Abbie found herself grimacing again, her eyes amused. "All I'm offering is pizza."

"Careful," he warned, eyes dead ahead. "Press corps at one o'clock."

Abbie followed his gaze with a heartfelt groan and forgot everything else.

Abbie had every intention of entertaining Michael in traditional style, with napkins and plates at a set table. She was even going to move her bike, long her only company in the kitchen for meals.

They ended up on the living-room floor with paper towels and sticky hands. Michael didn't seem to mind at all as he wolfed down three big pieces of pizza in quick succession.

Abbie noticed that he'd gone into the bathroom earlier rather then take another dose of codeine in front of her.

Probably force of habit, she thought, from years of police peer pressure. It just didn't do to actually admit to anyone that you were hurt or weak. He had what she always called the John Wayne Syndrome. Her brothers, though not cops, were classic victims.

"Michael Viviano sounds very Italian," she ventured, licking strings of cheese from her fingers.

Michael nodded. "Very."

"With your coloring, I hope you're going to tell me your mother was Swedish."

"French," he admitted.

Abbie's eyebrow rose. "Emotional household, was it?"

Michael gave her a grin. "Not really. The noisiest it got was when my father played his opera records."

"Opera?" Abbie's face said it all.

Michael found himself laughing. "It's an acquired taste, my father says. Like fine wine."

"And did you," she asked with some delicacy, "acquire the taste?"

She got another nod as he downed yet another mouthful and washed it down with Coke. "I have a subscription to the Lyric."

Abbie was impressed. Even to an uninitiate like her, that was quite an accomplishment. Chicago's opera company had a worldwide reputation, drew legendary talent and had been one-hundred-percent subscription for years. The joke at the hospital was that you had to be willed tickets to go at all.

"Who did you bribe for that?" she demanded.

"My father. It's a lot easier to share a set of tickets when you're an only child."

"Your mother?"

"Died when I was ten."

Abbie nodded, letting her eyes communicate all that was necessary.

"How 'bout your family?" he asked, warming with the easy camaraderie.

"Noisy all by itself," she admitted. "I'm the only girl in a great brood, as my grandmother calls it. Five brothers."

Michael gaped a little. "Five?"

She nodded. "My dad wanted to go for a baseball team. My mother said he'd have to be happy with an infield."

He was shaking his head. "No wonder you don't intimidate easily."

"How long have you been a policeman?" she asked, reaching over to pull another piece of pizza from the box. Sausage, mushroom and onion. Abbie's idea of heaven. She'd been pleasantly surprised by Michael's good taste.

He settled a little lower against the arm of the couch and took another sip of his soda. "About twelve years."

"You like it?"

She caught him with his fingers back up to his head in a gesture of pain and forced a rueful grin from him. "Some times more than others."

Abbie nodded absently, wanting to ask so much more and knowing she couldn't. "I don't really know that many police."

Michael grinned at her. "With a name like Fitzgerald in this city? Your family should be lousy with cops. Or ward politicians."

"We seem to be the exception to that particular rule." Abbie grinned back. "Solid white-collar, suburban vocations. The only thing my family's lousy with is accountants."

She was so relaxed. It felt as if Michael belonged here, had somehow slipped into the fabric of her life without leaving a wrinkle. When they talked it was without any of the stumbling uncertainties that usually plagued the early stages of male-female relationships. When they were quiet, it was a comfortable silence, with each acutely aware of the other's attraction. Michael didn't seem to mind when Abbie's eyes sought out the hard, clean lines of his face or basked in the crystal green of his eyes. Abbie couldn't bring herself to object when Michael's gaze tended to roam lazily over her, from the curls that tumbled over her forehead to the calluses on the soles of her bare feet. Somehow, even when she wasn't watching, she knew just where his eyes rested. There was a savory tingling, the feeling as if someone had swept careful fingers just beyond her skin, their electricity charging her.

There were not a few times when she thought to caution herself. She knew this couldn't lead anywhere. She couldn't let it. That was a decision she'd made long ago, and one she'd never had trouble living with. Until now. Until this fascinating man with hypnotic eyes mesmerized her with no more than a smile. She was going to have to pull herself away; and she was going to have to do it soon.

"Why aren't you married?" Michael asked after a considered pause.

Abbie's eyebrows raised. "Isn't that a rather chauvinistic question?"

His grin was a complacent one. "Probably. I'd still like to know."

So would I, she thought with a dour grin. "I was thinking about that very subject when I last had a gun to my head," she admitted.

"When you decided to have an affair?"

She nodded. "It suddenly occurred to me that I never had one satisfying relationship in my life. I guess I do best when I concentrate on one thing at a time and, until now, becoming a doctor was it . . . Why am I telling you all this?"

Michael's response was a reflective smile. "I bet you're a good doctor."

She smiled back. "I bet you're a good cop."

He shrugged. "I guess. That's what my wife said when she asked for the divorce five years ago."

Abbie saw the pain that still lingered behind those words and wondered that Michael was comfortable enough to allow it. She thought how much she wanted to sit on the floor and tell Michael all her dreams and plans, the frustrations life had dealt her, and the story of what had happened when a fourteen-year-old girl had walked into the middle of a grocery store holdup sixteen years ago.

Abbie saw Michael's hand instinctively stray to carefully rub at the pain that refused to go away and thought, yes, I'm going to have to pull away soon. Soon. But not quite yet.

Chapter 4

The throbbing irritated him, tracking his sleep with relentless persistence. He was uncomfortable. Cramped. Fleeting pictures crowded his sleep, making no sense, forming no pattern, exhausting him. Then the ringing started. Damn, his head hurt.

"Michael?"

Michael felt the gentle touch to his shoulder and sat bolt upright. He blinked, struggling for coherence. He wasn't at his apartment. He was sitting on a couch in his jeans and shirt. Abbie's couch. What was he doing here? And what the hell was she doing, standing there in not much more than an oversize T-shirt? Just the sight of her sleep-softened eyes and tousled hair sent a hard ache through his gut.

"The phone," she said simply. "It's for you."

Michael turned his head a couple more times, still trying to piece together a reasonable explanation. None came. Giving up, he pulled himself to his feet and walked to the kitchen. He was dizzy again, and his head hurt. It was morning. He hated mornings. He'd always figured people were shot at sunrise because who wanted to live at that time of day?

"Yeah, what?" he snapped into the receiver.

"Michael? It's Swann."

Michael pushed a hand through his hair, still trying to assemble his senses. "How'd you know I'd be here?" Hell, he didn't even know how he'd ended up there.

"Lucky guess." Swann's voice was dust dry. It was also amused. "You really take your job to heart, Viviano. I like that in a cop."

"You're pushing it, Swann."

"Me?" Michael could envision those teeth flashing in a quick grin. "Hey, man, you're already in what I'd call the above-and-beyond category. Italians must heal fast."

"You're about to find out if blacks do, too. What do you want?"

"To do you a favor. Lieutenant's lookin' for you, and I have the feeling he's not in a very patient mood this morning."

Swann had his attention. "The lieutenant? What's up?"

"I haven't been called in yet, but I saw the guys from narcotics all over his office like a bad smell. And there was a guy from DEA in there."

"For me?" Something should have made some sense. What did he have to do with the Drug Enforcement Agency? Leaning the phone against a shoulder, Michael pressed fingers against his temples to ease the throbbing. The dizziness just wouldn't ease. Why couldn't they have waited a couple of hours to drop this in his lap?

"For you and your lady friend. Since I know what a good boy you are, Viviano, I'm gonna assume it has something to do with that show yesterday."

"When am I supposed to be there?"

"Twenty minutes ago. I'll tell him I just found you and buy you a little time. But don't waste it, ya know?"

Michael found himself scowling at the humor in the voice. "Swann," he growled, "stop smiling. It's unnatural this early in the morning."

"Later, man."

"Yeah, thanks."

Michael hung up the phone and took a minute to roll his head in a slow circle, trying to relieve some of the tension.

"What's going on?"

Opening his eyes, he focused in on Abbie. She'd managed to add shorts to her attire and stood in the doorway, those doctor's eyes assessing him with concern.

"Why did I wake up on your couch?" His tone of voice wasn't any more congenial.

Abbie shrugged. "Probably because you fell asleep on it. You were too heavy to drag to the elevator, and I don't give up my bed for anybody."

"Why didn't you wake me?"

She was losing patience with his brusque tone. "I didn't want to endanger the citizens of Chicago. You really weren't in any shape to drive."

Michael's eyes chilled. "That's my decision to make."

Abbie's eyes flashed right back. "Exactly why I didn't wake you. I know just what you would have done."

"Lady, you're not my mother!"

She found herself facing off with him, hands on hips. "Well, you're sure acting like a typical six-year-old. Your car keys are on the end table. Be my guest!" He would have to act like this at seven in the morning. Abbie didn't even have the patience to put up with sunshine at that hour. Her brothers had more than once informed her that breakfast would be more hospitable with Vlad the Impaler. And that was without the stress of the last couple of days.

"There's just one problem," Michael snapped back, his eyes tight with the pain. "You have to go with me. The lieutenant wants to see us down at the station."

Abbie allowed herself a smug smile. "Well then, that settles it. I'm not getting in a car with you again until you sit down and have some breakfast. Maybe then you won't be so dizzy." She punctuated the next words with her eyes. "Or so unpleasant."

"Abbie..."

"You can freshen up while I cook. How do you like your eggs?"

They stood faced off for a few more seconds; two tired, strained, terminally cranky people. Then, with a snap, Michael conceded. "On a plate."

Abbie caught the flash of a smile as he stalked past her.

As she went about throwing a quick meal together, Abbie thought about the man in her bathroom. He'd fallen asleep last night between slices of pizza. Abbie hadn't paid attention when he'd closed his eyes and relaxed against the arm of her couch. It had been a grueling day for both of them. She had taken notice, though, when he'd started to softly snore.

She'd sat across from him, completely flummoxed. Something like this had never happened to her before. Should she wake him and send him home? Should she let him stay where she could keep an eye on him? He certainly didn't seem to care to do it for himself. Could she even stay awake long enough to keep any kind of eye on him at all?

He'd looked so vulnerable resting there, his hair tumbled over the bandage, his features so relaxed and open. She'd sat for a long time just watching him. Then, after she'd pushed and pulled him up onto the couch and covered him with an old quilt, she'd found herself standing there just watching him.

He'd slept in that haphazard way that made men look like little boys and stole women's hearts. Rolled halfway on his side, he'd lain with an arm under his head and legs strewn over the cushions. Abbie had reached over and brushed his hair back to see him smile at the touch. Her heart had immediately been stolen.

Flipping the eggs with businesslike dispatch, Abbie set the toaster. She was going to have to watch those old maternal instincts. Nothing got a woman in trouble faster than that urge to comfort a man when he hurt. All she wanted to do when she saw that grudging flash of vulnerability was to hold him, to rock him against her and stroke his head.

The toast popped up, startling her. She pulled out the butter and painted a piece with it. Yeah, right. The maternal instinct. That was all involved here. The good old maternal instinct was what made her hands sweat when Michael got too near, what made her relive that kiss yesterday time and again until she was sure she'd read more into it than there was.

It surely hadn't been the maternal instinct that had taken her breath away this morning when she'd come in to wake Michael and seen the soft morning light play across his unshaven face. She hadn't wanted to rock him then. She'd wanted to jump his bones.

The residue of that moment still plagued her. She felt flushed and uncertain, her skin still unsettled from the sudden thrill of him, her heart still beating just a little too fast. A nagging knot and a sharp ache of anticipation had taken up residence in her chest, right under her breastbone.

You're playing with fire, she thought dourly as she realized that just the second place setting on her table pleased her. You've lost your mind, and you're going to pay for it. Even so, she knew that she couldn't quit just yet.

"Abbie."

Michael stood in the doorway, his hair damp from the water he'd splashed on his face, his eyes brighter and apologetic. Abbie's heart skidded at the sight of him. Good, she couldn't help but think. That's the perfect way to blow out the fire: memorize his features like he was the map to lost treasure.

"Sit," she offered, a hand to the table as she turned to get the coffee. "I'm going to down a couple cups of caffeine so I'm a little more civilized. Want some?"

She heard a chair scrape behind her. "Thanks. Do you always work evenings?"

"Do you mean am I always this charming in the morning?" she countered. "Yes. I've been called Anastasia the Hun."

Michael chuckled as he accepted a cup of coffee. "Well then, at least I didn't surprise you. My partner says I'm so bad he won't even talk to me before ten."

Abbie took her seat. "I can see why." She considered her plate a moment without much relish. She really wasn't hungry, but she had a feeling it was going to be another busy day.

"Anastasia?" It was a question.

Abbie nodded. "My full name."

"After the Russian duchess?"

She shook her head with a grin. "After the wife of a potato farmer. Irish tradition holds that a first daughter is named after her maternal grandmother. My mom's that kind of old-fashioned lady."

Michael's features eased into a warm smile. "It's a beautiful name. How'd you get Abbie out of it?"

"My brother Tommy. Anastasia's not the easiest name to pronounce at age two. He got as far as Abbie, and it stuck."

"Are you old-fashioned?" Michael asked. He, too, seemed to be forgetting the food on his plate for the coffee. Abbie gave him a refill and left the pot on the table.

She shrugged, intrigued by the question. "Selectively, I guess. I'd probably have to do a case-by-case evaluation on it."

Michael nodded to himself, taking his time over his second cup of coffee.

Abbie watched him, thinking how soft the early-morning light from her tiny window was on him, and that she was digging herself an even bigger hole just enjoying the sight of him like this. Wondering why at that moment she didn't care.

She set her coffee cup down. "I wasted all that good food, didn't I?"

Michael looked up at her, then at his plate with a quick scowl. "You're not going to start lecturing me about breakfast being the most important meal of the day, are you?"

She shook her head. "Not me. This is the first attempt I've made at it in about a year."

"Now you tell me."

"It probably wouldn't hurt you to eat something, though. Especially if you're still feeling a little shaky." She picked up her cup again, eyeing him carefully over the rim. "Are you?"

His impatience surfaced in a quick grin. "I've felt better."

"Even Fred Astaire wouldn't be dancing this soon after getting shot," she assured him with a lazy grin. "Especially after spending the night on a strange couch."

Michael scowled again good-naturedly. "Yeah, here Swann thinks I took you up on that affair, and all I was doing was getting a sore neck."

Abbie's coffee cup landed on the table again. "Detective Swann knows about that?" There was a definite chill in her voice, her eyes widening with warning.

Michael gave her an offhand shrug. "Sure. Do you want to change before we head over? Swann said the call was ASAP."

She was not to be put off. "What do you mean, 'Sure'?" The temperature in the room had dropped a few more degrees. "Swapping stories in the locker room, or is this going to be on national TV?"

Michael couldn't believe how much sarcasm Abbie could pack into one sentence. He wanted to grin at the outrage that stiffened her posture. He didn't. "No. No locker rooms, no TV. Swann's the only one who knows, and he's very discreet. He thought it was a pretty gutsy thing for you to come up with while looking down a gun."

Abbie wanted to throw something at him and wasn't quite sure why. To be perfectly honest, it was something she'd intended to share with her friends. But somehow, everything had begun to subtly become more complicated. She found that the matter had become a personal one, not something to be chuckled over. It upset her that Michael could.

"Eat your eggs," she snapped, and stood to leave. "I'm going to change. I'll be back when I can overcome the urge to get even for that smug look on your face."

"How long will that take?" Michael asked as she reached the next room.

She turned to see him finally go for his cutlery, amusement crinkling his eyes. It made her even angrier. "Probably about a week."

She came back out in a yellow-and-black print cotton sundress that made her skin glow and Michael's skin tingle. It had narrow tank-top shoulders and a scoop neckline that revealed the soft recesses of her throat, the ridges her collarbones created. A yellow belt caught her waist, and the full skirt swirled around her tanned legs. She'd pulled her hair off her neck into an untidy knot that spilled curls. Michael felt that ache ignite in his gut again and remembered why she was so dangerous: he wanted to taste that smooth skin.

"Abbie." He caught her at the door, his hands grasping her slender shoulders.

Abbie stilled at his touch, her eyes lifting to his with wary response. She didn't need to tell him that his unexpected intimacy set her heart racing. He could see her quickened pulse throbbing at her throat. She wanted to ease closer, to test the solid strength of that chest and curl her fingers into the hair at his neck. She even wanted to feel the rasp of his day-old beard against her. Brushing the so-sensitive skin of her belly, her thighs...

"What?" Her answer was abrupt, a ragged catch of breath. How was it he could set her off in such unexpected directions without any warning? He was like a spring wind that spawned sudden tornadoes. The reaction seemed to surprise him, too. His eyes had widened, gone dark and smoky with desire. He'd begun to knead her arms, the unconscious motion disturbingly intimate. Abbie wanted to tell him to stop. Might have if his hands weren't working fire throughout her. For just a moment the two of them seemed to move together beyond their worlds into one neither had ever experienced. And neither of them—though both knew better—wanted to stop.

"I was going to apologize," he managed, trying to pull his whirling thoughts back into order. He couldn't. She'd changed her perfume—a slight, soft fragrance that seemed to belong only to her—and it was seducing him.

"A nice idea," Abbie breathed, her eyes locked into his.

A smile was born in his eyes that seemed to envelop her. "I have a much better one."

This time he took her gently in his arms. Carefully, as if afraid she'd break. He let one arm slide around that cool, soft cotton dress and brought the other up to cup her face in his hand. He'd meant to bring her to him. He needn't have bothered. Without any urging, she lifted her face to his, sought his mouth with her own. Her eyes slid closed against the languorous heat that filled her. A sweet fire flared.

It was a different feeling than the last time Michael had kissed her. There was no urgency, no shock of recognized passion. This was more a savoring. She felt his warm breath against her and tasted the coffee he'd just finished, a smoky fullness that her tongue slowly sought out. His lips were soft, searching. They explored her face as tenderly as if it were a precious treasure. She felt his open hand fit against the small of her back and settled closer against him.

Abbie couldn't get her mind to work. She couldn't get past the assault on her senses: the steely strength of Michael's body, hard against hers; the tense desire just his kiss surprised in her; the musky, slightly disheveled feel and smell of him. She was falling, more than her knees buckling in his tender embrace.

Michael heard a small whimpering noise of protest from her and straightened up. "What's the matter?" His voice was a little rough with restraint. He wasn't a user, but he was no saint, either. She was driving him crazy.

Abbie managed to open her eyes, their lingering light of desire battling with a look of distress. "You're not being fair." She laid her head against his chest and couldn't object when his hand went to her hair.

"I don't seem to have a choice."

"Easy for you to say." Her heart still beat like a reggae band against him, and she found herself with a foolish grin on her face. So what did Michael Viviano have that lit her fuse so fast? And when had that fuse suddenly gotten so short? She felt like stretching to ease that tight, sprung-wire feeling in her pelvis. She wanted to feel bare skin against Michael's. That was after only knowing him a little more than a day. What would her mother say?

"What would my mother say?"

"She'd say that you had good taste."

Michael was grinning, too—a silly grin that was telling. He was fast losing control of an already out-of-control situation.

"She'd say I was nuts." With an effort, Abbie pulled away. It would have been much easier to handle if all she saw in Michael were the fireworks. She wasn't the kind of person who settled just for that. But when she looked up, she saw the humor, the sense, the compassion that colored those green eyes with their cool light. She saw the lines concern had carved and patience had tempered. He was a special man, and that was dangerous.

"Wish I'd done that last night." He smiled, a finger playing along her cheek.

"Last night you would have fallen asleep halfway through it," she retorted with a shaky grin.

"I sincerely doubt it."

"Michael," she said, the sincerity in her eyes quieting him. "This just isn't my style."

"It's kind of a surprise for me, too."

"But I don't think it's a good idea." When she found herself wanting to ease back into the comfort of his arms, she pulled away from his touch. Then she tried a rueful grin. "I told you. No affair."

"Because you don't respond to me." His deadpan delivery even got a smile from her.

"Because I just don't think it's a good idea."

His eyes softened. "Does this mean that after today I don't get any more free passes to the couch?"

"Not even a free pass to the elevator."

He looked down at her for a moment longer, a certain resolve growing on his features. She thought she'd never seen such a strong, kind man. "Abbie, I have the feeling that there's something you want to tell me about. And that that something is what you're also afraid the press will get." Michael saw the truth of his assumption in her eyes. "I'm not going to pressure you, but I think you should talk to me about it before they find out on their own. They will, ya know."

She nodded. "I know." How do I best avoid the pain, she wondered, wanting very much to be able to sit down and tell him the story. Afraid he'd react just like her parents still did. "It's not bad, Michael. Just ... annoying. It still pops up when I don't want it to." With a smile, she finally pulled away. "Everybody has their dreary little secrets that don't seem so important to anybody else. This is just mine."

The only distinction between the hall outside the interrogation room and this one outside the lieutenant's office was that the lieutenant had a nice nameplate on his door. Abbie paced outside, another cup of bad station coffee in hand as Swann watched her from one of the chairs he'd pulled out into the hall.

"They'll be in there a few minutes," he offered laconically, his eyes surreptitiously straying to Abbie's legs. He'd been right. They went from here to the border and back.

"But what am I doing out here?" she asked. Abbie didn't wait well. The occupational hazard of E.R. physicians. They just weren't trained for it.

"Waiting." Swann seemed to be more inured.

Abbie shot him an acerbic look. "Why can't you go in?" she asked. "Did you misbehave?"

He smiled slowly and took a drink from his own cup. "I've heard it all before. I offered to keep you safe from the wolves out here while the lieutenant talked to Viviano."

"Why is he in there? Did *he* misbehave?"

"I doubt it. Viviano's too white-bread for that."

Abbie found herself chuckling. Turning back on the passive face of the detective, she finally gave up and took the other seat. Swann was about Michael's age, but heavier. He had no visible flab, just muscle and menace—although she had the feeling that beneath that concrete front was a cop who wouldn't misbehave much, either.

"Do you have a first name?" she asked.

Swann shot her a sharp look. "Why?"

Abbie shrugged. "Only football players and drill sergeants are called by their last names."

"And me."

She nodded with a smile. "Okay. Have you known Michael long?"

"We used to partner when I was on the street. He saved my butt when I was a rookie."

For some reason, that did and did not surprise Abbie. "Why is he still on the street?"

Swann took a moment to appraise the fresh, open face next to him. Viviano was already showing signs of some serious intentions toward this lady, which, under the circumstances, could be a bad move. Swann couldn't fault him, though. He liked her too. "He likes it better out there. Been workin' off and on with some of the street gangs. They trust him."

Abbie looked over toward the door, as if to better imagine Michael in there. Yes, she could definitely see him bringing his calm brand of reason to the streets like that.

Swann was looking the same way. "He won't be out there much longer, though. Burnin' out. Lieutenant wants him in a suit bad, too."

"A detective?"

He nodded. "He's real good at it. Fools everybody with that boy-scout face of his."

Abbie laughed at the assessment. She could just see it. She sipped at her coffee for a moment, thinking how alike coffee was in hospitals and police squad rooms: awful.

"Detective Swann?" she started.

"Just Swann."

Abbie felt herself given a compliment. "Michael was married before." Swann nodded without comment, but Abbie's purpose faltered. She'd impulsively wanted to ask him about it. He must have known. Michael didn't seem as if it were something he wanted to talk about. Like Abbie and her holdup story. But she wasn't sure she could ask his old partner something that personal. She found herself studying the dregs of the coffee in her cup in embarrassed silence.

Swann wasn't the lieutenant's favorite detective for nothing. He assessed the situation with one look. "How long you been a doctor?"

Abbie looked over in surprise. "Four years."

"Ever wish you were something else?"

She shook her head. "I'm too old to go out for ballet, and there isn't a whole lot of call for cowgirls in Chicago."

Swann grinned briefly. "Viviano's wife didn't want to be married to a cop. Too much time and trouble, she always said. Too many nights alone and days when he'd come home whipped from what he did." With a shrug, he delivered the judgment. "Happens with cops, ya know? We don't have the prettiest job to bring home."

"Was he a policeman when she married him?"

He nodded.

Abbie felt angry at the woman she'd never known. "She must have known how he felt."

"Guess she thought she could change him."

Abbie snorted rather unkindly. "That would be like asking me to become a plumber so I wouldn't leave work with blood on my hands."

Swann looked over at her expression of offense and nodded to himself. Yeah, she might be real good for Viviano. She understood.

And Abbie, sitting next to him, felt worse as she realized that if she let herself feel more for Michael she, too, would be tempted to ask him to change.

Chapter 5

"What do you mean, you're not bringing him in?"

Michael Viviano was the only one standing in the lieutenant's office. Lt. Capshaw, his heavy features set in a neutral mask, sat passively behind his old oak desk. Two guys from narcotics were draped over a couple of the chairs, looking more like bad guys than good guys in their grubby clothes and unkempt appearance. Leading the band was a very well-kept bureaucrat from the DEA who made demands and kept his own counsel as if he were the only one in the room with brains.

It had all started when he'd complained that Michael had interfered with a nationwide drug investigation when he'd rescued Dr. Fitzgerald at the hospital. It seemed that the criminals, Percy and Marlow, though small-time in their own right, had landed the perfect connection to pad their collective nests for the foreseeable future. They had set up a transaction between a Colombian seller in Florida and an American buyer in Chicago. The problem was that only Percy and Marlow knew who the buyer was and when and where the shipment was due to arrive. When Officer Mendlesohn had shot Percy defending Michael, he had dead-ended the DEA's link to the whole operation. The DEA man, ever one for solutions, had come up with the perfect alternative—if he could only get Michael and the good doctor to cooperate with him and the gentlemen from narcotics.

"We know where Marlow is," he'd said without noticeable inflection, "but don't feel it would be wise to bring him in. If we did that, we'd lose the connection altogether. And we've been working on this too long to lose it for one lousy arrest."

Michael had made his predictable objection. The DEA man was not impressed by the uniformed officer's outrage.

"It was all over the news that there was a second man at that holdup and that we're looking for him," Michael went on, not at all happy with the direction things were taking. They wouldn't have asked Abbie down here just to beg her pardon for risking her life for a few kilos of heroin. "And I'd bet my badge that Marlow has an idea he was made. What's to keep him from trying to shut up a couple of witnesses?"

The look the DEA man gave questioned Michael's courage. Michael was long beyond rising to bait like that. "We have him under constant surveillance," the man said. "He can't go anywhere we don't know about. We have to leave him out on the street so he can make contact with the buyer. But we can also push up the timetable by turning up the heat on him."

Michael stopped his pacing in front of the suit. "With the witnesses."

"Witness. We feel that if we could make a lot of noise about finding a second man, he'd get jumpy. But if we let him know he's been made, he's gonna go underground." The man had eyes like a day-old fish that he leveled on Michael. "A cop would know him. A civilian wouldn't."

"No."

"He's gonna smell something fishy if we go any other way."

"Were you going to ask her permission?" Michael demanded. "Or just hang her out in the wind?"

For the first time since the DEA man had begun to state his case, the lieutenant spoke up. "I had suggested you talk to Dr. Fitzgerald. Detective Swann said that you'd developed a rapport with her." Michael could tell his superior wasn't happy about the situation. But he had the feeling that the lieutenant's hands had been tied. "Unless you can think of something better."

Michael tried. He stood in front of the old desk and thought the situation through. It stank from beginning to end. It also, in its own warped kind of way, made sense. The deal had to be big-league if the DEA was sweating bullets about it. That made him wonder how two rookie dealers like Percy and Marlow had gotten involved in the first place.

But to put Abbie at risk again was unthinkable. There would be no way to protect her from Marlow, or from the cold disregard of this man who only wanted his collar.

Without warning, Michael turned and bolted. All eyes followed with confusion as he threw open the door.

Abbie and Swann, by now well into their second cups of coffee, looked up in surprise as Michael appeared in the doorway, his eyes intense.

"Abbie, you're a doctor," he began.

She couldn't help it. "Better than being a cab, I guess." Swann almost choked.

Michael was not to be put off. "I've been shot in the head. I can have amnesia, can't I?"

"You can have anything you want." She saw that Michael wasn't in the mood for levity and stopped. "Sure," she said. "It's not at all uncommon for someone with a concussion of any degree to have what we call retrograde amnesia about the incident. It usually clears after a while.... Why do you want to know?"

He smiled and shut the door again.

"There's no reason to involve her any more than she is," Michael was saying inside the closed room. "She never did get a good make on Marlow anyway. All you have to do is say that I saw him, but that because of my...retrograde amnesia from the injury, I can't remember what he looked like. You can even say that I heard Percy say something before he went down. Something the doc didn't get because she was too scared. Retrograde amnesia's temporary, so we're just waiting for it to clear to ID the perp.''

The DEA man didn't know Michael very well. "You'd be willing to do that?"

The DEA man missed the look on the lieutenant's face in response.

Michael's expression was unforgiving. "Rather than serve up an innocent bystander for slaughter? Yeah, I think I would."

He didn't think it necessary to confide to these gentlemen that Abbie had long since become more than an innocent bystander to him.

"Have Dr. Fitzgerald come in," Lt. Capshaw suggested. The DEA man got the door this time.

"Is it true that retrograde amnesia is temporary after a head injury like the sergeant's here?" the lieutenant asked her when she hesitantly joined them. Swann and Michael ended up flanking her, as if to protect her from the plan that had almost been hatched in this room. It wasn't necessary.

Abbie looked from one person to another before answering. "You called me down here to ask me about head injuries? Don't you guys have your own doctor for that kind of thing?"

Three of the participants had trouble keeping straight faces. "It's more expedient to ask you, Dr. Fitzgerald," Lt. Capshaw managed. "If you don't mind."

"Heck, no," she shrugged. "But I don't understand. Sgt. Viviano didn't display any symptoms of it at the time. Forget your badge number or something, Sergeant?"

"My badge number's fine, thanks. This is purely hypothetical."

She shrugged again. "In that case, I'll tell you what I told the sergeant. Retrograde amnesia is not at all uncommon in the case of concussion. It usually involves incidents that occur during or immediately prior to the injury. A lot of people in car accidents who are knocked out can't remember getting into the car.''

"How long does it take for their memory to come back?" Lt. Capshaw asked.

"There's no real set time. Some, right away. Some, a few days. Some—never.''

"Thank you, Doctor. And for your own protection, you'll have someone keeping an eye on you for the next few days. Until we arrest Percy's accomplice.''

Abbie thought she was confused then. She wasn't really mixed-up until she and Michael walked straight into another onslaught of press a few minutes later.

"Just follow my lead,'' he hissed in her ear and turned to the microphones. She blinked a little stupidly and braced herself.

Then Michael served up the new story, and she was stunned.

"They call it retrograde amnesia,'' he was explaining as if he hadn't just thought the whole thing up. "A blank spot where the shooting occurred. I can't remember what the accomplice looked like, and I was the only one in a position to see him. As soon as my memory returns, though, I think we'll have ourselves an arrest.''

"But I saw him,'' Abbie protested a few minutes later as Michael helped her back in the squad car.

"Not for the press you didn't.''

She waited until he climbed into the car to respond. "But why?''

"Marlow's still out on the street somewhere,'' he answered easily as he started the car. "The lieutenant just thought it might be safer for you if he figured you didn't know anything.''

"Then why the baloney about amnesia?''

Michael grinned. "He also thought it would be safer for me. The press already knows there was a second man. We just forgot what he looked like for a while.''

Michael's explanation didn't sit precisely well with Abbie, but she couldn't think of a particular objection. She should have remembered what Swann had said about that boy-scout face.

Abbie didn't return to work for two more days. It wasn't her idea; she'd wanted to go back after the first session with the lieutenant. But she and Michael had ended up having to meet with the mayor to receive commendations, and with the governor because he happened to be in town. They were asked to appear on the news and were recommended for citations. The more Abbie wanted to get away from Michael to get her bearings, the more she was paired with him for city functions.

Abbie couldn't figure it. It was nothing more than your average armed robbery gone wrong, but in this week when nothing major managed to happen, she and Michael had become the Fred and Ginger of law enforcement. She sighed and Michael cursed and Swann kept his silence—until one of papers demanded a repeat of the now-famous kiss on the station steps; then Swann offered to show them his legs instead.

Other than that, nothing much was happening. John insisted that she take the time off she needed, since it was all good publicity for the hospital, which gave her a citation of its own. She often felt as if she were being watched, but considering that she was, it wasn't much of a surprise.

She supposed she should have felt grateful. After all, Marlow was still out there somewhere. She wasn't all that sure that he watched the news to know that she wasn't supposed to have seen him. Even so, the thought that nothing she did was private was an unsettling one. She simply didn't like the idea that she was never alone.

The Friday Abbie finally got back to work was a busy one. It was just as well. There was nothing better to clear the mind of pressing notoriety and a handsome escort with electric eyes than a busy summer night in the E.R. She figured that she'd just immerse herself in other people's problems and forget her own.

It worked for a while. She had a wide variety of complaints and traumas to choose from in keeping herself occupied. But then Phoebe Turner came on duty, and Abbie found herself right back with her own problems.

Phoebe was one of the nurses who'd worked there as long as Abbie. A small, soft woman with pretty features and unusual compassion, Phoebe was just days away from her first pregnancy leave. She also had a husband who worked homicide.

Abbie found herself surreptitiously watching Phoebe as she worked and wishing she could ask Phoebe how she did it. How did a woman marry a cop and survive the day-to-day fear? Do you wait out each shift, never turning on the news for fear you'd see your husband on it? How do you handle the dread that you'll open the door to his captain and police chaplain? That the next call will be from his partner at the hospital?

It had to be possible. Phoebe never seemed to dwell on it. She went through life regaling everyone with Ralph's sillier stories and unabashedly boasting about his accomplishments. When Ralph made a good collar, the staff at the E.R. knew about it before the press.

But there wasn't any way Abbie could think of to approach the subject. She couldn't face that beaming, anticipatory woman and ask how she dealt with the fact that the child she carried might grow up fatherless.

Michael reached Abbie's apartment building close to midnight. He'd spent his shift bristling at the desk, confined there until the police surgeons said he could go back on the streets. Two of the gangs he'd been helping to control had clashed tonight. He should have been there to prevent it, and the lieutenant hadn't let him. On his way home he'd decided to stop by and make sure that at least Abbie was okay.

"When did she get home?" he asked the "taxi driver" parked across the street.

The man pitched a spent cigarette onto the pavement and stretched. Baby-sitting was not his favorite job. "'Bout twenty minutes ago. Her lights are still on."

Michael knew from their comparisons of late-night preferences that Abbie wouldn't be thinking about bed for at least another couple of hours. He walked into the building. There was no answer when he buzzed her. Shower, maybe. He tried again. Then he pressed others, hoping somebody was up and not being cautious. He was let in.

By the time he pulled open the elevator, a teenage boy was leaning out one of the doors.

"Hey," the boy protested. "You're not Artie."

"No, I'm not," he agreed, and rang Abbie's bell. The boy would have ducked back into the apartment, but Abbie didn't answer. Michael tried again with a little more force.

"Roof," the boy said with a nod upward.

Michael found himself looking the same way.

"She says it's her sun deck."

Michael tried the roof.

Initially, he couldn't see a thing. The light from the hallway first slashed out into the night, then disappeared when he closed the door. There were no lights up here, nothing but black tar and air vents.

Beyond the edge of the roof, Chicago crowded the sky in a glistening panorama that vied with the starlight for beauty. Michael could see the modern sweep of the Lake Shore Drive high rises to his right and, far down toward the Loop, the tallest of the city's skyline. A couple of blocks beyond the building, the city stopped abruptly at a black void that seemed to consume light: the lake. Michael couldn't see any boats, so it seemed like one of those great black holes in space that supposedly sucked in space ships and planets.

If it hadn't been so dark and he hadn't been a cop who didn't trust the dark, he would have enjoyed it a lot more.

After a minute of standing against the wall, he found himself able to make out something more on the black roof: a line of clothes hung out to dry, a small box of tomato plants, and, at the far edge of the big rectangle, a lawn chair.

"Abbie?"

He got no answer. He could see now that she was sitting in the chair, a darker form in the dim light. She didn't even move at the sound of his voice.

"Abbie? Is that you?"

He moved closer, the hairs on the back of his neck up. Instincts made him wary. Experience made him automatically fear for her. If he'd gotten to the roof this easily, so could anybody else. His hand sought the gun he carried under his jacket as his eyes swept the silent, still roof.

When he got closer, he could see that she was back in her jogging clothes, stretched out on the chair as if sunning herself. He couldn't see much else in the dimness, except that she still wasn't moving.

"Abbie." He touched her shoulder and she came off the chair like a shot. Michael was sure that Dixon down in the taxi could hear her scream.

"Hey, whoa," he soothed, hands up, the relief more intense than he'd expected. "It's just me."

"My God, Michael," she gasped, a hand to her chest where the shock still pounded. "Why did you sneak up on me like that?"

"I did not sneak up," he protested. "I called your name twice."

She still couldn't manage an even breath. She did summon an apologetic grin as she lifted the small earset she'd been wearing. Michael instantly understood. Even now he could hear the heavy beat of guitars and drums. Pumped directly into the ears, it would have been assaultingly loud.

"What *is* that?" he asked, motioning more to the music than the equipment. The gun had been back in place before Abbie ever saw it.

She sat a little heavily back in the chair. "Van Halen." With the benefit of a few moments' recovery, she was able to offer a more enthusiastic smile. "My pacifier. The roof, the lake, and rock and roll. I can't think of anything more relaxing than lying here watching the sky and listening to music."

Raised on the greats in classical and opera, Michael didn't think it wise to inform Abbie that in his home, rock and roll had never quite been considered music.

"I'm not so sure that sitting out on the roof is such a good idea right now," he offered casually.

She squinted up at him. "How'd you get up here?"

He shrugged. "The way all cops do it. Press all the buzzers until somebody answers. Your neighbor was expecting Artie."

"Then *what* are you doing here?"

He scowled, but she caught very little of it in the darkness. "Checking on your security. I'm glad I came. Would you mind walking back to your apartment for a minute?"

"I told you," she warned lightly, "no passes for the couch."

Michael smiled at her, thinking that even the small breeze up here did provocative things with her hair. The starlight twined itself in its chestnut depths and glinted red.

"No couch. This visit is for professional reasons."

"Yours or mine?"

This expression she saw. He grinned like a little boy with a secret. "Yours. I need some treatment."

"Why couldn't Tim take these out?" she demanded a few minutes later as she zeroed in on Michael's stitches with the tiny Iris scissors he'd managed to procure from the resident in question.

"Because I decided that I wanted you to take them out. You don't mind, do you?"

She made a face and snipped another hairlike thread. Tim had done a good job. In a few months Michael would hardly be able to tell that he'd ever had stitches here. "I usually prefer to leave my work at the E.R."

She was so close to his face, trying to concentrate on the delicate stitches and finding herself distracted by his eyes. This close they were an even more intense green. Abbie had never had much of a thing about eyes before. Suddenly they seemed the most fascinating part of a man. Of this man, she amended. If she weren't careful, she might just find herself leaning over a little too far and falling right into them.

Once she was able to move beyond Michael's eyes, she saw the strain in his face. The line of his jaw was like steel.

"Did you have a bad night?" she asked, surprised by the protective ache in her chest. She found herself wanting to erase the taut lines on his forehead.

Michael kept very still as he turned his eyes over to her. "I rode the desk. That's boring."

She nodded passively. "You look like you're ready to chew wire."

He shrugged carefully. "I don't like being cooped up. I'll be in a better mood when I'm back on the street."

The street. Something clicked way back in Abbie's brain. She'd helped take care of three street kids who'd come in tonight with knife injuries. Not serious, they were just flexing muscle . . . as one had said with a cocky grin. She wondered if Michael knew them.

"I had a busy night," she admitted. "Full moons and summer heat make for a lot of fun in my business." Snip, snip. "I took care of three fifteen-year-olds who were sharpening their knives on each other. Members of the Blood, I believe. Great jackets."

She'd struck gold. She could see it in the set of his jaw. But evidently Michael wasn't in the mood for confidences.

"Sounds like you had more fun than I did. Are you about finished?"

The message was implicit. No man's land for communication. Abbie wondered why. It obviously bothered him. She wondered whether she should try and get him to open up.

"Swann said that you worked with some of the street gangs."

"Sometimes."

Abbie sighed. She was getting nowhere fast. "There. That's the last one. Want to take a look in the mirror?"

Michael shook his head. "No thanks." He watched her put her instruments away with agile hands and thought how very soft they were. He remembered how refreshing they'd felt against his forehead when she'd cared for him the night he'd been shot. And how disciplined they were in her work. It amazed him that such tools could belong to a woman who sunbathed at night and listened to rock and roll for sedation. It fascinated him.

Sometimes he wished that he could succumb to the healing of those hands, her elegant fingers comforting him as she listened to the frustrations he needed to share. Her eyes would melt, just as he'd seen them do, and she'd understand. Michael needed someone to understand, someone besides Swann and the crowd down at the local watering hole. Someone who wasn't a cop. But no one who wasn't a cop could understand. If there was one thing he'd learned from his marriage, it was that.

"How would you like to see an opera?" he asked with a grin.

Abbie found herself thrown a little off balance. The tension from the unshared problem still radiated from the set of his jaw. But the smile he proffered was open and friendly. And absolutely out of context.

"An opera?" She made a face at him. "I really don't think so."

"Don't be so closed-minded. It's Mozart's *The Magic Flute*. I think you'll like it."

Abbie was far from convinced.

"They're doing it in English," he coaxed.

She shook her head. "I don't care if they did it in the nude. I just don't think I'm opera material."

"You'll never know unless you try."

Abbie couldn't believe this was the conversation she was having. But then again, she had had difficulty believing she was taking out stitches at one in the morning. "I thought the Lyric didn't start its season until September."

His grin broadened. "It doesn't. They're doing a concert version up at Ravinia."

Ravinia. Abbie had been there once. It was an outdoor amphitheatre where the symphony had played a summer season. Well, at least if it got boring she could bring her headset and watch the sky.

"Why?"

He grinned at her. "Because my father decided he couldn't come. Besides, you're still under surveillance, and it would give some of the other guys a night off."

She had to ask. "What if they never catch Marlow?"

"They will."

He seemed so sure. Abbie just knew that she was beginning to long for her privacy. "When?"

"I don't know when they'll catch Marlow. The concert's a week from Saturday."

"I'm going to see the Cubs."

"Fine. We'll go see the Cubs in the afternoon, get some dinner and then go to the opera."

Abbie's expression was dubious. "Ought to be an interesting day." It did occur to her that she was finding it more and more difficult to say no to Michael. He'd begun to cast lines of involvement: the crooked, bright-eyed smile that she waited for like sunrise, the compassion that colored his expression a different shade than most police she knew, the stresses he refused to share.

Something made her want to pull those from him. She wanted to be the one to ease that tightness, the tension he'd carried away with him from work and couldn't seem to unload. And then, she realized without much surprise, she wanted to make slow and deliberate love to him.

His body beckoned to her, the lean lines of it fashioned to fit hers. The scent he wore tickled at her memory when he was away and enticed her when she was with him. Still too close to her, its tang lingered over Michael's skin and evoked dark fires in her belly. Michael would be gentle, she knew, and thorough. And very, very loving. It was in those crystal-green eyes of his. She thought that she could be the one to soothe with her hands the pain that still rested there.

"All right," she conceded, refraining from reaching out to stroke away the new lines he'd brought with him. "You win. One opera won't hook me, I guess."

She was an idiot. But when he smiled she realized that she didn't care—at least for the moment, when his elation stirred such exhilaration in her.

Chapter 6

By Wednesday, Abbie was really beginning to feel the pressure. It wasn't just the fact that Marlow was still out there; the lieutenant had assured her that the situation was under control. But the strain of being followed had gotten worse.

A feeling of claustrophobia haunted Abbie as she walked to work or waited with her friends to catch the bus back home. Somewhere in the shadows, just beyond her reach, there was someone waiting. Someone watching everything she did.

Occasionally, she saw the policemen who constantly kept pace with her, slipping by in a dark sedan or walking past with careful nonchalance as she stepped into the hospital. Sometimes she didn't. They were always there, though. She could always feel their eyes on her.

What she couldn't understand was the disparity of the men she did see. A couple of the men who followed her looked as much like cops as Michael and Swann, all business and wary eyes. But one of the guys she kept seeing looked more like the narcotics officers she'd met in Lt.

Capshaw's office. She guessed everybody was pooling resources for some reason.

What made it all worse was that Michael was unintentionally pressuring her. He'd show up at the Emergency Room on dinner break or take over for the surveillance team when she was jogging through Lincoln Park. Any precious objectivity she'd ever been able to manage with regard to him was beginning to disintegrate. Soon, she knew, she'd have to tell him why she kept discouraging his advances. And soon, she knew, she wouldn't have the strength left to discourage them anymore.

Abbie had never been the kind of doctor who distanced herself from her patients. She refused to get into the habit of referring to them by their complaints and sometimes even called them when they got home to see how they'd done. It made her popular. It also made it more difficult when something went wrong.

When Hector Ramirez was brought in, she knew this would be one of those times. The Bloods, the gang she'd treated a few nights earlier, had finally broken out of their turf and gone after the neighboring gang, Hector's Guerillas. Hector was brought in around dinnertime with a gunshot wound to the chest. Two hours later, he died.

No matter what magic tricks Abbie tried to pull out of her bag, no matter how many surgeons she called in or which stopgap measures she desperately tried, Hector's life slipped steadily away. Abbie couldn't let go of a fifteen-year-old life without feeling some responsibility. She walked away from his grieving family, turned into the staff lounge and began to throw things.

"He didn't make it?"

She whirled around. Intent on venting her anger and frustration, she hadn't seen the quiet figure in the corner of the half-lit room. Michael sat behind her on the couch, coffee cup in hand. He was in uniform and looked very rigid.

"No." She glared, daring him to come closer and offer comfort. If he had, she probably would have hit him. Abbie often desperately needed to vent her anger, but nobody ever respected that. They smothered and coddled and worried over her, and she couldn't stand it.

Michael slowly stood, nodded and approached her. Abbie was about to yell at him when he handed her his own now-empty ceramic mug with the word Sarge imprinted on it.

"Here."

She stared at him. Then at him.

"It has to break to really feel like the throw was worthwhile."

That act deflated all her anger like a spent balloon. She felt herself sagging, the weight of that young life still on her but easier to bear. She held the cup a minute, balancing it in her hands. Then, with a grin of appreciation, she handed it back to Michael.

"Be my guest."

He looked at the cup a minute. Then, with a hurl that would have broken major-league pitching records he heaved the mug. It shattered with an impressive crash that brought a couple of passersby to the door. They got there to find the policeman and the doctor grinning at each other in a silly kind of relief. Then they just closed the door and left.

By the time Abbie got off work that night, she was exhausted and jumpy. The pace had never let up long enough for her to assimilate what had happened between her and Michael, and he had left again before they'd ever had a chance to really discuss it. She did realize that his reaction to Hector's death weighed on her as much as hers. He'd been there for her, had silently done a little venting, but he hadn't talked about what it meant to him, what kind of loss he felt. Abbie knew all too well that this wasn't healthy.

It didn't occur to her that she needn't worry about Michael, or that by wanting to help him she was involving herself even further. She only felt a tight ache in her chest that carried his name as well as her own. She instinctively knew that Michael carried the responsibilities of his work much as she did, and that they suffered equally from it.

She got to the bus stop too late to stand with all the homegoing evening shift. That usually wouldn't have bothered her since it was right next to the side door of the hospital. But lately the shadows had become more ominous, the waiting more tense. A car waited across the street, and two men walked down the sidewalk talking. They were no one she recognized. Someone was there, though, just out of sight. She could feel it. It gave her shivers.

There must be a full moon beyond the cloudy sky, she thought with a disparaging scowl. I'm acting like one of the psych patients who sees FBI agents in the microwave. Even so, she turned to scan the pitch-black alleyway next door, and thought for sure she saw a movement in the impenetrable shadow. Where was that bus? Did it always take this long to get here? Abbie had never realized how vulnerable this spot was.

Another car slowed down at the bus stop and she thought she recognized the driver's face. It was the atypical cop. The one who looked as if he should be staking out drug deals. He smiled briefly. She returned it with some relief. The man waiting across the street observed passively and checked his watch. He must be waiting for somebody to get off duty, she thought.

She was just beginning to feel a returning sense of security when she heard a rustling behind her coming from the alleyway. She whipped around, her heart in her throat.

"What an anachronism. A doctor waiting for a bus."

Michael. Abbie didn't know whether she wanted to kiss him or hit him over the head. Her first impression was that he looked as good as ice in August. He was wearing an open-neck oxford-cloth shirt with the sleeves rolled to his elbows and chinos. The deep shadows cast his face in dramatic geometrics, all clean lines and grace. It made her smile when she didn't want to; the pleasure of seeing him lodging in her chest and radiating a most delicious heat.

"I really wish you'd stop doing that," she protested with feeling. "I'm jumpy enough as it is."

He shrugged agreeably, but Abbie could see that Hector's death had already carved cruel lines along his mouth. "You shouldn't be riding the bus at one in the morning."

"I don't have a car. Would you rather I walked home?"

He grinned. "I thought all doctors drove Mercedes."

She grinned back a little dryly. "I'm saving myself for a Jag. What excuse do you have for being in an alleyway at one in the morning?"

"Relieving Martin. He wanted to go get some doughnuts. I told him I'd baby-sit the pretty young doctor." He made Abbie smile when she hadn't all night.

"The guy in the car?" she asked.

Michael nodded. "Yeah. Let me go tell him to go on."

Abbie looked around for the departed policeman, but couldn't see him. She was just about to ask Michael about it when he strolled across to the waiting car. She opened her mouth to protest.

He was a cop? He was new to her. Michael laughed as he bent over the car, and then straightened up, giving the car door a parting slap. The driver grinned his goodbyes and started the engine.

When Michael returned, she gestured. "I don't know him."

"I know." He took her arm and started her down the street. "We do that on purpose. That way the bad guys don't get a make on the same cop."

There was an undercurrent to tonight's banter. A tension leaped between them. It made Abbie want to pull Michael close to her, to buttress her pain with his strength and salve his with her hands. She just wanted to feel the vitality in him. In old war movies, lovers defied death in each other's arms. She understood why. After having to face the loss of life, she found herself needing to reaffirm her own. She needed to be with Michael tonight because he understood. He'd faced the same loss, suffered the same pain. She was glad he'd appeared in her alley.

"Where do you want to go during Martin's break?" Michael was asking as he helped her into his own car, a vintage midnight-blue Mustang that had seen quite a lot of action in its time.

"Well, what about going for doughnuts ourselves?" Abbie asked. He'd have to pay the penalty for mentioning sugar around her, especially after a bad shift.

Michael slid into his seat and offered her a particularly grim scowl. "I'd rather be shot again."

Abbie showed her surprise. "I thought all cops snacked on doughnuts and coffee. Most nights there are more cop cars at the Donut Hole than at the station."

"Which is why I hate 'em so much. I've ridden with two addicts, Swann and Mendlesohn. If I so much as hear the word cruller, I could get violent."

"All right." She shrugged elaborately. "Be that way." He looked so drawn out, tight as piano wire. The familiar ache ignited in Abbie's chest to battle with the one his nearness set up everywhere else. This is not the time to be aroused, she thought disparagingly; but she was. He looked so handsome in the half-light a streetlamp scattered through the windshield. Damn it, why couldn't life be simple?

"I'll tell you what," she finally offered with careful neutrality. "I have some wine and cheese at my place. You want to stop by for a bit?"

Michael looked over, his eyes betraying the battle in him. Then he nodded and turned the ignition key. "Anything but doughnuts."

Michael wasn't sure why he'd sought out Abbie. Usually he would have been down at the station's favorite bar, the Precinct, rehashing the evening with everyone. He'd have had a few drinks too many and told bad jokes and traded stories. And then he would have gone home alone to deal with Hector's death.

But tonight, for some reason, he couldn't bring himself to walk into that smoky, frantic place. He didn't think he could find enough solace in any amount of liquor or relief in false cheer. The idea of returning to that empty apartment where his only entertainment would be to sit in front of the TV and think about what had gone down didn't appeal to him at all.

He'd found himself, instead, at the hospital. Waiting for Abbie.

He hadn't been able to get her out of his mind. Her soft, fragrant body, her electric eyes that had slashed at him with such fierce intensity when she'd come upon him in the lounge. She'd fought Hector's death as if it had been a personal adversary, and had mourned him as if he'd been her child. The lady had guts, he thought. She had class.

It surprised him how much he wanted to just hold her. Not necessarily to say anything. Not to rehash or boast or joke. Just feel that incredibly life-filled body in his arms. God, he thought, I haven't felt like this in too long. It scares the hell out of me.

"First of all, I want to say thank you." Abbie gave Michael a glass of Vouvray and curled up next to him on the couch.

Michael's eyebrows went up. "You're welcome. For what?"

"Not...hovering when I was in the lounge. I needed to scream and you let me."

He shrugged. "It wasn't that much."

Abbie shook her head as she sipped at the liquid in her glass. "Oh, yes it was," she disagreed with feeling. "More than you know."

Michael looked over to see her expression colored by something she had to look inward to see. Her eyes were clouded with it, her face just a little slack. He had a feeling she was reliving the chaos in the E.R. tonight. What he'd seen of it had been bad.

Without realizing it, Michael settled a little closer and easily wrapped an arm around her shoulders. They were stiff, as if better to brace herself against what she saw. He bent down and brushed gentle lips against her cheek.

Abbie hadn't even noticed herself easing into the comfort of Michael's hold. It had been enough to feel the solid warmth of his body against hers, the unspoken support of his arm around her. The touch of his lips against her brought tears.

"There is nothing worse," she said very quietly, her voice trembling with the effort to stay calm, "than walking up to the parents of a child and taking away their future."

With gentle hands Michael put the wineglasses aside, and then eased Abbie into his arms, his head close over hers. She talked on, her words sporadic and angry, the pictures she painted those of desperate frustration.

Michael felt her trembling against him, felt the warmth of the tears that splashed against his chest. He didn't answer, didn't offer advice, didn't deny the rage she brought him. He knew what that rage felt like. It boiled in him, too. Worse. Abbie hadn't known Hector.

When she ran out of words, Abbie closed her eyes and leaned against Michael, letting his strength seep into her. For that moment, safe in his arms, she couldn't imagine having to forfeit them again.

"Better?"

Abbie nodded with a rueful grin. "Been a while since I've cried like that." She turned her streaked face up to him with a smile. "Thanks." When she saw his face, she stopped.

There was a war waging behind that concerned expression. Abbie could see it as easily as if Michael were shouting at her. His eyes seemed to melt when they met hers, the pain he felt and his concern for her fusing in that soft green. He seemed to be holding his breath, torn by what he needed and what he feared. It was the same terrible conflict Abbie recognized in herself.

God, she needed him so much. She hurt for him, and she hurt for herself. More than anything, she was terrified.

"Michael?" Unbidden, her hand lifted to his cheek. She could feel the taut muscles beneath, the cost of control.

Her action paralyzed him. He found himself wanting to confide in her. To tell her what had gone on out there tonight and what it was costing him. There was such a guileless compassion in those eyes. But he was afraid. The rage in him burned black and ugly, swelling out from the battlefield he had to face every day. Michael didn't want the pictures he carried in his mind to drive Abbie away as they'd driven Maria away. Abbie wasn't a cop. She didn't live with it, surviving minute by minute out there, enduring the cancerous frustration. She didn't understand. How could she possibly survive?

For a moment, Michael didn't answer. He simply held Abbie's gaze as if he could draw from her what he needed without words. Then he shook his head a little. "I think it's just about time to take the lieutenant up on his offer of a desk" was all he could say.

Talk to me, she wanted to beg. Please, let me give you what you gave me. Let me help carry the pain. She couldn't think of a way to make him do it, though. She commanded his eyes and knew that he wanted to confide in her, and yet he wouldn't. Somewhere during his life, Michael had been taught that it wasn't wise to allow the sharing of that kind of suffering. And that made him suffer more.

Unable to think of any other way to ease the anguish she saw in Michael's face, she raised her lips to his mouth. Instinctively, he bent to her. She kissed his lips, his cheeks and the line of his jaw where the tension radiated. She kissed his eyes shut and then returned to claim his mouth.

His arms gathered her to him. She tasted the salt of his skin and the soft flavor of wine on his lips. Seeking to ease his pain, she discovered her passion.

Michael brought his hands up to her face, cupping it to him as he returned her kisses, his lips lingering over her closed eyes. He tangled his hands in her hair and pulled her tight against him. The soft urgency of Michael's lips ignited a hot, thrilling pain that flared along her limbs and settled in her belly. She drew closer, knowing that Michael was the source of the heat, and that the heat was healing. Her breasts stiffened against the solid planes of his chest. She felt his hand drift from her hair and took hold of it with her own. His hands were so strong, so capable and callused. They were hands that worked hard, yet cradled compassion like a rare gift. Abbie wanted to feel those hands against her skin; needed to bring them—to bring Michael—to her where he could find the sweet oblivion of her passion.

Michael turned her hand over and brought his mouth down to it. Gently, so very gently, he kissed first her fingers and then the tender palm. When he brought his eyes up to hers, he saw her tears and bent to kiss those, too.

Abbie's heart started to skid again, battling the pounding of Michael's against hers. It pulled the breath from her and sapped the strength from her limbs. She brought his mouth back to hers.

There was such a sweetness, such a hungering intimacy, as their tongues danced in among soft, deep recesses. Abbie felt Michael's tension ease with her fingers and tasted his need with her mouth. His hand swept along her throat, searching, savoring, his fingertips trailing an even hotter fire. She shuddered with dreadful anticipation.

Michael's fingers found her breast. Hesitantly, hungrily, they sparked rippling chills that only served to feed the flames. Abbie arched closer, aching for the rasp of his fingers against her skin.

She let her own hands search, sliding along Michael's shoulders in to the hollow of his throat. Her fingers tickled against the hair that curled along his chest.

Michael's hand lifted then and dipped, slipping down beneath cotton and silk. His hand cupped her breast, eliciting a surprised sigh from her. His fingers, trapped warm and snug against her skin, followed the throbbing of her heartbeat. His thumb coaxed her nipple to tingling hardness. His mouth surrounded hers and drank in her soft moans. Resting her hands along his throat, she trapped the quiver of his pulse with her fingers.

The molten delight of him coursed through her. The sweet urgency of his embrace drew her. Their pain softened and lost shape within the enclosure of each other's arms. Then Abbie let her hand stray just a little too far.

She jerked upright, by turns shocked, dismayed and repulsed.

"Abbie?" Michael drew his hand away. His eyes were still steeped in passion, languid and smoky. He looked more puzzled than upset.

Abbie turned to face his confusion, her own heartbeat still matching his.

He wasn't sure what do. "What's wrong?"

"Michael," she began, feeling very uncomfortable. "I'm not sure how to ask this, but...well, are you glad to see me, or is that a gun in your pocket?"

Michael's straight face lasted all of thirty seconds. Then he burst out laughing.

"I'm serious," she insisted, her mouth compressed for fear of catching the urge. She knew she'd lose before she ever spoke. "This is important."

"I am glad to see you," he managed, and then broke down again. It took him a minute to get to the rest. "And yes, that is a gun in my pocket."

He pulled it out, still laughing. It was a small piece, probably foreign, and very lethal looking. Michael held it out with two fingers and then dropped it on the table.

"Stop that," Abbie insisted, the chuckles already bubbling up in her even as the sight of the gun made her want to flinch.

"I can't help it," he gasped. "You really know how to break up a party."

She giggled. "I didn't bring a gun."

"You brought it up."

"It's kind of hard to ignore."

He laughed even harder. "I thought I'd made a bigger impression than that."

"Michael, you don't understand." She tried again, conversation getting more difficult with the silly laughter that cascaded through the two of them. She found herself help-

lessly shaking her head. "Talk about your tension break-
ers."

"I'm a cop," Michael announced, trying to keep a
straight face long enough to display mock severity. "My gun
is my life."

Abbie hit him with a pillow. She was as out of control as
he was now, wiping her own tears and holding her sides.
"Put that thing away."

Wrong thing to say. Michael dissolved all over again. "I
assume you mean the gun."

Abbie pointed halfheartedly at the offending weapon as
she joined him. "If you knew how psychotic I was about
those things, you wouldn't be so cavalier about it." Somehow the threat got lost amid the giggles.

"Well, you'd better damn well tell me," he warned, "because I can't see the police department doing away with guns
for a while."

Abbie succeeded in reining herself in then. The laughter
between them began to ebb as she considered Michael,
trying to gauge what his reaction would be.

"Oh, all right." She finally surrendered. "But don't say
I didn't warn you." Searching the space beyond Michael for
inspiration, she tried her best to ignore how very much depended on his understanding.

"Should I get popcorn?" Michael smiled softly.

She managed a small grin in return. "More like No-Doz."

All the same, Michael slipped his arm back around her
shoulder. She appreciated it. Even with the silliness still
buoying her, this wasn't Abbie's favorite story hour. She
reached over to retrieve her wine and spent a moment sipping it. Michael held his peace.

"It's late," she told him after a moment. "I'll give you
the *Reader's Digest* version."

He shook his head. "You'll give me the whole thing."

She shrugged. "You asked for it." Then, with a final sip,
set off on her story. The unabridged version. "One day
when I was fourteen, I walked into our local grocery store.
It was when we lived on the south side of the city. Anyway,

while I was there, two guys storm in with big guns and ski masks to rob the place. When the police showed up at a wrong moment, a fourteen-year-old girl turned out to be a useful hostage.''

She looked over to see that she had Michael's complete attention. She didn't see any pity, though—only understanding. Going on wasn't as difficult. "I spent an unforgettable eight hours with the gentlemen in question," she continued, eyes back on her wine. "Then the police decided to play a little decoy game. They sent two officers in— one to negotiate, the other to surprise the robbers and get me free." Now that the second robbery was behind her, the pictures had once again dimmed, the terrors slipping back into the shadows where they belonged. If it weren't for Michael, she could have gotten on with her life again.

"Only the officer who was supposed to get you free got killed," he offered.

Abbie nodded, her eyes closed, her chest rising in shallow, rapid movements as she remembered. "It's funny how similar the two setups were. He was hit in the head. Went down right next to the robber. But he never got up." Finally, the pain surfaced in her voice. "He was married and had two little kids."

Michael's voice was incredibly gentle, a reassuring caress. "And you blamed yourself for what happened."

She shrugged a bit helplessly. "His wife did the honors for me. I decided that I had to go to the funeral home, and she came at me like one of the Furies. Said that if it hadn't been for me, her husband would still be alive. Which, of course, made perfect sense to me at the time."

Michael drew her a little closer. "Sounds like it was bad."

Opening her eyes away from the faces she could still see, Abbie nodded. "It was awful. Fourteen is not the best age to deal with guilt."

"And that's why you don't date cops?"

She couldn't face him with her answer. This was the admission that hurt them both. "Cops get killed. I saw what that does to people. I don't want any part of it."

"Not all cops get killed."

She grinned ruefully. "I know that. Here." She pointed to her head. "But here—" she touched her heart "—is not so rational. Every time *you* get too close, it screams, 'get me an accountant!'"

At least they could both grin about it. Abbie was thankful that she'd finally told Michael. Far from reacting with that smothering pity that so imprisoned her, he'd met the story with pragmatic empathy. She felt as if he'd released her from the years of hiding.

She was also glad they'd opened it up now. They were both in the mood for handling it with all the respect it deserved, which to Abbie was none. She had never had any patience with her own neuroses.

Michael dropped a soft kiss to her forehead. "Yeah, well, I can understand why. Is there any way I can help?"

"Short of becoming an accountant?"

He grinned. "Short of becoming an accountant."

Abbie considered. "I don't know. I want to say just understand, but I don't know if that's enough. I really don't know if I want to get involved." She sighed. "Which stinks, because I..." I'm falling in love? she thought. God, I am. Fast, hard and hopeless. The realization ignited fresh pain. "I care for you an awful lot. You're just such a...cop."

"I'm sorry." She was glad he was still smiling. "I wish I were altruistic enough to say I'd respect your wishes and back off. But I can't." The humor faded a little with the effort of telling a truth that Abbie was still too scared to speak. "I have the most uncomfortable feeling that I'm falling in love with you."

Abbie turned to trap that truth in his eyes. She saw a rueful smile, as if the admission were one that surprised even Michael. And she saw a sweet tenderness that pierced her, the immobility of a past pain that imbued his words with courage.

I want to love you, too, Michael, she thought—sure he could see the conflict in her own eyes. I wish I had the courage you have to at least admit it. Her eyes strayed to the still-ragged slash along his temple, a graphic reminder of the price of involvement, a fresh memory that robbed what strength she had. She found herself relying on a wan smile.

"You've got your uncomfortable feelings mixed up."

He smiled back. "No such luck."

"Which means, I suppose, that you're not going to do the noble thing and vanish from my life so I don't have a collapse over you."

"You've been hanging around doctors too long," he retorted with laughing eyes that cushioned the truth they skirted with their humor. "There's nothing noble about cops."

Abbie laughed at that. "You've been hanging around cops too long. There's nothing noble about doctors, either." She summoned her own courage to go on. "Well—" she sighed elaborately, "—if you're going to hang around, do you think you could at least do something with that gun?"

"And what do I tell the lieutenant when we have inspection?" he grinned. "Sorry, sir, Abbie had me make my gun into a lamp?"

She grinned back with a shake of her head. "It's not when you're in uniform so much that the gun bothers me—the whole *uniform* bothers me, the gun's just part of it. But when you're in civvies, I can almost forget that you're…you know." The tension of their admissions seemed to dissipate just a little with the bantering. Abbie guessed that it was the way they were going to have to handle it from now on. "Do you really have to wear it all the time?"

"I'm supposed to. And with all this going on, I just feel better having it on around you."

"But I have all those baby-sitters," she protested. "Surely two guys on a shift can do enough."

Michael stopped. "Two guys?"

"Sure. Like tonight."

He shook his head. "There was only Martin."

Abbie straightened, unease tickling her stomach. "What about that other guy? The one who looks like he works narcotics."

"Who are you talking about?" Michael asked very carefully. "Nobody from narcotics is working this job."

"But he is," Abbie insisted. "I see him all the time."

For a moment, they sat very still. Then Michael took Abbie's hand and retrieved her glass. "I think you have some mug books to look at, Ab."

"Wait."

He'd stood, but turned back to the tight fear in Abbie's voice.

"I know how you can help," she said, her stark eyes focused on the gun he'd picked up, her resolution already forgotten.

Michael sat back down and took her hand. "I can't leave the gun here, Abbie."

"No." She shook her head, the insistence one of urgency. Of making him understand. "Be careful. Just promise that no matter what, you'll be careful."

For a moment Michael looked bemused. Then, facing Abbie without reservation, he nodded. "I promise."

Abbie looked at the sincerity on that face and believed him. She should have known better.

Chapter 7

Abbie decided that she was spending far too much time at the police station these days. It had gotten to the point where the desk sergeant greeted her by name when she walked in. Swann no longer felt compelled to escort her when Michael was busy, and no one so much as looked up when she served herself coffee from the station pot. She had the feeling that one of these days, she was going to find a ceramic mug hanging alongside the others with the inscription Doc on it.

She'd spent the better part of the previous night back on the mug books, succeeding in scaring up a headache and not much else. Michael had even made her go through a police file. The man she'd mistaken for a cop hadn't been in any of them. At least she didn't think so. After your hundredth out-of-focus black-and-white picture, everybody started looking like the same bored suspect. Even the cops.

When Lt. Capshaw had found out about the late-night session, he had requested a return engagement for both of them before Abbie went in to work. So once again she sat outside waiting for Michael to finish consulting with the powers that be. Only this time she did it alone. Swann had been on the invitation list.

A lot had happened since the last time she'd sat staring at that nameplate. She thought about the savage delight Michael had awakened the night before, the laughter they'd used to fend off desperation, the simple understanding with which he'd met her story. It should have made her feel better. She realized, at least, that her secrets were safe with Michael, her traumas cared for without suffocation. He delighted her and cherished her. But the fact that he carried a gun when he came to her apartment terrified her to tears.

He was a policeman. Not all policemen were killed, exactly as he'd said. Enough were, her irrational subconscious said. Just enough that you would spend your waking hours waiting for the worst, dreading even the sound of the phone. Even the time she spent in the station with him was tearing her apart, because she saw how much he loved what he was. How he excelled at it. How he would never understand when she asked him to give it up.

Rubbing absently at the new fire that gnawed her stomach, Abbie sipped coffee and made it worse. She watched the closed door, wondering how she could ever get up the nerve to tell Michael she just wasn't going to see him again.

"He's not one of Marlow's people," the DEA man was saying on the other side of the door. The positions were virtually identical, with Swann joining the narcotics guys on the chairs.

"A free-lancer, maybe?" Michael asked.

No one seemed to know.

"Well, whoever he is, he's been tailing Abbie. She's seen him four or five times in the last few days."

Lt. Capshaw turned to the narcotics officers. "Sound familiar to you guys?"

They weren't very helpful either. Swann consulted his fingernails. "Should we bring him in?"

"And let him know we've made him?" the DEA man demanded. "No. He hasn't made a move for her. He's just watching."

Michael shot him a look of disdain. "Were you always this considerate, or did it take a lot of training?"

Capshaw scowled. "Viviano..."

"You're putting her at risk for the sake of one drug bust."

"The biggest bust this city's ever seen," the DEA man snapped back.

Michael's eyes widened. "Well, the DEA does need all the good publicity it can get." Without waiting for a rebuttal, he turned to the lieutenant. "Since nobody else seems to give a damn about Dr. Fitzgerald, how 'bout giving me a little time off, and I'll stick to her?"

"Getting a little too involved here, aren't you, Viviano?" DEA asked, with only a slight air of distaste.

"That's all right," Michael answered evenly. "It balances out you guys. You aren't involved enough."

"She has surveillance," Capshaw retorted.

"Yeah, and they let this guy through."

"You can't, Viviano." The lieutenant sought inspiration in his desktop for a moment, which was unusual for him. Michael threw a look at Swann who met it with neutral eyes. "You might have jeopardized her already." Michael turned back to see that the lieutenant was dead serious. "Mr. Magnusson here informed us this morning that things are heating up with Marlow. He's getting jumpy enough to talk putting a hit on you."

Michael waited for the rest.

"It's a good sign," the DEA man was saying. "It means that the deal is going down soon, and he doesn't want you screwing it up."

"Marlow's a penny-ante operator," Michael protested instinctively. "A hit's out of his league."

"So is this deal."

Michael finished the logic to its conclusion. "And if you pull me off the street, he'll know we've been yanking his chain."

Mr. Magnusson of the DEA nodded his head, anticipation bubbling up. "It would be the whole game. Our man on the inside is holding him in check so far, but we can't predict this guy. We can keep an eye on him though. We'll know when he puts it out.''

"And the doctor?"

There was no equivocation in his answer. "You have to stay away from her. Especially if you want her safe."

Michael took a moment to walk over to the lieutenant's window. There was nothing to see out of the grime and wire, but at least he wasn't facing the vulture in that three-piece suit.

"Swann?"

"Done."

Michael nodded to himself. Whatever else, Abbie would be watched more closely than Swann's own kids. Michael thought of how afraid she'd be if she knew what he was letting Magnusson talk him into. There was nothing he could do about it, though. This was his job. He could pretty well take care of himself—as long as he knew that she was safe.

"Just keep her out of it," he said.

"All right." The lieutenant nodded beside him. "Would you like a few minutes to explain this all to Dr. Fitzgerald?"

"No." Michael turned to him, his eyes intense. "She doesn't need to know what's going on. This has been bad enough on her already."

When the room had cleared of everyone but Lt. Capshaw, Swann and Michael, the lieutenant shut the door and turned to them. "He's right, Viviano," he said simply. "You are a little too involved."

"We kinda took care of that just now," Michael countered without much inflection, "didn't we, Lieutenant?"

"What I want to know is, should I yank you off this completely before you get yourself in trouble?"

Michael nodded with understanding. "A cop who doesn't pay attention is a buried cop." It was one of the lieutenant's favorite expressions. "I'll do my job. I just didn't want Abbie lost in Magnusson's damn bureaucratic shuffle."

Capshaw appraised him for a minute with severe eyes. Then he nodded. "All right. But no heroics. And no screwups, understand?"

Michael flashed a crooked grin. "You're too good to me."

The lieutenant flashed one right back. "I know. Now, if you don't mind, I'm going to invite Dr. Fitzgerald in and explain that we'd like to ignore the bad guy tailing her."

Swann drove Abbie to work. Michael said that he had to stay and clear some things up before his shift. Abbie had said goodbye to him with the nagging feeling that something was wrong. Over the next few days, the feeling got progressively worse.

It began when she got off duty to find that Michael wasn't waiting for her. He didn't show up the next morning when she huffed and puffed through Lincoln Park, nor did he call during dinner break. Abbie found herself looking over her shoulder for him, and starting when she saw the blue uniform shirt or the checker-banded police hats peculiar to Chicago.

Since she'd discovered that the shaggy-looking guy following her wasn't a cop, she had ended up with two babysitters on each shift, and a rented car to keep her off the bus. She'd seen them all there waiting for her—the two policemen and the bad guy they wanted to leave on the streets in hopes he'd lead them to Marlow. She'd seen Swann at least once a day. But she had not seen Michael.

At first she was puzzled. She couldn't begin to understand why Michael had suddenly disappeared from her life, especially after what he'd said to her that night in her apartment. Then, even though she had just finished telling herself that it would be much better for her not to see Michael again anyway, she was angry.

Just what did he think he was pulling, anyway? It would have been one thing to come to her and say, "Abbie, maybe we'd better cool things off for a while." After all, maybe his time and attention were taken up by his work again. Michael worked his streets the way she worked her hallways. There was no leaving them there and going home. She understood and respected that. But it was another matter entirely to simply disappear and not say why.

For Michael's part, he was getting so hard to live with after five days of separation from Abbie that the entire precinct was taking bets on just how long it would take him to explode. There was no bet on who the intended victim was to be. Everybody involved already knew.

When Michael came too close to losing Swann's bet, the black detective treated him to an after-hours visit to the Precinct.

The bar was a madhouse that Thursday night. Michael and Swann threaded their way through the crowds to a battered old table in the back where they could nurse their drinks in peace.

Michael carried a triple Scotch straight up, knowing even that wouldn't douse the fire in his gut tonight. He hated lying to Abbie, hated not seeing her. But nothing would have been worse than seeing her hurt because he couldn't stay away from her.

Abbie's surprise tail had been spotted almost immediately, with everybody not tied down trying to figure out where he came from. An ex-con from Joliet, he was a skinny, greasy-looking guy with pock-marked skin and a fancy for knives. So far he hadn't made contact with anybody but a waitress down at a local greasy spoon. Magnusson preached patience, and Michael had none.

"You almost lost yourself some hard-earned stripes tonight," Swann offered from the other side of a beer.

Michael impatiently waved aside the concern. "Magnusson needs a leash."

"I don't care what his mother bayed at," Swann conceded. "He's still the man with the plan. And we're just the defensive line."

"I'm not in the mood for metaphors, Swann."

Swann shook his head slowly. "If you're this bad after only being away from her for five days, do us all a favor.

The minute this is wrapped up, drag her off and marry her before she realizes what she's getting herself into.''

"It's not just being away. It's not knowing if she's all right.''

"She's all right.''

Michael sipped at the amber liquid in his glass and thought about the past few days. He'd had a lot to contend with, between the new tension among the gangs and trying to work his beat with an eye constantly over his shoulder for the bad guy Magnusson was so sure was under control.

He'd tried to deal with it all the same way he had for the past twelve years. He worked his shift, gathered with his friends at the Precinct, pitched the odd softball game for the police team. Then he'd go home alone to his apartment, just as he had almost every other night for the past five years. It was a routine that had worked well enough for him in the past.

But this week had been different. Like the prisoner who gets his first taste of sunlight, he'd met Abbie and begun to depend on her. It wasn't just that she set off such a reaction in him, although just the sound of her voice generated shock waves. She had invited his confidence, offered a comfort he'd never known in a woman's arms. Now, when the stress got to him, he found himself thinking of her. The old routines that had gotten him by for so long just didn't seem to work anymore.

If she were kept safe, he thought, then this whole song-and-dance act he was doing would be worthwhile. But if she were hurt in any way because of Magnusson's monumental ego, Michael swore that the smarmy DEA desk jock was going to pay for it.

"All I have to say," he finally said with a frustrated sigh, "is that Magnusson damn well better wrap this up soon. I've just about had it with him.''

"Men should be shot," Abbie snarled at work the next night. She didn't stop to consider the fact that one of the group she addressed was Phoebe Turner, the cop's wife.

Abbie had gotten a message on her answering machine that Michael was going to have to cancel their Saturday plans. He hadn't been available when she'd called back to ask about it.

"Nice to see you in such a good mood, Abbie," someone cracked.

Abbie scowled. Michael's behavior was crawling around in her belly like an unwanted snake. There was something she didn't like at all about it, and she didn't want to even consider what it was.

"You wouldn't have been talking about Michael Viviano, would you?" Phoebe asked a little while later as she and Abbie sat alone over dinner. Abbie hadn't planned it that way, but when she looked up at the patient understanding in the older woman's eyes, she was glad.

"You know Michael?" Abbie asked cautiously.

Phoebe smiled with a nod. "Sure. He's a real honey. Did he do something wrong?"

Abbie didn't know what to say. There was so much whirling around in her that needed to be said, and so much that couldn't be said to Phoebe. But if not her, who else?

Finally, she shrugged. "He stood me up for a date tomorrow. Nothing earth-shattering."

"From what Ralph says, you two are the talk of the station," Phoebe said, smiling. "The Doc and the Sarge. They say Michael's turned into a regular white knight over you."

Abbie felt her stomach take a plunge. Everyone saw it, then.

Phoebe's next question was directed with just a hint of protective determination. "What do you think about him?"

Abbie was surprised by the rueful little smile she had to offer. "He scares the hell out of me."

What surprised her even more was that Phoebe nodded right back with recognition. "He definitely redefines the word dedication when it comes to his job," she commiserated. "Which in a cop can border on obsession." Her smile broadened. "Of course, you're the same way about medicine, so you have the advantage of understanding. Most women don't have that edge in dealing with their..." She faltered a moment. She was about to assume too much and say "husbands." Instead, she shrugged with a half apology and went back to her salad.

"What was the hardest for you to deal with?" Abbie asked before she had the chance to chicken out. "With Ralph, I mean."

Phoebe considered a moment. "That, I guess. I was never a fanatic about nursing, ya know. But since I've spent most of my career in the E.R., I can understand the down side of what cops face. The most common complaint they give about spouses is that they feel they can't confide in them—only in other cops, because they have to deal with so many awful things. Since I deal with a lot of the same kind of rotten behavior Ralph does, he never feels he can't tell me what he sees and feels."

"I understand that Michael's wife was... like that."

Phoebe rolled her eyes. "Oh, the worst. I don't know who she thought she was getting when she married Michael. Maybe somebody who did crowd control at the theater and arrested purse snatchers. She flat-out told him that she didn't want him to bring any of his work home. No sordid little stories from the street, no bad moods." The shake of Phoebe's head was frustrated. "Poor Michael. I don't know how he survived her. She finally left him for a dentist. I'm sure she's wildly happy now, talking about tooth decay and dentures."

Abbie couldn't help a chuckle at the unknown woman's expense. She liked Phoebe's attitude that "only real women can marry police." But it didn't answer her most pressing question. What about the fear?

Abbie wasn't sure whether it was just Phoebe's day for ESP, or whether her own expression was so telling, but Phoebe returned to the subject with deadly aim.

"But after the way you two met, I have a feeling those weren't your top priorities."

Abbie proffered another rueful grin. "Tied for dead last, I'd say."

Phoebe cocked her head a little, her soft brown eyes brighter. "Then you *are* ..." Her smile made the rest of the message implicit.

"If I weren't," Abbie retorted with even more honest eyes, "I wouldn't be so scared."

Phoebe nodded, as if coming to a decision. Then she leaned forward, her message from one woman who loved a policeman to another. "I'm not saying it's easy at first," she admitted. "But it's something you learn. Can you imagine Michael doing anything else?"

Abbie shook her head, a small smile giving away her thoughts about accountants.

Phoebe nodded again. "There is nothing worse than having to give up doing what you really love." Even closer, her eyes punctuated her next words. "Nothing. It's a trade-off. I'd rather Ralph died doing something that gave him real purpose in life than have him die a slower death by giving up what he loves for me."

Abbie found that for just a moment she had to look away. Come on, she thought to herself, sink in where it counts. You know damn well she's right.

Phoebe spoke up again and forced Abbie's attention back. "Even after what happened that day of the robbery, would you quit being an E.R. doc?"

Abbie's reaction was an instinctive shake of the head. "It's the only medicine I like."

Phoebe shrugged with a knowing grin. "Well, if you think about it, you were in much more danger than Michael. He's trained and armed for that kind of situation, but somebody here will undoubtedly face it again. Maybe by being untrained for that, we have the more dangerous job."

Abbie smiled back. Her relief was gained from the knowledge that she could always come to Phoebe for support if she needed it. But a fresh fear was born from the knowledge that Michael had been sincere. And that if he had, he wouldn't have just left her at the station and walked off without explanation.

"Abbie, you're in the news again."

Abbie and Phoebe looked up to see Beth Sommers drop her tray alongside theirs. The young nurse settled into her seat before continuing. "Your friend the sergeant is getting his memory back. The press wanted to know if you'd heard the same thing he did. Did he have memory loss? I don't remember that."

"Heard what same thing he did?" Abbie's stomach lurched. The situation had just changed again, and she wasn't sure in what direction.

Beth shrugged. "Beats me. Something the guy they shot said before he died."

Beth was intent upon asking more questions about the sergeant's faulty memory, but Abbie was already on her way out the door to the telephone.

"Swann, what's going on?" she demanded.

"Doc?"

"You're damn right it's the doc." She stood at the lounge phone seething. "Since nobody bothered to fill me in on the latest chapter in this fiction, you want to tell me what I'm supposed to have heard during the robbery? The only things I remember were some vague threats and a request for transportation."

"Nothing."

"Then what was Michael supposed to have heard?"

There was a pause. "If anybody asks you, just say you don't remember hearing anything."

Why did that make her so much more frightened? "I want to talk to Michael, Swann."

"Well, talk to him."

"He won't answer my calls. You want to tell me why not?"

Another pause. Abbie became very still. "I'll get him to call you, okay?"

Michael called just as Abbie was about to head home for the night. Abbie snuck back into the lounge where nobody ever had the time to lounge, and sat down.

"Are you all right?" she asked without preamble.

"Stitches are healing just fine," he answered without noticeable stress.

Abbie took a long breath to calm down. Her reactions were so irrational to this that she had to make sure she handled it as calmly as she could. "Then what's this about our missing our big date tomorrow?"

"It's unavoidable. Department canceled my day off."

"Call in sick. Everybody does when the Cubs are playing."

Abbie heard a pause, and found that she was gripping the telephone more tightly. She didn't know what she wanted Michael to say. Whatever it was, he didn't say it. "I can't."

"Has that been the problem all week?"

Another pause. Abbie had enough time to envision Michael as he spoke, his uniform drawn over his lean frame with crisp creases, his cap lined up low over his eyes. Just the picture ignited the vivid sensation of his fingers over her skin. She stiffened against the pain that brought.

"More or less. I'm afraid I'm going to be pretty busy for a while yet." She didn't see that Michael stood as rigidly, rubbing the strain from his forehead with trembling fingers. Nor did she see Swann standing behind him to offer support. "Okay?"

"No!" Her reaction was instinctive. "Michael, what's going on? You're avoiding me, and I want to know why."

"You're the one who doesn't want to get involved with cops."

"Don't give me that." How could he be so calm when she was so upset? He was hurting her, and Michael was not the kind of man to hurt anybody. "Tell me the truth."

"The truth," he answered wearily after another pause, "is that I've been putting in overtime with the Bloods and Guerrillas. When things settle down a little, I'll call you."

"What about this deathbed confession you were privy to?"

"Oh, that." His voice sounded disparaging. "Don't worry about it. The detectives cooked it up when they were bored."

"But it doesn't make any sense."

"It will. Don't worry, Ab. Everything's under control."

Then why did she still feel so afraid for him? "I saw that guy again today."

"I know," he answered quietly. "So did your escorts. There's nothing to worry about."

Abbie spent a moment in silent frustration. She wasn't getting anywhere with him. Damn him. Damn all cops for having such a secretive attitude. When she spoke again, it was with resignation. "Okay. I'll expect to hear from you soon."

"Do you want to?"

He surprised a hesitant smile out of her. "Yes."

"Soon, then. Everything's all right, okay?"

"Okay."

Abbie hung up the phone and stared for a long time at the wall, wondering why she had to fight tears. Because, she thought, she didn't believe him. Everything wasn't all right, and no one would tell her why. And if anything happened to Michael, she honestly didn't know what she'd do.

At the station, Michael held the phone for a minute after Abbie had hung up. Then he hurled the receiver from him and walked away.

There had to be a better way to spend Saturday night. Abbie hadn't noticed it so much before, but she didn't do that much on her days off. She jogged—but that was punishment for the sweets she ate—and she went to see the Cubs. One or other of her brothers often stopped by to take her out. But tonight they were all busy, as her friends were, as she was supposed to have been. She found herself left in an empty apartment, a heavy-metal marathon on the stereo and a quart of Häagen-Dasz in hand. A lot of very unsettling thoughts about Michael impelled her.

He'd sounded fine on the phone. Why was she so sure he wasn't? And why, after knowing him such a short time, should that really matter so much to her? Abbie paced back and forth licking chocolate chocolate-chip from a spoon and conjuring up Michael on the couch again. Back in her arms.

She couldn't believe how very perfectly they'd fitted together. It was as if someone had gone to the trouble of tailoring them to enfold her as perfectly as a crisp blue-uniform shirt. Even more, she couldn't believe how the memory of his touch still quickened through her like heat lightning. Her pace faltered a moment, her eyes closing against the certainty that grew so inexorably in her.

How long had she known him now? Just how quickly could a person really fall in love?

For a mind trained in science, it didn't make any sense. There had to be precedent and reason and recognizable patterns. There had been in her other relationships. But Michael... She had never known a man with such sweet eyes or such clever hands. He was the only person who instinctively knew when to come close but respected her need for room. He gave such a damn about what he did. And he brought humor and strength to her like beautiful gifts.

But he was a cop.

He was a cop.

Abbie hurled her spoon at the far wall and watched with some satisfaction as it left a brown splotch on the cream paint. Then she shook her head and walked in to get the rag to clean it up. Even Van Halen wasn't helping tonight.

She tried the TV next, but the only thing on was the news, and she was on that again. It was a bigger bore than cleaning ice cream. As she had an eye on a piece about city development the buzzer went off. She half turned to the sound, wondering who could possibly be downstairs at this time of night. It sounded again. She gave the TV screen one last look before answering, and froze.

For just a split second, she thought she saw Marlow on the screen. Maybe not Marlow, she thought. Maybe just someone who looked like his well-suited twin. Her heart leaped with recognition at the face of a man who stood at the back of a crowd on the steps at city hall. But then he was gone, and the buzzer sounded again.

"Yes?" she said into the intercom.

"Dr. Fitzgerald? It's Officer Dixon. I, uh, need to talk to you. About Sgt. Viviano."

Abbie stopped cold, suddenly unable to breathe. "Michael? Is something wrong?"

"I'm afraid so."

Without thinking about anything else, Abbie buzzed the officer up.

The Donut Hole was crowded with people out trying to get their Sunday doughnuts a little early. At the counter, a middle-aged officer laughed with the salesclerk as he paid for a bag of crullers and two cups of coffee. Out in the lot, his partner watched the Saturday-night crowd with tired eyes and took a last drag from his cigarette before flipping it out the window.

He had just reached for the gearshift, anticipating his friend's return, when the radio came to life.

"All units in the vicinity. Report of a possible 211 at 323 Fullerton. Officer requests backup."

Michael froze in his seat. Three twenty-three Fullerton. That was Abbie's address. Oh, God, no.

"Mendlesohn, move!" he yelled out the window, throwing the idling car into gear and hitting the lights and siren.

Mendlesohn tumbled into the other seat as Michael spun the vehicle into traffic. "What's up?"

"Abbie."

"It's out of our district, Michael."

Whipping in between two cars waiting at a light, Michael swung onto Clark and headed north. Mendlesohn was hanging on to the open window for support.

"If you'd rather, I'll let you off here."

Mendlesohn shook his head with grim determination as he picked up the mike. "Let me just tell them where we'll be."

Chapter 8

When Michael pulled the car up before Abbie's building, just about every other cop on the North Side was already there. The street throbbed with flashing lights and the chatter of radios. He didn't bother to wait for Mendlesohn before he jumped out and ran for the building's open door.

A knot of policemen filled the small lobby. "What happened?" Michael demanded.

"Don't know, Sarge," one of them answered. "We just got here. I hear some perp's being chased over the roofs."

"Maybe you'd better see what you can find to do to help out."

He didn't wait for the officer's puzzled reaction before heading for the stairs.

The fourth floor sported its own blue herd, most of them gathered outside Abbie's open door. Not open, he realized as he got closer. Broken down. He almost came to a stop, too afraid to discover what waited for him inside.

"Hi, Sarge," came the greeting, followed by silence as Michael failed to acknowledge it. He rubbed a hand across his jaw and forced himself forward.

Dixon and Walters, the two men on tonight's shift stood inside. They were facing the couch. Michael stepped over the shattered door and into the room.

"Michael!"

The breath he'd been holding escaped in a relieved rush. Abbie jumped up from where she'd been sitting on the couch and ran for him. Oblivious to the reaction of others around him, Michael seized her. She was okay. He couldn't believe it. He wrapped her into his arms and brought a trembling hand up to stroke her hair.

"What happened? Are you all right?"

"Yes." The word came out in a sob. She was shivering and her face was wet with tears. Michael had the feeling that her knees weren't all too sturdy. After the scare he'd had, his weren't either.

"It was that guy," she managed in a rush. "He...he said he was Dixon, and that you were hurt. I let him up...I'm so dumb. But I was so scared for you..."

"Shh," he soothed, "it's okay. I'm here."

"It's funny." she grinned lopsidedly. "I handle these little surprises much better at work. I'm a wreck."

"You did fine," he assured her as he guided her back to the couch to sit down. It wasn't until they'd made it that far that he saw the bruises that had begun to form on her face. At her jawline and left eye.

"Abbie?" A hand instinctively went to them.

"Rescued just in time again," she demurred. "If I hadn't been so stupid..."

"Let me get you a glass of wine," he offered. "Okay?"

She smiled, her eyes devouring him. "Okay."

He got to his feet with a pointed look for Dixon. The plainclothesman followed silently to the kitchen.

"Okay," Michael spat, spinning on him. "What the hell happened?"

Dixon stood uncomfortably by the table, a hand on the ten-speed bike that rested against it. "He got by us. We screwed up. I'm sorry, Michael."

"Sorry almost didn't count. How'd he get to her?"

"Just like she said. He walked in shaved and groomed, and we didn't recognize him. Buzzed up claiming to be me with news about you." He nodded toward the couch. "If your lady weren't so alert, it would have been worse. She checked him out through her peephole and called out the alarm. But when she didn't answer the door right away, he busted it down. Had her by the throat when we showed up."

"He got away." The words were accusing.

Dixon nodded. "Out the window to the fire escape. They're after him."

By the time Michael made it back into the living room with Abbie's wine, not only Mendlesohn but Swann, too, had made it up the four flights of stairs.

Swann was not one for revealing emotion. He said that bad guys didn't respect you as much if they were always sure what was going on. Michael would have come down a lot harder on him tonight if he hadn't seen the distress in the flat, black eyes.

"Doc? You okay?"

She looked up from the wine Michael had just handed her. "All this attention." She grinned feebly. "It could turn a girl's head. I'm fine, Swann. Thanks." All the same, she had some difficulty getting the glass to her lips without spilling some of the contents.

She hadn't exaggerated about being a wreck. She felt as if her body were disintegrating around her. It had been enough to think that Michael was in trouble. But when she'd peered through that peephole and seen that fish-eyed view of her shaggy shadow out in the hall, she'd almost lost it completely. There hadn't been any way to alert the guys down on the street. She hadn't even known if they were all right. Not knowing what else to do, she'd finally pulled whatever wits she'd had left about her and dialed for help.

It hadn't ended there, though. She'd hardly made it off the phone when the first blows had reverberated against the door. It had taken three to break it down. And he'd never said a word to her. Not one word.

Abbie sipped at her wine without really tasting it. Michael was here. Here and safe, and that was all that mattered. If only the feeling of relief could work its way through the rest of the jumbled emotions that plagued her.

"That's it, Swann," Michael was saying with barely repressed anger. "I'm taking her with me."

"Just settle down a minute, man . . ."

"Don't you dare tell me to settle down. I told them that I didn't want her involved. I told them I'd do whatever they wanted as long as it didn't hurt Abbie. Fat lot of good that did."

Abbie's wineglass came to rest on her thigh. She was having some trouble following what was going on. There was no doubt about Michael's feelings, though. He was quaking with rage.

"You know we have to get the okay from Magnusson," Swann reminded him.

"Magnusson can go to hell. Abbie can't stay here, and she's not going to be bait anymore."

"You can't take her with you," Swann insisted. "You're a bigger target than she is."

Abbie caught that. She came to her feet with more force than she'd thought herself capable of. "What are you talking about?"

Both men looked at her as if she'd witnessed some minor indiscretion. Then Swann scanned the exposed hallway where not a few neighbors had begun to mingle with the police.

"Why don't we talk in the kitchen?" he suggested.

"Why don't we just?" Abbie retorted.

She followed them into the tiny room and took up the spot Dixon had vacated. "Now," she began, "target for what?"

Swann answered. Michael kept his distance for the moment.

"Those guys you met from narcotics weren't there because of the robbery," the black man said. "They were working on a big drug bust that Marlow and Percy were involved in. When Percy went down, the only line they had to the thing was Marlow.''

"Was Magnusson the mannequin in the suit?" she asked.

Michael tried to stifle a grin. "Yeah. He's from the Drug Enforcement Agency. This whole operation's his."

"And where does the word target fit in?"

So Swann explained. Michael let him, because Michael himself couldn't manage an objective word about any of it right now. He couldn't take his eyes from the blossoming purple along Abbie's jawline, or the sick pallor of her skin. The danger had come too close this time. He couldn't let her be at risk again. He'd realized, on that agonizingly long ride over here, that he loved her far too much to lose her—no matter what it cost him.

Swann reached the part where Michael had set himself up as bait. When he explained why, Abbie turned on Michael with furious tears in her eyes.

"How dare you?" she demanded, her voice quivering. "How dare you put your life at risk like that for me without letting me know about it!"

Michael reached out to her, taking her gently by the arms. "You'd been through too much already, and Magnusson was just going to offer you up. I couldn't do that, Abbie."

"You couldn't even tell me?"

Neither of them noticed that Swann had edged beyond them out the door. "I didn't want you to worry."

She almost hauled off and slapped him. "Damn you! You disappear for five days without bothering to tell me why, you promise me you'll be careful when I find out you've just finished painting a big target on yourself, and you tell me you didn't want me to worry!" The tears coursed down her cheeks now. She saw through them that Michael's eyes were still liquid with fear for her. "Just what the hell did you think I was doing?"

"Abbie," he said tightly, "it isn't as if I'm walking blindfold into an ambush. It's my job. I'm trained for it. I've done it before. When they gave me a choice of who to set up as a target for a professional criminal, of course I'm going to pick me." He shrugged. "It's not something that I thought I needed to burden you with."

Abbie could only shake her head. He just didn't understand. "And you didn't think I wouldn't worry more when I was left in the dark, spending those five days knowing damn well something was wrong, and not being told what?"

"I told you not to go near her, Viviano!"

They whipped around to find Magnusson at the door, more emotion on his face than anyone had ever seen. It was all anger, and it had Michael's name on it.

Michael let go of Abbie and turned on him. "You bastard! She was almost killed tonight!"

"The police department's fault," the man retorted acidly, "not mine. You keep showing up around Dr. Fitzgerald, though, and you're going to blow our case and her life. That hit's definitely going out, Viviano. We just don't know when."

Abbie blanched. "Hit?"

Nobody heard her.

"You can just count her out from now on," Michael warned. "She's done enough."

Magnusson at least nodded. "That's why I'm here. I'm taking her to the safe house. Before Marlow gets to you through her."

"You're not taking her anywhere."

"I don't think you want to cross me, mister." The man's tone was implicit. Michael gave him a smile that failed to reach his eyes.

"What are you going to do," he asked with a carefully level voice. "Take my job? Put me on suspension? I'm your case, remember? Without me, you have nothing but loose ends."

Abbie watched the argument in stunned silence. She could see that Swann had stayed close by. It made her wonder how many times this had happened already. Michael stood by her as if Magnusson were a physical danger to be fought off. When she looked at him, all she could think of was that word *hit*, and pray it was some kind of sick joke.

"Who says I'm going with either of you?" she finally ventured.

Michael swung back on her, his words urgent. "You have to leave here, Abbie. He's tried once. There's nothing to keep him from trying again."

She turned her glare on Magnusson. "What about the guy who beat me up?"

Magnusson nodded. "Him, we can put away. But it's Marlow that's the problem, Dr. Fitzgerald, and we can't pull him in yet. Until this is finished, he can make Viviano here vulnerable through you."

She felt as if she were floundering. "So, what do I do?"

"Come with me. We have several safe houses in the area we can lodge you in."

"For how long?"

If there was an answer no one seemed to be able to find it. Magnusson even searched the tips of his shoes. Michael slid an arm around her shoulders.

"I'm sorry, Ab. I tried to keep this all from you."

She saw the pain in his eyes and knew that he'd done it for the right reasons. It still didn't make it any more palatable.

"Will you all excuse us for a moment?" she asked.

Magnusson hesitated, but he and Swann backed out of the kitchen, leaving Abbie and Michael alone. Abbie folded herself into Michael's arms to hide the new tears. It took her a moment to gather enough courage to keep from screaming.

"Will you be able to get in touch with me?"

He bent his head to hers, his hold on her fierce. "I'll make it a point to. Forgive me?"

She managed a watery little smile. "I'll let you know when you get in touch with me." Suddenly, her composure faltered. "Oh, Michael, I'm so scared."

"Don't be, love. They'll take good care of you."

Raising her head, she met his eyes without flinching. "But who will take care of you?"

Michael ran a thumb along her lips, trapping the tears that lingered there. "I promised I'd be careful. I will. You just have to believe that."

She shook her head a little. "I've been trying. Come get me soon, Michael. I . . . I can't . . ."

Michael silenced her with his mouth. Abbie stretched up to him, her arms around his neck, her lips open and greedy. Michael collected her small sobs and shared his own sighs. His sure, sensitive hands encompassed her waist and suffused her with their strength. His lips inflamed her need with their tender exploration. Abbie clung to him, as if she could carry the sweet ache he ignited in her away with her. As if the memory of his touch would color the lonely hours with a little light.

Thirty minutes later Abbie walked into the living room with a packed bag and her softball bat. She had called to reassure her family and apologize to John at the hospital. And then, even though Magnusson had promised she'd only be gone awhile, she'd packed her tapes and every book she could find, along with her variety of shorts and shirts. This was not a formal safe house, she assumed. Swann had stifled a grin.

He stifled another when he saw the bat.

"No offense to any of you," Abbie smiled sweetly, "but after tonight, I'll follow Franklin's adage about help coming to those who help themselves. Just a bit of insurance, you understand."

"Well, I don't know," Magnusson demurred.

"Oh, come on." Michael grinned with delight. "If things get boring, she can play fungo."

"What's your batting average?" Swann asked. Swann was the coach for the team Michael played for. They didn't win that often.

Abbie flashed him a smug smile as she headed past, out the door. "Four-fifty."

Swann swung on his heel as Magnusson ushered Abbie into the elevator. "You take real good care of her, you understand?"

The safe house would never make *Better Homes and Gardens*. Wedged into a lower-class neighborhood on the South Side, it was a brick, two-bedroom affair with grills on the windows and a steel-plated door. The narcotics officer who showed her around explained that it had once been set up as a rock house. Cocaine. The DEA made use of whatever little windfalls came their way. Abbie hoped that the original owners wouldn't be intent on getting their house back.

By the time she settled into the saggy old twin bed in the back bedroom, it was close to three. By the time she fell asleep, it was closing in on five. The two men baby-sitting her had played a few hands of gin with her and tried their best to involve her in innocuous conversations. She hadn't minded the lame jokes and listless cardplaying so much as she had the cloud of cigarette smoke that hovered in the room like smog over L.A.

When she finally gave in and went to bed, they just antied up again, promising her that they'd stay put right where they were all night if she needed anything at all. She smiled, thinking that the only thing she needed was Michael, and that that was the one thing they couldn't provide.

After a lot of pressure, Magnusson had finally come clean about the hit. Abbie had listened to him explain it all in his sterile tone of voice and understood why Michael hated him. She also understood why Michael would want to keep it all from her, especially after her little revelation the week before.

She didn't know what she was going to do. Michael Viviano bubbled in her blood like fine champagne. It had been Michael she had prayed for when the man had burst upon her, and Michael she'd wanted when she'd been rescued. Even now, as she lay alone in the dark, she conjured him up next to her, his words crafted only for her, his touch awakening her like Pygmalion's creation. Her body actually thrummed with the anticipation of him.

But battling with the exhilaration, the fierce desire and sweet promise, raged the terror. He was beyond her reach, and he was risking his life. Just the thought that she could spend these isolated, empty days waiting for him only to lose him, paralyzed her. He could be killed before she ever saw him again.

And every day she spent with him would be like that.

Abbie brushed impatiently at the new tears that welled up, and turned on her side. Her hand instinctively reached out to make sure the bat was safely next to her. Not much security, but she'd take anything she could get at this point.

She must have slept. She remembered dreaming. Michael had shown up, sliding into the room in the soft shadows of early morning to take her into his arms. He'd told the baby-sitters to take a hike, that he wanted to make love to her. She remembered that she hadn't been surprised, and that the men hadn't been happy, but they'd complied, picking up their deck of cards and cigarettes and dragging their chairs out the front door.

The front door that made such a flat metallic click when it closed.

Her eyes came open. It was dark, the house still. There weren't even any birds that braved this side of town at this time in the morning. Abbie's heart began to pick up speed. Had she been dreaming, or had she really heard the door? She couldn't hear the officers talking, or smell their smoke anymore. The place was just too quiet.

She sat up, her hand on the bat handle, and swung her feet over the side of the bed. There wasn't enough air in this grimy little room. She heard footsteps. Soft, careful, just outside her door. She knew that it was probably the officers. Even so, she brought the bat with her when she slipped out of bed.

The doorknob was turning. Abbie's heart thundered in her ears. The bat came up without her realizing it. The door began to open. When the head slid around the edge, Abbie went into her backswing...

"Abbie, wait!"

"Michael!"

Abbie froze just in time. She'd been within inches of giving Michael a whole new set of stitches. He strode up to her and took the bat from her numb fingers.

"A little apprehensive, aren't we?" He grinned, dropping a kiss to her gaping mouth.

She threw herself in his arms. "You keep sneaking up on me!" she protested, although the force of her argument was lost as she buried her head in his shoulder. "Don't do that again!"

"I promise." His hand came up to her hair, and they stood there for a moment, both of them just content to be back in each other's arms.

"Does Mr. Magnusson know you're here?" Abbie finally asked without moving.

Michael grinned into the darkness. "He will soon enough."

Abbie's head came up. "What are you up to, Michael?"

His eyes glinted with wicked amusement. Abbie immediately thought of a boy playing hooky. "I'm springin' you from this joint, baby."

She straightened. "What are you talking about?"

"Don't be so noisy," he warned. "The fuzz might hear."

"Don't they know you're here?"

"Sure. They just don't know where I'm taking you." His grin broadened again in anticipation. "Swann and I don't like this place. We found a better one."

"What do you mean?"

"I mean that since the guys out front are our guys instead of Magnusson's, we're taking advantage of it. Now, let's get going."

"Michael," Abbie spoke up a while later as Michael pulled his car into another drive. "This is the Ambassador East Hotel."

Michael looked up. "So it is." Then he pulled the car to a halt. The sky was lightening toward morning, and there were birds in this part of town. The sky was crowded with well-kept buildings and carefully planted trees. A porter approached to open the door for her.

"What are we doing here?" she asked, still looking up at the impressive Georgian architecture of the hotel. To her left she saw the tall windows of the famous Pump Room where the elite fought for the privilege of being seen in Booth One. In a few hours, brunch patrons would be munching on delectable croissants and watching the passing parade of life along the residential neighborhood of State Street and Goethe.

Abbie looked around at the elegant brownstones and high-rise apartments and thought how very romantic a stay here would be. She'd been one of the brunch patrons at the Pump Room on a regular basis, but she'd never had a chance to stay overnight.

"I told you." Michael smiled as he joined her. "Swann and I liked this idea better."

She couldn't help but grin. "Does this mean that you're a little old-fashioned, too?"

He just grinned at her as he guided her in the door and up the steps to the lobby.

The first impression one received of the hotel upon entering was that of high ceilings and crystal chandeliers. Pale salmon-pink walls complemented the verde antique marble floors. Twin square columns separated the comfortable seating area of overstuffed furniture and Oriental rugs. Between them rested the focal point of the room, an antique gallery table with peach marble top and scrolled legs that bore a huge vase of fresh flowers.

The room always reminded Abbie of quiet elegance and the reassurance of history. It had been showcased in Alfred Hitchcock's *North by Northwest*, and had known the celebrities of some six generations. She couldn't believe Michael had gone to the trouble of finding a room here for her.

"Good morning," Michael greeted the clerk, a pretty young woman who looked as if she'd been waiting for them to arrive. "You have a reservation for Mr. and Mrs. Smith."

The woman smiled and bent to her book. Abbie giggled. "Mr. and Dr. Smith, if you don't mind."

Michael laughed back. "Snob." After the past few days of unrelieved tension, they were beginning to discover a holiday atmosphere.

The clerk finished her search. "Of course, Mr. Smith. Walter will take your bags for you."

She waved Walter over, and all three headed for the elevators.

"At six in the morning, you get a room at the Ambassador East?" Abbie demanded.

Michael pulled her into his arms and kissed her. "You don't have an affair with a doctor at just any hotel. I wanted only the best for my Dr. Smith."

Walter was paid not to notice. Abbie giggled again at the improbability of it all and kissed Michael back. "Dr. Smith is duly impressed."

She had spoken too soon. The elevators opened, and Walter led them to a door across the hall that had some kind of plaque on it. Abbie wasn't paying attention. "Do you think they'll bring up my softball bat?"

Michael followed her through the door. "You think you're gonna need it?"

That was when Abbie realized where she was. Michael had not just gotten a room at the Ambassador East; he'd managed to book a suite. They walked into the living room, a classically designed room with Early American traditional furniture covered in soft gradients of grays that complemented the warm-peach accents. Abbie circled the softly decorated room and tested the couch, sinking into the gentle velveteen with a sigh. She was already planning what to do with the stationery she'd swipe from the desk against the far wall.

"I couldn't manage a really big suite," Michael apologized. "Those were already taken. I hope you don't mind." He dropped a bill in Walter's hand, and the little man backed out the door.

Abbie jumped up and headed in to check out the bedroom. "Mind? I've never been in a place like this." More soft grays and warm wood. There was a four-poster bed with a deliciously plump goose-down comforter designed in warm peach colors, and two chairs by the window. A live schefflera sat by the chest of drawers. She felt as if she'd stepped into a fine old home. The bathroom was all marble, with an old freestanding sink that added even more atmosphere.

"Oh, come on," Michael scoffed from behind her, the smile on his face reflecting her pleasure. "You can't tell me you've never been to a place like this. You're a doctor."

"A doctor who's still paying off school loans," she assured him, her voice echoing from where it was poked into the bathtub. Ceramic, and with a cloth shower curtain. This certainly wasn't like any Holiday Inn she'd ever been in.

"How did you manage this?" she demanded as she turned again and again around the bedroom. "And don't tell me your father has tickets."

"Connections" was all he'd say. Michael stood in the doorway to the bedroom and watched the delight sparkle in Abbie's eyes, her enthusiasm infecting him. He'd been the one to come up with the idea, the one to execute it. But he'd had no idea of its consequences until this moment. He'd never realized before how provocative enthusiasm was in a woman's eyes.

"Dr. Smith?"

Abbie turned back from where she'd been poking her head out the window to take in the awakening street twelve floors below. "Yes, Mr. Smith?"

"Come over here and thank me for getting you out of Magnusson's clutches."

Her smile growing lazy, Abbie sidled over to where Michael waited. "But now I'm in your clutches," she protested without much fervor.

Michael smiled down at her, his hands sliding down her waist and pulling her to him. "Exactly."

Chapter 9

When Abbie eased into Michael's embrace, she knew exactly what she was doing. No matter what else happened to them or between them, she knew that she couldn't manage another step without the sustenance of Michael's life-giving touch.

He lowered his face to hers, his eyes bare with need. Soft, hypnotic, compelling, they mesmerized her, drawing her to him like a sorcerer's incantation. Abbie didn't even realize that she'd lifted her fingers to touch him. She only saw them rest against his face as if to test him, his presence, his strength—his passion. She was barely breathing, her heartbeat synchronous with the staccato of his.

The silence stretched taut between them, the world around them dropping away. There was only the two of them, only the electrically charged atmosphere of this moment. Only the light that danced and sparked from their eyes.

"Abbie . . ." The word was an entreaty, Michael's voice harsh with the pain and longing and fear they had shared and survived.

She managed a smile in return, her own eyes melting in accord. "I need you, Michael."

Without another word, Michael scooped her into his arms. Abbie wrapped her arms around his neck, her fingers sliding into the soft hair at the nape of his neck to pull him to her.

He'd shaved before coming to pick her up. His cheek was soft against hers, and she could smell the woody tang of his cologne. She sought his lips, her eyes wide with efflorescent hunger. And he, his eyes as dark as hers, met her.

Within that instant, an act born of need and sharing erupted into one of desire. Just the soft contact of Michael's mouth against hers forced a surprised gasp from her. Her body, nestled in Michael's sure, safe arms, woke from its self-imposed slumber, the force of the fire in it rocking her.

Michael felt it, too. He'd meant to cross into the bedroom with her. That one kiss brought him to a standstill. He closed his eyes and crushed her against him, the hard knot of longing flaring into his arms and down his legs. He'd known he'd needed this, needed her; but God, he hadn't known how much. Just the feel of her in his grasp set off a fire storm he'd never known before. The world shrank into the taste and sensation of the slight woman he held.

Suddenly he knew without a doubt that any pain he carried with him from the streets, any uncertainty or frustration, could be lost in Abbie's arms. He buried his face in her wild, fragrant hair and found release.

Michael settled Abbie onto the rich, soft comforter and eased himself down next to her, his eyes never leaving hers. She lay beneath him smiling, inviting. Waiting. Bending to reclaim the soft treasure of her mouth, he slid his hand slowly up her slim leg. Soft, smooth, firm. She began to move beneath his ministrations, urging him on. He eased his hand up under her cotton top to test the gentle roundness of her belly, the sensitive skin below her breasts. Her body rippled in response to him, and he realized that it begged to be tasted.

"What's this?" His voice was breathless, amused. He was striving to maintain control. Abbie's soft chuckle quivered deep in her, vibrating against his hand.

"Lesson in life," she managed, pulling him back to punctuate her words with a long kiss that sapped the strength from his legs. "Twenty stitches for trying to jump a fence in a dress." Another pause that was not silent. "Can't you keep your mind on business?"

He lifted his head a little, the glint in his eye wicked. "I just wanted to know what it was before I kissed it." He saw her eyes widen and felt their heat knife through him.

Abbie hadn't felt him unbutton her blouse. It lay open now, framing the soft lace bra that restrained her breasts. Dipping to drop a light, tantalizing kiss on the material that kept him from each stiff bud, Michael unsnapped the clasp between them. The bra fell away to reveal the firm, erect mounds beneath.

Abbie shivered with the intensity of Michael's delight. She let him slide her shorts down, and then the soft blue panties that matched the bra that now lay in a jumble on the floor. And when she was undressed, he praised her with his hands.

She arched against his touch, pressing hard against him as he traced her breasts with trembling fingers and her throat with his tongue. She struggled to free him of his own clothes, anxious to feel the delicious rasp of his hair-roughened body against hers. Pain and need and loneliness swirled in her to heighten her passion. She ached for the pain she could exorcise from Michael's eyes, and sobbed with the immersion of her own.

"Well," she gasped as his lips found her breasts, "at least there's no gun."

Michael, now as naked as she, chuckled against her. Abbie couldn't seem to satiate herself with the feel of him. He was so lean and hard, his chest tight against her belly. Yes, she thought with a giddy smile, he does feel delicious against my stomach. Against my thighs. His hands swept over her, waking an exquisite life where they traveled. Abbie felt the shock waves to her toes. He circled the backs of her knees with rough fingers and pulled more moans from her.

"Michael, please..." She didn't know what to say, what to ask for. She wanted release from such torment, more pleasure that only he could unleash in her. Just satisfy that terrible fire in me, she thought, deep in me where no one can reach.

Michael reached it. He found it first with his fingers. Abbie moaned and rocked against him. Michael lifted his mouth from tantalizing her breasts and returned to claim her moans, his tongue ravaging her mouth. She could do no more than hold on to him, her tongue seeking as desperately as his.

He was rigid against her. Barely in control, his breathing ragged, his belly on fire. Yet he waited until his fingers brought her to agony. Her head came back against the pillow, and her eyes went liquid. Never taking his mouth away, Michael shifted his weight onto her. She arched, her legs circling him, Michael's name lost in the ferocity of their kiss.

Michael felt the sweet warmth of her envelope him, and the fire in him exploded. He called out to her, her name mingling with his, their soft cries of release escaping and trapped again by hungry mouths and feverish hands. He drove into her as if he could purge himself in her. As if the agony she ignited would cleanse him.

Abbie strained against the power of him in her. Strove to pull him deeper within her where he would never be lost again. She sought his rhythm and matched it until the world dissolved into molten, sweet fire and she fell back, his name on her lips one last time.

Michael fell beside her, his face cradled into her throat, his breathing heavy and intimate against her. She brought a hand up to his back, and he one to her breast, and there they slept.

Abbie woke with the early-afternoon sun in her eyes. Even in the soft, semilucid stage just before waking, she knew where she was, and that she was with Michael. His weight had shifted a little, a leg sprawled across hers, his head next to her on the pillow. She smiled, her eyes still closed, at the wonderful intimacy of that feeling of somnolent weight against her.

She didn't want to move, to disturb him. For just a little while, she wanted to believe that this hotel room was the universe, and that what had happened this morning was all that mattered.

Very carefully, she turned to look at Michael's face. He had that same haphazard look that had stolen her heart before—that open, innocent appearance that only sleep seemed to allow. Her hand came up to brush an errant strand of hair back from his forehead, and she found herself wanting to just wrap him in her arms and not let him go again.

"You're crying," he accused gently without even opening an eye.

She smiled through the tears. "They didn't make you a cop 'cause they liked the color of your hair."

He looked up at her, the sleep still heavy in his eyes. She smiled again for him, because she loved it when he looked like this.

"Are you in a better mood than the last time I woke you?" she asked.

He smiled now. "I think I can guarantee it." Already his finger had begun circling designs around her breast. Abbie felt the nipple go rigid and scowled at him.

"You probably have to go on duty or something this afternoon, don't you?" All the same, she didn't move away when he pulled himself up on an elbow and bent over to kiss her awake.

"Probably. What time is it?"

"About one, I think."

He nodded against her, which was a pleasant feeling. His beard had begun to grow a little, chafing deliciously against her skin.

"I have time."

"Michael..." He trapped her protest and turned it into a new little moan as his hand settled against her breast and began to tease it. She brought her own hand up.

"No," he said, taking hold of it and kissing it. "Lie still."

There was much giggling for a while, and then the escalating sounds of satisfaction.

The next time Abbie tried to bring up the time, she lay nestled against Michael's chest, the fires in her once again banked and glowing. She lay entwined in the sheets with him and watched the afternoon glitter off the city out their window.

"What time do you have to go in?" she asked, her mind more on the comfort of Michael's leg intertwined with hers.

"Tonight at eleven."

She lifted her head to glare at him. "Well, why didn't you tell me?"

"Why?" he demanded. "Feel like you've been wasting your time?"

"No, I've been worrying about you getting into trouble."

His eyes refused to be serious. "No chance."

"Speaking of which," she went on, resting her chin on the hand that had been exploring his chest. Her face was just below Michael's. "Just what is the story of my abduction?"

His eyebrows rose as he slid his other arm under his head. "Abduction? Is that any way to be? After all the trouble I went to..."

"And are going to get into."

His nod was nonchalant. "My cousin is public relations manager here. He owes me one. As of fifteen minutes after we signed in, there was no one in this suite. We are invisible."

Abbie's head came up. "What did he owe you for? Saving his family from a terrorist?"

Michael grinned. "Saving him from marriage."

Abbie managed a scowl. "Sounds like someone I'd love to meet."

"He's the third baseman for the family softball team. What were you crying for?"

Abbie pretended she didn't hear him. "If we're invisible, how do we eat?"

"What?"

"Room service. I'm hungry."

Michael scowled this time. "It was only so big a favor."

"I'm a doctor," Abbie reminded him with a playful kiss to the chin. "I can at least afford room service." Then she straightened a little. "Just how long am I supposed to hide out here?"

Michael shrugged. "As long as it takes. Three, four days."

"And just how was I going to eat if you weren't going to provide room service?"

Michael had obviously thought about it, and was proud of his attention to detail. "White Castle."

With an exaggerated groan, Abbie rolled off him and onto her back. "White Castle? Are you kidding?" Notorious among the midwestern states, once airlifted to the marines in Beirut as a treat, White Castle hamburgers were the size of flat meatballs and carried every calorie and carbohydrate Abbie so assiduously avoided. It was beside the point that they were almost tops on her list of favorite fast foods.

"Well, what's wrong with that?" Michael demanded without offense. "It's sure cheaper than this."

"Only if you can jog it off," Abbie reminded him. "Which I assume I can't."

"Not unless you want to run into Magnusson."

Abbie found herself back at the crux of the matter. "If he doesn't know where I am, how are you going to avoid being court-martialed, or whatever they do to police?"

"Don't worry about it." Swinging his feet over the side of the bed, Michael reached for the phone. "All you have to know is that you're safe here, because nobody followed us, and nobody in their right minds would think of the police putting somebody up in the Ambassador East. You have specially chosen baby-sitters, and the staff on this floor is personally picked for discretion.''

Abbie couldn't help it. ''Bring girls here often, do you?''

He gave her that lopsided grin. ''They line up outside the door.''

Abbie feasted her eyes on the lean lines of Michael's back, the strong outline of his arms as he used the phone with one hand and pulled a hand through unruly hair with the other. She remembered what those arms felt like against her hands and smiled.

While Michael consulted with his cousin, Abbie hopped out of bed to wash up. And when she wrapped herself in a sheet to receive the breakfast cart, Michael did his washing.

He must have been right about the staff, because the bellboy barely blinked at her outfit as he set out the silver coffee service and uncovered the croissants. There was fresh fruit on china, and a pink rose in a crystal vase. Abbie looked at the elegance of such simple fare and decided that she should have come to this place sooner.

Michael came out smelling like soap. Abbie pulled the tray onto the bed with her so she could eat her croissant lounging in the buff. It seemed so decadent and delicious. The icing on the cake was to be able to watch Michael pad around just as naked as she was.

She just couldn't get enough of the sight of that strong body. The gold-tipped hair that fanned across his chest and narrowed to a tantalizing line that trailed down his torso. His slim hips and steely thighs. And yes, she thought as she nibbled on a strawberry, he does, in fact, have a great tush.

Michael turned just in time to see Abbie taking a delicate bite from a large strawberry. His reaction was immediate and obvious. He didn't think he'd ever seen anything more sensuous than that tousled vixen clad only to the waist in a soft white sheet and pursing her lips around the succulent fruit, a little juice sliding down her chin.

''Good grief.'' Abbie mugged, seeing him. ''Don't you ever get tired?''

"Not around you," he admitted, and slid into bed next to her.

"Here." She giggled, the delight in his eyes arousing her. "Have some fruit." She shoved a slice of melon into his mouth. Then she picked up another strawberry and began to nibble. Michael took the melon out of his mouth and leaned over to lock his teeth around the other half of Abbie's treat.

Her eyes widened, the soft fragrance of him enveloping her, his greedy eyes giving her no room. She worked toward his mouth and ended up sharing the last piece between them, their tongues wrapping around the tart, strawberry taste and mingling with delicious abandon. Abbie found herself leaning forward, a hand against Michael's chest so that she felt his heart accelerate just as hers did. She felt the warm sun on her shoulders and his cool fingers on her belly.

"We're going to knock over the coffeepot," she whispered, moving against the pressure of his hand.

"So what?" Michael grinned offhandedly. "We don't have to clean it up."

She giggled again, and then pulled back. "Yeah, but then I won't get any coffee. Let's eat first."

Michael's grin broadened, but Abbie didn't give him a chance. She plugged the melon back in.

"I have a question," Michael said sometime later. He was on his stomach next to Abbie, propped on elbows. She passed him a cup of coffee and a croissant.

"Don't ask questions," she advised easily. He didn't feel the quickening of her heart.

Michael paid no heed. "You're like a different person today, Ab."

Her answering smile was knowing and tinged with sadness. "Footloose and fancy-free?"

"Something like that. It's like you're purposefully ignoring all those things you told me about my being a cop."

She concentrated a moment on her coffee. When she answered, she couldn't quite face him. "But I am." The gesture she used encompassed the suite. "The minute we walked in here, it was like walking into another world—a separate universe where nothing can go wrong. It may sound stupid, but I invented us a magical kingdom. Here, I can love you just like I want without having to worry about the consequences."

Michael shook his head a little. "But they're out there."

"I know. But for a little while, I'm pretending they're not. I need you too much right now to let all that interfere."

He kept his silence for a moment, his eyes unfocused. Then he turned to her, flashing a crooked smile. "You love me?"

Abbie offered her own grin that had gone a little watery again. "Dumb, isn't it?"

He leaned over to deliver a heartfelt kiss that hurried Abbie's tears. "I think it's pretty wonderful."

She shook her head a little impatiently. "But Michael, that's only something I can tell you here, don't you understand?"

"I can't get killed in the magical kingdom?"

"Don't make fun of me."

He set down his cup and saucer and reached over to take hers. Rolling over, he came to a sitting position next to Abbie. Then, with gentle hands, he drew her to him. "No, Abbie, I'm not making fun. I understand." His finger drew a slow pattern down the side of her cheek. "We'll just make the most of our time here, and then deal with the outside when we get there. Okay?"

Tears spilled over onto Michael's hand as Abbie gave him a hesitant smile. "Michael, I want you so much."

"Well—" He smiled back, kissing her tears "—you have me. I've been falling in love with you since you first fainted in my arms."

Abbie didn't mean to giggle. "That did it, huh?"

He nodded, his eyes softening again.

Abbie let her grin broaden to wicked proportions until her eyes rolled up in her head and she turned for a dramatic dive. She landed on her back, firmly caught in Michael's capable hands, her head over the side of the bed.

Laughing, Michael looked down at the sleek lines of the body in his arms, the breasts pointing high, Abbie's hair tumbling to the floor. Even though her eyes were closed, she couldn't keep the grin off her face. Michael had other problems.

"Excellent placement," he grinned, and dropped his mouth down on her breast.

Abbie's first instinct was to jump. Her next was to stretch against the sweet pain Michael's touch ignited in her. He held her very still against him so that he could take his time teasing her breast to an agonizing stiffness. She could feel his lips—so soft and wet, sliding along the susceptible skin—then the warm rasp of his tongue to circle her nipple and give way to the nip of his teeth. He brought his hand up to her other breast to consume its pliant curves.

Michael's eyes were on Abbie's face when she opened her eyes to him. He saw passion take hold of her features and soften them, saw smoke rise in the sky of her eyes. When she smiled up at the heat she discovered in his eyes, he pulled her back up to him.

"I might be late for work after all," he admitted.

Abbie grinned. "Well, you did say we should make the most of our time here."

He smiled, his kiss a soft, lingering taste of commitment. Then, a smile back in his eyes, he lifted Abbie to her feet at the foot of the bed so that he faced her. "Now," he mused, his eyes at a level with her taut breasts, "where was I?"

Twelve hours later Abbie lay on the same bed wide-awake and waiting for Michael to return. Her mystical universe of safety had lasted only until Michael had walked back out the door. From that moment, she had paced and worried and paced some more. She'd pulled the headset out and made good use of Santana and Led Zeppelin, but even the driving rhythms that usually purged any of her ghosts only forced her to pace faster.

She had wanted so desperately to beg Michael not to go back out on the street where he was a target. She'd wanted to hold him back from ever going out that door again. But that was the one thing Abbie had no right to do.

Michael had given her a number where she could reach Swann if she had to. More than once, she found herself studying it. Once she'd had a finger on the phone ready to dial. All she wanted was news. Reassurance.

She agonized for hours, and then finally returned to the rumpled bed that still carried his scent, the impression of his weight where he'd last slept. And there she lay awake listening to the city and worrying.

She loved him. There was no sense trying to hedge around that truth any longer. This day when she should have been cowering in a corner in fear for her life, she had discovered a whole new Abbie Fitzgerald—one who blossomed in the presence of a police sergeant, who lived for his smile and dreaded his departures. She had known an abandon today that she'd never hoped for in her life; she felt so comfortable with Michael that it hadn't seemed at all unusual for her to wander the room naked with him or confide her innermost thoughts and feelings. He knew her body better than she ever had, his deft fingers seeking and inciting until she had recognized a completely sensual self she'd never acknowledged before.

They'd played and laughed and slept in each other's arms. They'd been quiet and spent time just watching the life ebb and flow in each other's eyes. Abbie had never spent a day like that, wasn't sure she ever would again. No matter what happened, Michael had brought her to life, and she would never be the same again.

Michael slipped back into the room just after dawn to find Abbie sideways across the bed, the sheet bunched up around her hips. The sight of her bare breasts, her mouth slightly open in sleep, set off that hard ache in him. She looked so vulnerable. So small and soft in sleep that he wanted to gather her into his arms and hold her.

He pulled off his shoes and padded across the carpet. He was tired. It had been the worst of nights, between Magnusson shrieking around the station like the mother of a deflowered daughter and the lieutenant demanding explanations. A bad situation on the streets had allowed Michael to fend them off for most of the night until the lieutenant gave up and went home. But then the news came in about the safe house.

"Michael?"

Her voice was thick with sleep. Michael turned at the door to the bathroom to see that her eyes were barely open. She looked as if she'd managed about as much sleep as he had last night. Damn. Well, he wasn't about to make it worse for her. Bad news could wait.

"I'm here, Abbie. Go on back to sleep."

She huddled over to one side of the bed. "You, too."

Smiling, he bent over the bed to drop a kiss on those soft lips. "I'm coming."

He thought she'd be asleep by the time he got back. But when he walked in in his jockey shorts, Abbie was sitting up, the sheet draped over her knees.

"Welcome back," she smiled sleepily. "I've been keeping your spot warm."

He sat down with a heartfelt groan. "I appreciate it. The way I feel, I'm going to sleep until Thursday."

Abbie reached over to pull him down next to her. Michael followed without protest. "Bad night?" she asked, nestling against his side.

He wrapped an arm around her and nuzzled against her hair. "Magnusson was not pleased."

"Tell me about it."

"On Thursday—" he yawned "—when I wake up."

"Anything else go on?"

"Nah." He kissed her. Abbie felt the strain in his shoulders, saw the ridge of his jaw, and knew that he was lying. "I love you."

"I love you, too."

She watched as he fought for sleep to overtake him, the tensions he brought robbing him of peace, his body taut and uncomfortable, and realized that for the first time since she'd come into this room, she was angry.

When Michael woke up, he was alone in the bed. He'd turned over, expecting to bump into Abbie. The sheets weren't even warm next to him. He blinked a couple of times and struggled up. Whatever sleep he'd managed hadn't helped any. He still felt as refreshed as a muscle cramp.

"Abbie?"

There was no answer. He swung off the bed and walked over to the bathroom. She wasn't lounging in the bath. He backtracked toward the living room where he could now hear the faint throbbing of music. What Abbie called music, anyway.

He sidled up to where she sat curled up on the chair by the couch. She pulled out an earphone. "Need a sedative?"

When Abbie turned to him, she wasn't smiling. Her eyes were pensive, unhappy. Michael saw them and settled down next to her on the couch, wondering why her eyes scanned him so intently.

"What's the matter, honey?"

This finally brought a smile, though it was a weak one. "You."

He brushed an errant curl back from her forehead, thinking how very vulnerable and attractive she looked, sitting there in just that oversize T-shirt. His smile was meant to be sympathetic.

"Any problem of yours is a problem of mine. Want to talk?"

"Actually," she countered with a frustrated little sigh, "it's kind of the other way around."

Michael didn't follow. "What?"

Her smile didn't gain any humor. "I was just thinking that your problems were my problems."

"Are you talking about my job?"

She shook her head. "I'm talking about your inability to confide in anyone."

Now she really had him confused. "I think I'm missing something here, Abbie. You want to start at the beginning?"

Abbie found that she had to give vent to the emotions boiling up in her. She'd started with anger, then progressed to frustration and finally pain. It had been a long few hours alone while Michael slept and she couldn't, and she had spent them thinking about what she knew of him. It all ended up painting a picture of a man who couldn't rely on the woman he loved to offer him support and solace when he'd needed it. Finally, she decided, he had given up trying. She could see him spending his off-hours in a bar with the other cops, substituting their camaraderie for a healthy relationship at home. And now he probably didn't know how to open up. He had offered her sympathy and strength, and then shied away when she had sought to do the same for him.

She supposed that she should have let Michael gradually open up to her, building his trust until he could confide in her as easily as he allowed her to confide in him. But Abbie's instincts told her that he wasn't dealing well with the stresses he faced. He had brought his pain home alone too long now, and he was in real need of someone to help bear the burden. It was even more imperative now, when Michael couldn't tolerate being distracted by unfinished business; he didn't have the luxury of entertaining his troubles for a few weeks until he could wade through them.

Abbie walked over to the window where she could look down on the afternoon pedestrians on Goethe. A mother with a baby carriage, a few couples out scouting the summer day, a well-dressed gentleman carrying dry cleaning. Directly below sat a familiar-looking cab, and poised alongside, a blue-haired matron and her beribboned poodle. All quiet, everyday activities. Life went on around the Ambassador, and Abbie felt as if she were smothering in the climate control of the twelfth floor.

"Every time I see you," she said without turning, "you're about as tense as a guide wire. I can see it. But when I ask you about it, you won't say anything. You wouldn't even talk when Hector died.'' Turning, she impaled him with the pain in her eyes. "And I have a feeling I know what he meant to you. Who do you talk to, Michael? Who's there for you?''

Michael got to his feet, but couldn't quite go over to her. "I have friends on the force, Swann, and Mendlesohn.''

She nodded. She'd been right. He was keeping his distance now, because that was the only way he'd ever known. "Has that been enough?''

"It has to be.'' He gave no ground with his answer or the set of his jaw. "It was something I understood when I became a cop.''

"Us against them?''

He shrugged. "Not everybody understands.''

She came a step closer, so afraid to make such a commitment. So afraid she'd be rejected. "Did your wife?''

Michael's head came up like that of an animal that smelled danger. "Why should she? Maria didn't have to face it day after day.''

Abbie nodded. "I know.'' He still defended her, even after all these years. He still considered it his fault that she hadn't been a strong enough person to share the stress of his job. Abbie took another step closer, gaging him carefully. "Why wouldn't you tell me about the deal Mr. Magnusson was cooking up for me?''

"You didn't need to know about that,'' he retorted. "It just would have...''

"Upset me?'' She stood right before him, her head back a little to face him squarely. "What I don't know won't hurt me?''

She could see by the surprise in his eyes that she'd struck home. He tried to escape, the cant of the conversation a sudden threat to him. The hotel room had become as much a fantasy place for him as for Abbie and now reality was setting in. "How 'bout we just go back to bed and worry about all this some other time?'' he asked, trying his best to camouflage his tension with a tight smile. "We've got enough problems without asking for more, my lovely doctor."

Abbie shook her head. "That is part of the problem, my handsome sergeant." She took a gentle hand to the steel edge of his jaw. "I can't abide being helpless about something. And I find, much to my surprise, that it matters more to me when it concerns you than anything else. I can't bear to see you rip yourself apart like this."

She saw the ambivalence surface. The struggle between sharing and protecting. Fear of the unknown and a greater fear of what Michael did know. He didn't think he could trust Abbie with the ugliness of his job, and she didn't know how to make him. The air between them crackled with the escalating tension.

His answering grin was poignant. "You're not going to do the noble thing and stay away from this, are you?"

"Michael." She reached out to touch his arm. "I'm not Maria. If you have pain, I want to share it. Let me help, please."

It took Michael a moment to answer. He finally reached out to take her by the arms, his touch and tone of voice more harsh than he'd intended as he tried to put twelve years of training into words.

"Abbie, I don't think you understand. It's not like I'm an accountant or a retail manager. When I have a bad day, it's not because I had a heavy audit or slow sales. I deal with twelve-year-old dope pushers and gang warfare. And that's on a good day. Why should I bring that back to you?"

She smiled then, because she knew the answer. "Because I love you. And because I understand what a really bad day is like." He tried to protest, but she placed a silencing hand to his mouth. "Michael, why do you think I meet so many police at work? It's not because we sell doughnuts, that's for damn sure. When that twelve-year-old overdoses, I'm the one you bring him to. I was the one in there trying to save Hector, remember?"

He couldn't think of an answer. The conditioning was too great, the same pressure that made him such a stoic too deeply ingrained. Survival meant retreating within the ranks, and Maria had only proven it.

Abbie held her breath, praying he'd understand.

In the end, it was just too much to hope for. Michael let go of her, turning away, his agitation telegraphed by the swift shake he gave his head. "No." Abbie tried to protest, but Michael turned on her, his eyes in agony. "I can't, Abbie. I can't afford the possibility that I'd drive you away, don't you understand? Just having you here with me is too vital to me. If I forced you away, too, I don't know what I'd do."

Abbie couldn't help the tears that threatened. "Michael, if I can't help you, I can't stay. It's the only way I know how to be."

"You might think you want it," he retorted, "now. But it wouldn't work. I know."

She reached for him, fear driving her voice upward. "I am not Maria!"

"And you're not a cop!" he shouted back. "How could you possibly understand?"

"Give me a chance, Michael. That's all I ask. Please!"

They stood faced off, trembling. Michael glared at her as if she had betrayed him. "All right! You want to know about work last night?" He came a step closer, and she fought the urge to back away from his turmoil. "It was a really rough night last night, Abbie. Remember those two cops who baby-sat you? They're dead. Somebody snuck in and blew them up in the safe house. Now you want to talk about it?"

Chapter 10

The minute the words were out, Michael regretted them.

"Abbie, I'm sorry..."

She'd gone ashen, standing so rigidly that Michael thought she'd break. He reached out to her, but she flinched, her action knifing through him. He'd been right. She shouldn't have to face this kind of thing. God, she shouldn't have to be involved at all.

The room fell into a stark silence, and they heard the city noises filling the background like the irritating buzz of insects. Abbie turned away, her head down, her eyes shut against the picture of those two men who had played cards with her and swapped opinions on rock bands.

They were dead. She couldn't comprehend the finality of it, even though it was her business to. Yet she couldn't quite move beyond the concept. The vagaries of life had never seemed more absurd or pointless than they did at that moment.

Her voice flat, she didn't turn to face Michael, "Tell me what happened."

He ached for her. She looked so lost. "They were still investigating it this morning," he finally said, the pain echoing in his voice. "But when we took you out, we asked the narc guys to stay on at the house as a decoy. Sometime last night, the house just blew up." He paused, seeking a way to comfort. "They never knew what hit them."

Abbie allowed a rueful little laugh. How many times had she used that particular balm? Death could be easier to take if the person involved were surprised about it. And how many times, she thought, had she been telling the truth?

She turned on Michael. "Did you know them?"

He shook his head. "Not really. The vice guys tend to stick together."

She nodded absently. "It was meant for me, wasn't it, Michael?"

"They're trying to decide now," he lied instinctively. "There might have been something the two guys were working on, a revenge angle..."

"Michael, stop it!" Her eyes glittered as she confronted him. "Lying to me isn't going to help. I have to know."

He couldn't stand to be separated from her any longer. Crossing the intervening space, he took her gently by the arms, as if it would ease his words, not just for her, but himself. He felt as if he were floundering. He felt pulled in too many directions at once when he should have been keeping his mind on the case at hand and Abbie's safety. It's the price you pay for involvement, he could hear the lieutenant say. Truer words, he thought, the distress on Abbie's face tearing at him.

She was trying to change the rules on him. And if you didn't have the rules, what did you have to go by?

"All right," he conceded with a nod, his eyes on hers, trying to anticipate her. Trying to protect her when he knew he couldn't. "They think Marlow was trying to shut you up. Or get to me through you." His grin was rueful. "The news of our relationship has evidently preceded us. I'm sorry, Abbie. I wish I didn't have to tell you. I'm sorry I told you like I did."

He saw his own torment mirrored in her eyes, and saw the deliberate softening in her posture as she eased a little closer, never taking her eyes from his.

"I understand," she said, her sincerity surprising him. She wasn't going to punish him for hurting her. There was only worry in her expression as she took her index finger and traced the creases of weariness that responsibility had etched on his face. "I wish there was some way I could make it all better for you."

He slid his arms around her, his body aching for her. Her words had anticipated his sudden need to share his frustration, to create between them a retreat from the harsh realities that awaited them outside this room. He'd been the one to ask those guys to stay. If he hadn't, they might still have been alive.

"There is a way," Michael admitted with more sincerity than he'd intended, his cheek nestled against the soft comfort of her hair. "But I promised the lieutenant that after I got a little sleep I'd bring you back in for a statement."

Abbie rested her head against his chest, her arms around to the smooth skin of his back. Even now the embers were stirring, the most delicious heat seeping through her limbs. It amazed her that just one day with him could so sharpen her appetites. It troubled her that that same day had made her so dependent on him. She knew she shouldn't have let that happen, with so much still unresolved between them.

"When do you go back on duty?" she asked, closing her eyes to the heady exhilaration just his fingers against her neck aroused. It was so good to be back in his arms. God, if only they could stay within the safety of this room, never having to go back out and face the problems, the danger. Taking a slow breath, she held on more tightly.

"On duty as in on duty," he answered. "I don't. Magnusson pulled me. Said that my working would be counterproductive now."

Abbie looked up, expecting relief and finding consternation instead. "What's wrong with that?"

He scowled. "There's a lot of unfinished business I have with the Blood and the Guerrillas. Things haven't gotten much better there." Satisfaction surged briefly in his eyes. "I did manage to collar the kid who killed Hector. Brought him in this morning."

Abbie smiled. "One less bit of unfinished business, at least."

Michael looked down at her with surprise. That was what he'd just been thinking. If he weren't careful, he'd begin to depend on her common sense. "Yeah, well, the rest of the unfinished business still awaits. And I'm afraid that Lt. Capshaw isn't as patient as I am."

Abbie stretched to deliver a long, soft kiss that ended her up in a fierce embrace. "In that case," she finally managed a bit breathlessly a moment later, "I'll just go get on my formal jeans."

Michael hugged her again. "Do it now," he advised, just as breathlessly, "before you don't get a chance."

She grinned. "I'd almost risk it just for the chance of seeing you explain the delay to the lieutenant. And Mr. Magnusson."

"The lieutenant gave up on me a long time ago." He grinned back, reluctant to let her loose. "And I'd be delighted to tell Magnusson—except he probably wouldn't understand what I was talking about."

Taking just a moment more, Abbie challenged the guilt in those taut eyes with her own healing. "It wasn't your fault, Michael."

He hesitated, surprised again by her perception. "Everything's my fault," he retorted with a wry look in his eyes, trying his best to joke past the tight pain of that early-morning news. "At least, that's what Magnusson says."

She refused to yield. With a smile born of love and understanding, she slowly shook her head. "You saved my life again." Then her smile widened a little. "When we're finished at the station, we'll find you something to throw."

* * *

The station hadn't changed any in the past few days. Abbie was beginning to hate its dingy walls and never-ending noise. What she really hated was the fact that every time she walked in, she was thrown back in with the mug books.

It was as if they figured that maybe this time the guy would look like somebody recognizable. Abbie hated to disappoint them, but he still didn't look enough like any of the photos she paged through hour after hour for her to point to it and say, "Yes, this is definitely the man who busted down my door and tried to throttle me."

Swann assured Abbie that a lot of people had trouble identifying bad guys, but Magnusson looked disgusted. She informed Magnusson that if his own men couldn't identify the guy when they were trained to, it stood to reason that she'd have a little more trouble.

"Do you think he's the guy who blew up the safe house?" she asked.

Magnusson shrugged. "It stands to reason. Especially since he already made one attempt on you." At that point, he'd delivered a scathingly unhappy look in Michael's direction. "I really think, Miss Fitzgerald, that you're running a greater risk letting Sgt. Viviano play hide-and-seek with you, than you would under our protection."

"That's *Dr.* Fitzgerald," she reminded him coldly, taking offense to his patronizing attitude, "and, may I ask, greater risk than what? Being blown up in your safe house?"

Michael actually laughed.

"Viviano..." The lieutenant's rebukes were beginning to sound weary.

"So, what do we do now?" Abbie asked.

"Nothing that will involve you, Dr. Fitzgerald," Magnusson assured her, accentuating the *Dr.* enough to sound peevish.

"That's what you said the last time," she reminded him, "and since then, I've been accosted, chased and almost blown up. I shudder to think of what would have happened to me if you'd set me out as bait, like you wanted to in the first place."

This time both Swann and Michael laughed.

"If there's one thing I'm learning," Michael warned, "it's that you can't very well keep anything from her."

So Magnusson told her.

"Another session with the press?" she demanded. "Michael, I'm sure glad you get along so well with them."

"It would be safer for you if you disavowed ever seeing Marlow," Magnusson advised her, ignoring the levity. "At least for now."

"I wouldn't think of stealing Michael's limelight." She grinned. Only Michael could see the tension build in her.

"It probably wouldn't hurt, though, if you were there with him when he made the announcement. The press is, of course, interested in your well-being after the incident at your apartment."

She gave him the sweetest smile she could. "So am I, Mr. Magnusson. So am I."

Michael stood to one side of her, Swann to the other, and Abbie recognized at least four plainclothes officers in the crowd when the press came to ooh and aah over her safety and Michael's latest news.

"Thanks to the information supplied by Officer Viviano," the lieutenant was saying in his prepared statement, "we now have a much better idea of who we're looking for."

"What caused his memory to come back?" one of the reporters asked. The lieutenant turned to Abbie for a medical ad-lib.

Abbie couldn't think of anything more impressive to offer than a shrug. She was tempted to say a hit on the head with a frying pan, but John would never forgive her. "It was bound to come back," she finally offered. "The timing involved is up to the whims of nature." Or the full moon, or the tides. Or the dictates of the DEA.

"And Dr. Fitzgerald," he went on, "you don't remember seeing the accomplice in question?"

She grinned. "I had eyes only for that gun barrel."

They were having their little talk in the press room at the station, merely a conference room with enough electrical outlets for all the equipment. The glass partitions allowed a view into the main station and out the front door, which was far more interesting to Abbie than the three-act musical they were putting on for the press. Magnusson, the silent director of the show, lounged out by the main desk, his eyes on the proceedings. Abbie was tempted to throw him a kiss.

She was about to turn her attention back to the next question about indictments and such that the lieutenant was answering, when she spotted the man again. Marlow. Wasn't it? He was walking toward the front door, and he was in a suit again. She looked around, but no one seemed to see him. She had thought they were going to bring him in this time. Why in God's name was he wandering the station?

"Michael." A surreptitious hiss in his ear. "Why is Marlow out there?"

Michael almost ended up with whiplash trying to find out. He missed him, just heading out past Magnusson. "Where?"

She did everything but wave. "He just walked out the front door."

"What?"

The newsmen heard that. Michael turned back to them with a guilty look and shrugged. The lieutenant offered him a scowl before returning to his answer.

"I thought you said he was a scum bag." Abbie kept the level of her voice intimate.

Michael looked a bit surprised. "He is. Why?"

"He was wearing a suit."

Michael didn't wait any longer. While the lieutenant thanked the press for coming over, Michael slipped down the side of the room and headed after Magnusson and the man Abbie claimed to have seen.

"Abbie says she just saw Marlow walk out past you," Michael accused. The look on Magnusson's face put Abbie's observation right where he thought it belonged.

"Marlow is at home with his lady." He had a real knack for sounding bored.

"Abbie says she saw him."

Magnusson raised an eyebrow. "And you think I'd let him walk right by me?"

Michael had no patience for him. "I think you'd do whatever's expedient for the DEA."

"What's this about Marlow?" Swann asked, coming up on them with Abbie in tow.

"He wasn't here," Magnusson repeated as if to a very slow class.

"Then who was it?" Abbie asked. "He looked just like the man I saw."

"Dr. Fitzgerald," Magnusson said with exaggerated patience. "What would Marlow be doing in the middle of a police station?"

She had to grin. "That's what I was wondering. But I also saw him Saturday night at city hall."

Michael turned on her. "What do you mean? Saturday was the night you were attacked."

She nodded. "The Channel 4 news. I just remembered it when I saw him again. I saw a brief clip of Marlow at the back of a crowd at city hall." A quick look at Magnusson's impatience robbed her of her certainty. "At least I thought I did. It was right as that guy buzzed up."

Magnusson pulled himself upright. "I'll tell you what. I have things to do. Let me know if he comes in again." About as likely as seeing Margaret Thatcher at a meeting of the IRA, his expression said. He walked on down the hall without waiting for an answer.

Abbie found herself glaring after his retreating figure. "I'm not an idiot, Michael," she protested, then turned to him. "Couldn't Magnusson be wrong?"

Michael slipped an arm around her waist. "This guy really looked like Marlow?"

"Enough that I felt my stomach kick over."

Michael turned to Swann, his eyes speculative, when the reporters began to file past. Abbie saw the purpose behind the banter, most of them offering Michael and her jokes and platitudes and hoping for bonus nuggets for their stories. She felt Michael's arm tense up. And as she'd said, she was no idiot. She smiled back without saying a word.

Michael must have given one of the TV guys some kind of signal. Everyone had cleared the door by a good minute or so when an anchorman she recognized sidled back in, a quizzical smile on his face.

Michael drew him unobtrusively to the side. "Want an exclusive?"

The man was no fool, either. "You can make promises like that?"

Michael smiled over at Swann. "He can." Swann smiled back.

He got a nod from the TV man. "What can I do for you?"

"We need to review some tapes from Saturday's ten o'clock news. Any problems?"

Abbie saw the speculation grow on the other man's face. "And my exclusive?"

Michael gave him a short nod of agreement. "When I can break the story, you get it first."

"Then that dog and pony show in there was just that?"

Abbie saw the charm of Michael's good-boy facade. "Just keep in touch."

The man consulted a watch. "I have a show to do. Can you be at the station at about eight?"

After a quick consultation with Swann, Michael nodded. They forwent a handshake. After the newsman walked back out the front door, Michael and Swann led Abbie back into the now-empty conference room.

"We have some talking to do," Swann said. "Where do you want to do it?"

Michael shrugged.

"Am I invited?" Abbie asked.

Michael grinned briefly. "If it's the only way to keep an eye on you."

"Then I say we eat."

"Eat?" he retorted, his eyes bright. "Is that all you think about?"

Her answering grin matched his. "No, but it's the only thing I can think of that includes the three of us."

She heard Swann make choking noises behind her.

"In that case," Michael agreed, "we'll eat. How 'bout White Castle?"

"Is that the kind of stuff you usually eat?"

"That and pasta."

Abbie shot Michael an appraising look as she slowly shook her head. "How can the boy possibly stay so thin?"

Michael's returning smile was a bit dry. "Aggravation," he assured her. "Now, what would you like to eat?"

"Anything that isn't served here."

That ended up being room service back at the Ambassador East. The three were just heading for the station door in a try for dinner when they were intercepted by Magnusson coming the other way.

"Oh, Viviano, good." He greeted them without noticeable enthusiasm. "I was hoping I'd catch you before you took off on another escapade."

Michael stopped to face the man, once again shielding Abbie from him. Abbie wondered what kind of reflex that was. "I wouldn't have missed saying goodbye to you, Magnusson."

"I hope not, Viviano. I got some news a while ago from my undercover. The hit's gone out. Out-of-town talent— you probably don't know them. A pair from Philadelphia. Pictures just came in."

As he handed the two black-and-white photos to Michael, Magnusson made it a point to cast a look at a now pale Abbie. "Their name is Traveleno. Interested in a safe house, now?"

Michael looked up as he passed the photos on to Swann, his expression unforgiving. "Thanks, no. I don't want your death toll going up."

He and Swann turned again for the door, the photos still in Swann's hand. Abbie didn't quite have enough wits about her to follow. She stood where she was, the life draining from her face.

She'd been doing her best to ignore the threats Magnusson claimed to be out toward Michael. Every hour she'd spent getting lost in the city going from point A to point B by route of point Q just to make sure they weren't followed, she'd concocted and delivered elaborate tour monologues, just to make light of her tension.

She couldn't do that anymore. The danger had materialized. It had a name. The Travelenos, whoever they were, were being paid to travel from Philadelphia just to kill Michael.

Magnusson saw the torment on her face and allowed himself a look of satisfaction. "I was making the offer to you, Dr. Fitzgerald. Would you like to make use of a safe house now?"

Abbie's head jerked up as if she hadn't seen the man standing there. Michael and Swann had turned back for her, Michael laying his hand on her arm. He didn't say a word, though. It was Abbie's decision to make.

"Mr. Magnusson," she said with as much iron as she could manage. "I wouldn't think of putting myself into the hands of someone who takes a person's life so lightly that he can't wait to tell him he's in danger of dying. You can go straight to hell."

The trip to the hotel seemed endless. Michael took Abbie south as far Burnham Park, just beyond the black behemoth of McCormick Place, and then west into Berwyn and Cicero before winding their way back toward State Street. When they reached the depressed lanes of Wacker—an underground world Abbie had always referred to as the Emerald City because of the green lighting—Michael pulled the car over and set the emergency lights.

"What's the matter?" Abbie asked, automatically apprehensive. They hadn't said more than a few words since setting out, Michael's eyes always alternating between the rearview mirror and the road ahead.

"This." He smiled and pulled her over for a kiss.

Abbie dissolved into his arms, the feel of his solid body around her enough to threaten tears.

"I've been wanting to do that since you told Magnusson off back there." He smiled, and kissed her again, his lips lingering over hers for a moment. "You were magnificent."

"I was furious," she admitted, a smile tugging at her own mouth. If she were so deathly afraid for him, how could she be so exhilarated? She felt as if someone were pumping hot air into her bloodstream. "He couldn't care less about you."

"That's what makes him such a good government official."

"Michael..." It took a minute to progress any further. "Isn't this kind of a dangerous place to be necking?"

"Nah."

Cars whizzed by in both directions, some coming within inches of their bumper. Quite a few were testing out their horns. Michael didn't even seem to notice.

"What if we're being followed?"

"We are," he assured her. "Swann's behind us."

Abbie straightened, craning her head around to see that Swann's car was just slowing behind them. He didn't seem particularly worried.

Abbie was mortified. Flipping off the emergency lights, she motioned to the ignition. "Get going, bucko. I don't intend to have someone peeking over my shoulder while I steam up the windows of an unmarked police car."

Michael laughed as he turned the key. But then he sobered for a moment. "Abbie." He turned to her, and she knew what was coming. "It might be safer for you to take Magnusson up on his offer."

She shook her head with more conviction than she really had. "If I have to be worried about you for the next few days, I'm going to be worried with you. Not across town. That would be asking too much, Michael."

He nodded, leaning over to deposit another light kiss. "Okay, hon."

"Well," Swann spoke up a while later, "if you don't have good taste yourself, hang around with someone who does."

He finished the last of his poached salmon and set down his cutlery.

"You saying you don't have any taste, Swann?" Michael grinned from where he was rolling linguine on his fork.

"I'm saying I almost ran out of hope for you, Viviano."

Abbie watched the two of them from where she nibbled on scampi across the table, and wondered at the humor that kept them going in a situation like this. Like the humor at work, she guessed. You had to laugh sometimes. It was the only way to stay sane. She wished she had the energy to try it, but the danger to Michael preyed too heavily on her.

"You really think this is better than hamburgers?" Michael was demanding, even though he'd made short order of his food.

Swann shook his head. "Man, maybe there isn't any hope for you after all. What do you think, Doc?"

Abbie couldn't offer any more than a small smile.

She let them trade good-natured insults during dinner, and then sat back with a snifter of Grand Marnier as they discussed their plan of attack.

"Magnusson's head's in the wrong place," Swann decided laconically. "I think he's lost touch with the street."

"Your snitches come up with something?"

Swann shook his head. "Just a feeling. How about yours?"

Michael took a drink of beer and shrugged. "Mendlesohn's gonna keep on 'em for me. There's got to be some news out there. You don't just get a shipment of this size without some shock waves. Especially when it's been as dry out there as it has been."

Swann nodded reflectively. "I put the word out on the Travelenos. We'll know something by morning."

"Thanks."

It was only seven-thirty, and already Abbie wanted to turn in. Maybe it was the liqueur, but all she wanted was to crawl into the warm security of that big bed where policemen and careful hotel employees protected her, and sleep for about a week. She just wanted to hide.

It was when she looked at Michael that she knew she couldn't. The strain was growing on his features, each day taking its toll. His jawline was rigid, the lines across his forehead almost never gone now. He spent most of his energy protecting her. How could she possibly back away when he needed her the most? When he gave her so much?

"Time to go, Abbie."

She nodded slowly and uncurled her feet from the couch.

The newsman met them at the door to the TV station. The corridors were almost empty in between shows, the only chatter coming from the weather station set up in a little closet just next to the control booth. Abbie spotted the weatherman she watched every day but without his toupé. She almost didn't recognize him.

They were led into a small conference room where a TV waited with four or five cassettes piled on top. The newsman motioned for them to sit down.

"What was the story?" he asked.

Abbie rubbed at her tired eyes. "Oh, something about city redevelopment. It was at city hall."

He'd evidently just been through the tapes, because he pulled one out of the pile and stuck it right in the machine. Abbie looked up just as the reporter began her voice-over.

There was the crowd—about twenty people meeting to formalize some kind of agreement about putting funds into the West Side. Along the fringes wandered people conducting their everyday city-government business, a number of bagmen looking for their fortune, and a couple who appeared to be sight-seeing.

"There he is." Within the space of an instant, Abbie's weariness vanished. The man parted himself from the back of the crowd and began to walk away.

Michael leaned forward. "Stop the tape."

The tape stopped, freezing the man in a three-quarter profile. Abbie imagined him angry, with a gun in his hand. Her stomach lurched.

"He really does look like Marlow," Michael was saying in awe.

Swann nodded, never taking his eyes from the screen. "Dead ringer, almost. No wonder Abbie spotted him."

"Marlow?" the newsman asked. "Is that a name I should know."

Michael never took his eyes from the set. "In a few days. Abbie, what do you think?"

Her voice was very small. "It's him."

"Is this to do with that robbery?" the newsman asked, a skeptical eye on the tape.

"You could say that." Michael relented.

"Then you have the wrong guy."

All three of them looked at him.

"Who is he?" Michael demanded.

"John DeRosa. Big-time developer. He's donating his time to help develop a blighted area program for the West Side. They're thinking of naming the park they're gonna put up after him."

"DeRosa?" Michael asked. "Never heard of him.

The man shrugged. "He came to town about five years ago. From out East. Since that time, he's made the right connections and the right noises to finance two office towers on Wacker and condos along Lake Shore. Big money."

Michael looked over to see that Abbie hadn't taken her eyes from the tape. "What do you think?"

It didn't make any sense, but the sight of that man was giving her the most awful chills. Maybe if some of those mug-book pictures could move like the ones on this tape, she could get a better feel for them. If she could see Marlow's eyes move, see him walk, he might elicit the same deathly chill.

"He looks so close," she protested, knowing she must be wrong.

"He's not the man I saw, Abbie," Michael said. "He's not Marlow."

"You're sure."

Both Michael and Swann nodded.

"I'm sure," Michael said.

Their host was all ears. "Marlow's the name of the guy you saw? The one the doc here was supposed to have missed?"

"The one she *did* miss." Michael corrected him with a deadpan expression, his finger toward the screen. "You can see for yourself that she identified the wrong guy."

"Why isn't Marlow a guest of Chicago's finest?"

Swann's expression was just as informative as Michael's. "We're doing our best."

The newsman smiled broadly, nodding with acquiescence. "Okay. But don't forget. I get the first word."

Michael got to his feet. "Deal." This time he held out his hand. The man took it with a knowing smile.

When Michael turned to help Abbie to her feet, he was struck again by the confusion on her face. She was really reacting strongly to this guy. Too strongly. Maybe she'd do the same when they finally got Marlow in, but he decided to play a long shot and not take a chance on it.

"Listen," he said, turning back on the newsman who was pulling the tape back out. "Will you do me one more favor?"

"Depends."

"Can I get your morgue stuff on this DeRosa guy? Just for curiosity's sake."

The man shrugged. "No skin off my back. But like I said, he's well connected."

Michael's grin was wry. "My boss can still arrest his boss."

Swann spoke up again when the three of them stood back out in the parking lot. Abbie couldn't believe the two of them weren't checking out every shadow.

"You know something I don't?" He was speaking to Michael.

Michael shrugged as he opened the passenger door and helped Abbie in. "You know me and my hunches. I'd just hate to overlook something."

"You want to make Abbie feel better?" He kept his voice low.

Michael's smile was enigmatic. "I want to make *me* feel better. I've got enough to worry about right now without having to worry about being blindsided."

Swann nodded thoughtfully. "Do you want me to follow you back?"

"Yeah." Michael stole a quick look at Abbie who was sitting in the front seat, staring disconsolately ahead. He kept his voice down. "Let's see if we can get this thing over with fast, Swann. I don't know how much more she can handle."

Swann just nodded again, his expression unreadable, his loyalty unquestionable. "I'll get to you tomorrow, man."

Michael turned back to him, his own expression offering his own unstated gratitude. "See you then."

When Swann was walking back to his car, he added a final warning: "And don't you be feeding that fine lady any more fast food, you hear?"

Chapter 11

Abbie didn't get much sleep that night. If it had been just her own uncertainty and fear she'd had to deal with, she might have managed at least a short doze. She was, after all, an E.R. doctor, used to dropping off no matter what was going on. She had trained herself to sleep even through a churning stomach and the tight breathlessness of apprehension.

She lay on her side, facing the window and watching the square of sky ease from late night to early dawn, keeping herself very still so that she wouldn't disturb Michael with her restlessness.

She needn't have bothered. Michael tossed and turned all night, the tension in him radiating like summer heat off a sidewalk. She was sure he never closed his eyes. He spent most of the night within inches of her, his body stiff and unyielding, a deliberate wall constructed between them.

She had tried to get him to talk to her, just after they'd given up on pacing around the suite and turned in. Slipping across the intervening space in the big bed, she'd nestled her head against his chest and wrapped her arm around him. He lay with an arm beneath his head, smoking a cigarette.

"Bad habit," she said softly.

Michael grinned tightly, still trying for humor. "Swann says I'm full of bad habits." Taking a last drag, he stubbed out the offending cigarette and brought his arm around Abbie. She settled closer, her hand against the rigid muscles of his chest.

"He also said that you started again when you got shot."

"Swann worries too much."

"That's all right." Abbie grinned just as tightly as Michael. "You won't let anybody else do it for you."

He didn't move. "I think we've had this conversation before."

Abbie wasn't sure if Michael heard her pause, the careful tone of voice she used to question him. "Is there anything I can do to help?"

He never hesitated. "No. Just get some sleep."

Lifting herself onto an elbow, Abbie faced him. "I'm scared, Michael."

"I know." His eyes melted for her, his growing love coloring everything else. Abbie realized that that was what scared her the most. He carried the responsibility of that love alone, and she was afraid that it would interfere with his judgment. Worried about her, he might not watch out for himself.

"You *don't* know," she answered evenly, fighting the constriction in her throat. It would be so easy to drive him further away. So easy to lose him completely. But having him like this was like only having part of him. How could she make him understand that unless they shared the bad as well as the good, they could never develop a viable relationship? How could she teach herself to be patient enough to let him work it out on his own, when she was so sure time was running out?

She sighed, seeing Michael's defenses go up the minute she wandered too near a vulnerable area. "Do you realize that I'm having more trouble talking to you than when we first met? We're in one hell of a situation here, and neither of us can seem to talk about it.''

Michael's eyes were indecipherable. ''I just don't want you to have to worry,'' he finally admitted. ''This is hard enough on you as it is.''

''Michael,'' she retorted gently, wanting so much for him to understand, ''I'm not going to lie to you. This whole setup scares the hell out of me. You're in danger, and there's nothing I can do about it. But the part that really frightens me is that you won't let me help. You treat me like Dresden china, when you should be able to rely on me. Don't you think I worry more, knowing that something's preying on you and I don't even know what it is?''

For a long moment, Michael studied her, his eyes veiled and dark. Abbie honestly couldn't say what was going on behind them. Then he brought his other arm around her and drew her back to him. ''What do you want to know?''

Abbie held her breath against hoping for too much from his offer. Her eyes were level with his arm, the strong biceps where the proud sergeant's stripes would stretch when Michael left her again. ''I want to know how much danger I'm in. How much danger you're in.'' It took her a moment to finish the rest of her request, since Michael's answer was so important to her. ''I want to know if I'm making it more dangerous for you by staying with you. And I want you to be honest.''

Michael tightened his hold on her, bringing his face close to the soft fragrance of her hair. Abbie kept her silence with difficulty as the moments stretched on before Michael answered.

''I'm not going to pretend,'' he said, although she could tell by the tone of his voice that he wasn't telling the whole truth even now. ''Until we nail Marlow, you're still on his list. Since we made such a point of letting him know you didn't see him, I think he wants you to get to me. He wants me pretty badly.''

''Hence the Travelenos.''

She felt his shrug. "I'm not too worried about them. Swann said he'd ferret them out."

"But if I stick close to you, won't that make you more vulnerable?"

"Not as vulnerable as I'd be, always worried about whether Magnusson was taking good care of you." Michael brushed a stray curl back from Abbie's cheek and kissed her. "If you want to stay here with me, I want you to. I'll take care of you."

Abbie closed her eyes, the gentle touch of his lips searing her. The answer was the one she'd hoped for, even though she knew it was selfish. Now if she could only measure another success. "Will you let me take care of you?"

She knew that Michael didn't know quite how to answer. "You do take care of me," he finally said. "Just by being here."

"I don't make it more stressful for you?"

"No." He was lying. "Now go to sleep."

"Michael . . ."

"You aren't very patient, are you?" he demanded playfully. Abbie couldn't hear much relief in his tone.

She edged closer to the support of his strong body, frustration crowding her. She'd wanted him to tell the truth. To tell her how her presence in this complicated everything; what he really felt about the threat to himself; maybe share his frustration over having to deal with Magnusson. He was right. She was impatient. She wanted him to be able to trust her now, when he needed to.

"No," she finally admitted with a small sigh. "I guess I'm not. But I am long on undying support."

Michael lifted her face to him, his fingers gentle against her skin, his eyes softening with a smile. "Did I tell you that I love you?"

She smiled back. "Did I tell you that I love you, too?"

He nodded. "Good. Since it's all settled, let's get to sleep."

He kissed her, his eyes closed, his arms tight and sure, meant to reassure in their own way. But he spent the night tossing and turning, retreating to the other side of the bed where Abbie couldn't reach him. Abbie spent a sleepless night thinking that of all people, Michael should have known that sometimes love just wasn't enough.

Michael finally gave up on getting any sleep about ten the next morning. Dragging himself out of bed, he pulled his watch from the table and scowled at it, thinking that it was still too early. But if he'd been on duty he'd already be past his first break. He was supposed to be at a seminar for the Gang Crimes Division tomorrow. He usually spent the day before sounding out his kids on the state of things on the street. Instead he was holed up in a hotel room with nowhere to go and nothing to do.

Michael turned to take in Abbie, lying on the bed. She lay curled on her side at the far edge, her hair tumbled haphazardly over her face, her chest rising and falling in gentle, even rhythm. She hadn't so much as moved all night long. Michael couldn't understand how she'd slept so well. After the talk they'd had, he hadn't managed fifteen minutes' worth.

Damn, he wished she knew what she was doing by tempting him like that. He'd come so close to just giving in, trusting those guileless eyes and offering up his troubles. He'd remembered that she hadn't flinched from his anger, hadn't rejected him for the unintentional pain he'd inflicted on her. Instead, she'd come back to comfort him. After the past few days, he needed that comfort. He needed her insights and understanding.

But history had taught him too well that the understanding didn't last long. The comfort slowly withered as the job began to crowd the rest of life.

Michael wondered whether Abbie would understand that as much as he dreaded walking back out on the street in search of Marlow, he couldn't wait for the hunt. The challenge. You pit your wits and reflexes against those of a criminal and bet that yours are better. Michael wanted Marlow. He probably wanted him more than that jackass Magnusson did, just because he didn't want some sleaze ball outsmarting him. He wondered if Abbie would understand his wanting to risk his life for that.

He looked down at her sleeping figure and thought not. She had seen what happened when reflexes weren't enough. He knew she didn't want to hear that Michael thought his were better. No, he thought, getting slowly to his feet and heading around for the shower; that was an addiction she wouldn't want to hear about. Just as she wouldn't want to face the day-to-day refuse Michael had to shovel. Or the fact that someday his reflexes might fail him.

Michael didn't see Abbie open her eyes and watch him walk past into the bathroom.

He'd thought a hot shower would help revive him. Standing under the stinging jet, he wasn't so sure it would do the job. His palms flat against the cool marble wall, he bent his head to the water, letting it cascade down his tired neck and back. Steam lifted around him in thick billows, and the marble echoed with the rush of the water. Michael closed his eyes and tried his best to escape into it.

Somehow, he heard the soft click of the door. Even as he stood halfway to a stupor, his instincts kicked in and brought him upright, his hand whipping the curtain back.

Abbie started, dropping the towel she'd been ready to wind around her head, a small look of mischief in her eyes.

"A little apprehensive," she chided, "aren't we?"

She was naked, her arms still up to her head so that her breasts lifted toward him. The steam had softened her skin to a pink glow, and she had a marvelous come-hither look on her. Michael stopped breathing as the hard ache of desire erupted in him.

"Were you going to join me?" he managed, his eyes sliding along her belly to where the soft, curling triangle of hair taunted him.

"Well," she demurred, "it is summer. We should conserve water, ya know."

His eyes returned to her face to find that she was actually blushing at his attention. It aroused him even more. Her smile was shyly pleased.

Michael held out his hand, the water dripping from his arm. Abbie saw droplets slide over the contours of his chest and glisten in his hair. Following him into the shower had been difficult for her, especially after the disappointment of last night, but when she'd seen Michael struggle to his feet as if the weight of the world were still on his shoulders, she knew she had to come to him. If this were the only way he'd let her help, then she would. The smile his flattering eyes gave birth to grew as she realized that she wanted to be here for more than just comfort.

She stepped over the rim of the tub, her hand firmly enclosed in Michael's, and slid in under the jet of water, the towel to protect her hair forgotten. Michael's eyes glowed in the indirect lighting. The water that splashed across his shoulders fell on her breasts, stinging them to life even before Michael brought a hand up to them.

Abbie reached up to run a hand against Michael's cheek. The soft rasp was delicious against her palm. She wanted to run her tongue along it.

"You didn't shave," she smiled a bit giddily.

Michael took hold of her hand with both of his, wedging her body closer to his in the small space. "No. Do you want me to?"

Abbie wanted to answer, but the slippery steel of his torso against hers was distracting. His skin was warm and rough, the water hot, the porcelain cool against her feet. Her hair began to unravel along her neck, water channeling from the curls down her back.

"Oh," she grinned, her eyes to her hand, still trapped within his. "I don't think so."

He grinned back, drawing her hand to his lips. He kissed her palm, and Abbie felt it all the way to her toes. It was like static electricity in the winter, sharp and unexpected. She didn't see her own lips part a little, even as her eyes widened in heady surprise. He took her index finger into his mouth and sucked the water from it, his tongue dancing over its surface. Abbie felt the strength oozing from her knees. She'd come to comfort him and here he was seducing her. And he'd touched no more than her hand with his mouth.

Michael took each finger into his mouth, all the while bending his face closer to Abbie's until he could feel her shallow breath against his skin. The veil of water surrounded them, its music sheltering them. Michael returned Abbie's hand to her, and then took gentle hold of her face, his thumbs drawing slow circles at the angles of her jaw. Abbie closed her eyes, moving her own hands to his arms to steady herself. Her heart thundered in her ears. She thought she felt the thrumming of Michael's as her breasts brushed against his chest. His lips skimmed her cheek. Abbie turned toward them, hers parted in a small moan of anticipation. She pulled him closer until her own soft skin molded against the unyielding warmth of his. When his mouth settled against hers, she stretched up to meet it.

Abbie surprised Michael with her fervor. Where he'd begun his lovemaking with gentle explorations, she'd met him with fierce need. She held on to him as if challenging his desire, absorbing his demons with her body since she couldn't with her words. To Michael's surprise, he realized that that was just what she was doing.

He bent to gather her into his arms and found himself drowning in the sweet smell of her, the darkly mysterious flavors of her mouth, the soft recesses of her body as it molded so surely to his. The world beyond their steamy curtain of water whirled away and disappeared, Michael's mind and body sinking deliciously into the fire of Abbie's touch.

He plundered the soft, secret places of her mouth, his tongue gliding over hers in provocative play. He crushed her against him, the very texture of her skin maddening his senses. His body ached for her. His hands fled over her as if satiating their own hunger. When he bent to taste her throat, she brought her head back, her hands caught at his waist. When he knelt to taste her breasts, she tangled those hands in his hair and held him against her.

Michael felt the dark, tight buds against his tongue and groaned, the fire in his belly unbearable. Teasing the nipple with his teeth and lips, he slid a hand along the velvet of her thighs, toward that triangle that beckoned him, the hidden fever that drove him.

Abbie gasped, her fingers pulling Michael closer against her breast. The assault on her senses was overwhelming. She had to move, arching against his suckling mouth and tormenting fingers. Tears mingled with the shower and were lost. She stopped breathing. Gently moving her hands, she lifted Michael's head so that he faced her. She drank in the languid light of his eyes like nectar.

He saw the water stream over her face and thought of tears.

Michael stood and took a hand to Abbie's cheek. He trembled with need for her. Bending to recapture her mouth, he lifted her gently in his arms. She wrapped herself around him. When Michael entered her, they shared soft moans of surprise. Every time they joined, the intensity of their pleasure in each other seemed a new discovery. Abbie never took her mouth away. As he filled her with that sweet, hot light, she held on to him, her fingernails raking his back in that most primitive of instincts. She rocked against him, her back now against the cool marble. Michael's hands clutched her to him, pulling her hard against him, as if no matter how close she was, she couldn't possibly be close enough.

Abbie's last, shuddering cry filled the small room, and then Michael followed, her name again and again on his lips as he spent himself in her, his head buried in her neck. Abbie smiled, her hand holding him to her, Michael's breathing ragged against her neck.

"I think somebody's going to complain about water usage in this room," she managed sometime later.

Michael grinned against her. "And I still haven't washed."

"Or shaved."

He laughed. "Or shaved."

They washed each other, using slippery hands to lather skin that still glowed with their lovemaking. Abbie watched her hand trail down the taut muscles of Michael's chest and wondered again at the beauty of his body. It was so supple and strong, so lean. She loved the feel of it next to her, never tired of exploring now familiar planes, her fingers dipping along muscle ridges and the tight rim of his pelvis.

The human body had always fascinated her in her study of medicine. An amazing machine that functioned beyond reasonable expectations and stood up to unbelievable abuse, it was one of the more impressive miracles of nature. She had just begun to appreciate firsthand, though, what a true work of art it was. And she had the feeling that she would never get her fill of this particular work of art.

As they knew they would, the gentle ministrations they performed on each other—massaging life into tired muscles and exploring the sensations of soap against skin, the slow savoring of a kiss under water—led them to make love again. Michael turned off the shower and lifted Abbie from the tub, carrying her back to the rumpled bed they had been unable to sleep in the night before.

And there they continued the explorations at their own leisurely pace, each completely immersed in the other as they took the time to learn rhythms and rediscover age-old instincts. Their voices were soft and hushed with new wonder as they instructed and laughed together and smiled their pleasure. And when they fell against each other, once again satiated, they slept. And this time they slept easily.

The phone woke them about dusk. Stretching at the discreet ring, Michael opened his eyes to find that Abbie was already moving to sit up.

"It's only Swann," he assured her, his eyes on the graceful curve of her body as she reached over to answer it. It didn't yet occur to him that he felt better than he had in days. More relaxed and well rested. More at peace.

Abbie grinned at the response Swann must have made to her greeting and handed the phone over. "He says you're a lazy good-for-nothing."

Michael reached up to pull her over onto him, inciting a round of surprised giggling. "He's right." Abbie tried to fend him off, but he landed a solid kiss that left them both a little breathless.

"Hello, Swann."

The voice on the other end was just shy of disgusted. "You want me to call back sometime next week when you can pay attention?"

"I'm not sure I'll be much better by then."

"Well, I hate to break up the party," he said without much enthusiasm, "but we have business to attend to."

The tone of Swann's voice cost Michael his smile. Abbie saw his expression change and felt her heart lurch. Their sanctuary had been breached again.

"What's up?" he asked into the phone, not seeing her anymore.

"I figure if we meet at Francis's during dinner breaks, we'll have plenty of company."

Michael understood. Francis's was a diner on Clark that the police favored. Crammed with Formica tables and businesslike waitresses, the small room was the kind of place people went for hearty food at good prices rather than atmosphere. The kind of place police loved. The place was solid blue during breaks.

"How soon?" he asked.

"I can make it in half an hour. What about you?"

Michael reached over to check his watch again, his eye straying toward the window in delayed surprise at the dearth of sunlight. "I'll be there."

When Michael hung up, Abbie was there waiting. "A powwow?"

He nodded, trying to decide what to do. "Just Swann and me," he assured her, his voice already distant. Abbie wanted to cry. "Why don't you stay here and get some sleep?"

"I just got some sleep," she reminded him. "If it's all the same to you, I hate to wait alone."

When he shook his head with that tolerant air, Abbie knew that he was protecting her. "It's not going to take that long, believe me. Swann just wants to fill me in over dinner on what I've missed today while I was . . . busy."

The smile Abbie gave him in return was less convinced. "I haven't eaten all day. And this place just isn't as much fun without you in it."

Michael finally gave in to her, although Abbie could see he wasn't pleased. It made her wonder what had gone wrong now. What he wanted to keep from her. She dressed quickly in a lightweight cream sweat suit and followed Michael out the door and back along the maze of streets that kept them safe from being followed.

Francis's was jammed to bursting when they arrived. All of the cops knew Michael on sight, and every one greeted him as he guided Abbie over to the table Swann had commandeered toward the back. Abbie saw them and thought of a cadre of bodyguards. As the men and women in this room laughed among themselves and worked their way through the buffet dinners they'd collected, they kept surreptitious watch over the occupants of the table in the far corner. It made her feel better and worse at the same time.

"Did you see yourselves on the news last night?" Swann greeted them without looking up from the crossword puzzle he was working in the *Trib*.

"It's all getting quite boring," Abbie assured him with a campy grin. He looked up to grin back, but the flat, black look in his eyes was one that Abbie had learned to interpret pretty accurately. Something was up. She felt her own smile stiffen and wilt.

"The price of celebrity." He shrugged. "I've been told the chicken and dumplings are good tonight." Setting aside his paper, he stood and led the way to the buffet line. The waitress had already deposited drinks for Michael and Swann, and accepted Abbie's order.

At first Abbie tried not to pay attention to the under-the-breath conversation the two men were having ahead of her in the line. After all, if they'd wanted her to hear it, they would have directed it to her. But then by degrees it began to irritate her. She heard just enough to realize that Swann was giving an update on the case—the same case that had driven her into hiding at a hotel.

The two of them had automatically gone into their police-mode jargon so that civilians wouldn't understand or appreciate what they were saying. Maybe it was a selfish notion, but Abbie thought Michael should now at least have the courtesy to know that she hated being left in the dark when she was involved. Which put her right back where she started with him, she thought with a frustrated sigh.

When she returned to the table, she set her plate down and faced the two men with very dry eyes. "Well," she said, smiling, "I hear it might rain Friday."

It took them a moment. Michael scowled and Swann's mouth twitched before he allowed a nod of tacit apology to be directed to Abbie.

"Whispers and rumors," Michael informed her. "Swann's spent his day with an ear to the ground."

"Good way to get run over by a bus," she retorted. "What did you hear?"

Swann directed a surreptitious glance at Michael before answering, obviously for the censorship opinion on the news.

"The word out on the street is that the shipment is due. We shouldn't have to play hide-and-seek much longer, Doc."

She nodded reflectively. "Anything specific at all?"

For that she got a matched set of shaken heads.

"Does Mr. Magnusson know?"

This time she got mischievous grins. She nodded again, her own grin tolerant. "I'm hardly the one to talk you out of showing him up, am I?"

Michael leaned over to drop a kiss on her nose. "Did I tell you she was a lady with sense, Swann?"

"A rare gem," Swann agreed dryly.

"Sarge." The three of them looked up at the softly delivered greeting to find a young patrolman hovering at the edge of their table awaiting Michael's attention. Michael gave it.

"Yeah, Burt. What's up?"

"I just got a call that you're supposed to contact the station."

Michael nodded and got to his feet, fumbling in his jeans pocket for change. The patrolman headed over for his own dinner, and Swann went back to his. Abbie waited for Michael to head over to the phone by the front door before she turned on the detective.

"Okay," she said simply. "Spit it out."

Swann looked up with feigned surprise. "Spit what out?"

An eyebrow arched. "The rest of the report. You know, the part that had Michael looking over at me like he'd just been handed a *Playboy* in church."

Swann allowed a dry grin as he carefully set his cutlery back down again. Then he spent a moment considering Abbie with calm eyes. "The Travelenos have made it to town."

Abbie prided herself on her control. She kept herself in her seat and maintained a certain calm in her features even as the floor dropped away and a deathly cold seeped into the room. "I assume somebody's watching them?"

"A lot of somebodies."

She nodded, watching Michael as he leaned against the wall, the phone propped on a shoulder as he jotted a message on a napkin. "He didn't want to worry me."

"No."

She turned back, knowing she was putting his friend back on the spot again, yet knowing that no one but Swann would understand as well. "How do I get him to open up to me, Swann?"

"A lot of this he shouldn't even be telling you." The detective defended his friend instinctively.

Abbie shook her head impatiently. "I'm not talking state secrets. I'm talking stress. He hasn't even had the chance to deal with the death of that young boy he knew, much less any of this insanity." She saw the protest rise and pointed an accusing finger. "And don't you dare give me that garbage about going to the bar and having a few drinks with the boys. All that does is make him drunk and depressed instead of just depressed.''

A brief flash of amusement crossed Swann's face before it settled back into more passive lines. Abbie didn't see the pain behind that look. Swann knew his friend and knew that what he needed more than anything was to be able to trust this lady. She could save his life. But Swann also knew what that would take from both of them.

He finally shrugged, his eyes locked into hers without yielding. ''You wait.''

Abbie frowned, her heart leaden because of the walls Michael needed built between them. ''It stinks, ya know?''

If Swann had been the kind of person to do it, he would have reached out to take Abbie's hand. As it was, she felt his support in his steady gaze. ''Time, my lady,'' he said. ''All he needs is a little time.''

''That's what scares me,'' she answered, her own fear surfacing only briefly. ''I'm just afraid that he doesn't have enough time to waste.''

Swann smiled briefly for her. ''Well, we'll just have to make sure he does, won't we?''

''Won't we what?''

Abbie looked up to see Michael slip back into his chair, a curious light in his eyes. Wary anticipation. Predatory. The look of a hunter who's caught the scent of his prey. She couldn't take her eyes from him, distracted by the sudden change.

Swann spotted it, too. ''Where's the canary, Viviano?''

''We might just be about to find out, my friend.'' Michael leaned forward, his eyes intense. Abbie saw Swann unconsciously match the posture. A policeman on the offensive.

''The Guerrillas wanted to express their thanks for my collaring Hector's killer,'' Michael began, his voice conspiratorial. Swann nodded him on. ''Alberto wants to meet me in an hour on neutral ground to give me a tip on a certain shipment due in any day.''

For the first time since she'd known him, Abbie saw Swann admit surprise. "What does he know about it?"

Michael shrugged. "I guess I'll find out."

"Where?"

"Mt. Carmel Cemetery."

Abbie couldn't help but shiver. "This guy has a great sense of atmosphere, doesn't he?"

Michael hardly noticed her. He was still facing Swann. "I figure if one of the guys here will drop Abbie back by the station while we go..."

"Now, wait a minute," Abbie protested, a hand up. The level of her voice succeeded in getting Michael's attention. When he turned to her, she proffered nothing but determination. "I'm going along."

Michael shook his head before Swann had the chance. "I don't think so, Abbie. It's too dangerous."

She smiled when she felt less like smiling than she had in her life. "You can either take me with you or explain to Magnusson why you don't plan to give him the information you're getting. He'll show up right after I tell him where you're going."

Michael looked wary. "Abbie, you wouldn't."

She just smiled again. "I'll sit quietly in the back of the car and not say a word. Don't make me go back to that hotel room alone, Michael."

His eyes were like steel. "Abbie, this is the way my life is. It's something you'd better get used to."

She nodded. "And this is not the way my life is. When I'm not completely isolated anymore, I'll deal with waiting for you. But right now, you guys are the only thing I have to hold on to. You're the only two I can trust."

It didn't really bother her that she wasn't telling the whole truth. She was hoping that when things got back to normal she could learn to handle waiting for Michael to come home. Right now she just knew that she had the most irrational fear that if she weren't with him, somebody would miss one spotting of the Travelenos and Michael would wind up dead.

Michael pulled out a cigarette and lit it. He shouldn't be letting her talk him into something so dangerous. Any number of things could go wrong. Swann said that the Travelenos were under tight surveillance, but what if they broke out? They were ruthless, and ruthless men didn't give a damn about who got caught in the cross fire when they went to work. An empty cemetery in the west side of the city wasn't the best place to be sitting at ten at night.

But Michael didn't want Abbie out of his sight right now, either. Just how many times could the department screw up and still keep her safe? He never wanted to go through the agony of discovering that broken door again.

"You won't make a sound," he bargained.

She slumped a little, so sure he'd turn her down. "Not a peep."

He shot Swann a challenging glare that the detective took with an agreeable nod, and then stubbed his cigarette back out. "I must be crazy."

If Alfred Hitchcock would have loved Abbie's elevator, he would have absolutely swooned at the cemetery. Set incongruously between two taverns and a closed bowling alley, Mt. Carmel Cemetery was an overgrown, unkempt square of ground that sported straggly trees and toppled-over tombstones. It had been here before the neighborhood had gone bad, but no one seemed to want to return to care for the spirits of ancestors foolish enough to have been buried in a declining neighborhood.

The blocks that spread out from the corner on which Mt. Carmel sat were crammed with decaying buildings, small stores bristling with grills and warnings, and a few Chinese take-out restaurants. No one strolled the streets on this late-summer evening. Abbie didn't really mind. The place was uncomfortable enough without an accompanying cast. She hoped that this was one of the places the city was planning to renovate. It could certainly use it.

Michael swung Swann's battered old Chevy into the entrance of the cemetery, and eased through a half-open gate.

Convenient, Abbie thought with some trepidation from the back seat. She was already beginning to think that maybe Michael had been right after all. She had nothing against seedy, run-down cemeteries in the dead of night, but the suite at the Ambassador East sure sounded good right now.

Michael pulled the car to a stop just under one of the more impressive trees when a shadow detached itself from all the other shadows and approached.

"Hola, amigo."

A young Latino man leaned in the window. Abbie could see shiny black hair and dark eyes, the handsome face of a youth who knew it. His eyes swept the car and rested on Abbie sitting quietly in the back.

"Hey, Miguel, man, who you got here?"

Michael opened the door, forcing the youth to back away. "The new police chief, Alberto. She doesn't date anybody under eighteen."

Alberto laughed. "Yeah, man. Sure. Looks like you got some other business to attend to tonight, you know?"

"She's the doc who worked on Hector when he came in," Michael told him, stepping out of the car and leaning against it. Alberto's eyes widened a little, and he nodded.

"You ever need anything, Doc," he offered back through the window. "You let Alberto know."

Abbie nodded. That seemed all Alberto needed.

"Hey, you guys are all screwed up again, you know?" Alberto danced around a little as he moved, from one foot to another. Cocaine, Abbie thought. Maybe uppers. She wondered that he would turn in his supplier, especially when things were so tight on the street. "Colombia! Man, somebody watchin' too much TV. These dudes comin' from Mexico."

Michael's head came up a little. "Mexico? You're sure?"

"Oh, ma-a-a-n." Alberto shook his head at Michael's skepticism. "My man Jaime's workin' the airport, and this heavy dude comes to him and offers a little extra on the side."

"Which airport?"

"Midway. That's why it's so funny. Everybody's gonna be at O'Hare waitin' for some big shipment from Florida, when it's comin' up into Midway day after tomorrow. Last flight from Houston, ya know?"

"Who's meeting it?"

Alberto shrugged. "Some Anglo. Good dresser. The bag's coming in to Gate A-Seven, a big brown plaid job. Name of Arthur C. Doyle. Jaime does a little diverting so the Anglo and this Doyle can take it with 'em to deal. Doyle's supposed to be baby-sittin' it in, ya know?"

Michael refrained from a grin. Somebody had a pretty good sense of humor. Arthur C. Doyle. Author Conan Doyle, creator of Sherlock Holmes, one of the world's most famous drug addicts.

"Midway just a transit stop?" he asked instead.

Alberto nodded, the distant streetlamp glinting off the oil in his hair. "Yeah, man. I don't know where they make the trade."

"This is the job Marlow's been working?"

"Oh, yeah. Way out of his league, but the word is somebody set him up in business. Family or somethin'." The succinct opinion of Marlow's competence that followed was enough to make Abbie grin back in the shadows. Alberto never thought to apologize for his language.

She watched as Michael completed the exchange with a series of nods and quick grins that seemed to mean more than a handshake. Then he turned to return to the car and started the engine as Alberto slipped back into the shadows, a wink and a leer his farewell to Abbie.

They pulled out of the cemetery and went along the side streets that would bring them back to Cicero Boulevard and the highway, and Abbie felt herself physically unwind. It would be good to get Michael back to the suite and give him the chance to relax before this all started blowing up again in a couple of days. She watched the taut lines of his neck as he drove, and knew he was planning. Anticipating. Then his fingers went to the remnants of his injury, absently rubbing at the healing scar. The tension had begun to build again.

"Four Adam One on tack two."

Swann reached over to pull the mike to him. Abbie felt the hairs stiffen on the back of her neck as he answered.

"Go."

"Swann? It's Dixon. We've lost them."

"Lost who?" Abbie demanded from the back seat, leaning up to hear better. Her heart was suddenly in her throat.

"What do you mean you lost them?" Swann barked, not noticing her.

"They slipped into One Illinois Center. Damn, Sarge, you know what a maze that place is. Magnusson's men were on them and lost them."

An underground network that connected four buildings along East Wacker and Michigan. Abbie knew it well. She got lost every time she went in there. The knowledge didn't make her feel any better. That chill was creeping back into the air, stealing her breath.

"Who did they lose?" she asked one more time, her voice very deliberate.

Michael never turned his attention from the street. "The Travelenos."

Chapter 12

You stay put in that fancy hotel until we catch up with them again."

Swann leaned into Michael's car with his warning, ignoring the traffic he was blocking. They were on Clark, just outside the now closed Francis's, where they'd left Michael's car earlier in the evening. Abbie sat silently alongside Michael, content to let Swann make the threats.

"I'm coming to Midway with you," Michael told his friend.

"That's two days away." Swann retorted. "By then, we'll have those guys wrapped up nice and neat."

Michael nodded without much conviction and started the motor they'd just spent the last ten minutes checking. For bombs, Abbie had realized, her stomach dropping away. How could Michael live like this, watching every shadow, checking every person and vehicle he came in contact with for danger? How could he do it day after day, knowing that somewhere out there somebody would always be more than happy to see him no more than a memory and a full-dress funeral. Abbie had been doing it for less than a week now, and she was already sure she was working on an ulcer.

Looking at him now, she saw the toll the past few days had taken. It ignited a new pain in her chest. He looked so tired, so strained. His eyes had grown so feral, the instincts of hunt or be hunted preserving him, but changing him.

It was when she found herself wondering how much Michael liked himself like this, that she realized something of what he felt he couldn't bring her. This was part of his job, a piece of protective equipment he wore when he faced the streets. When he walked the streets, he had to lower himself to the level of those he pursued. Think like them. Understand them. He couldn't possibly find that side of himself appealing. How could he think she would?

It simply wouldn't occur to him that she would understand. That if he brought that to her, she could soften it.

When Abbie found herself getting calloused at work, she retreated to the comfort of friends. Now, she realized that it was Michael she wanted to come to. Her friends were her friends, but Michael loved her. When he found himself becoming callous in his work, he should be able to do the same. Because she loved him, because she saw the good in Michael, she could help him keep the dark world he sometimes had to walk in in better perspective. If he could draw strength and peace from her, the dark side he had to face wouldn't trouble him so much.

"Abbie?"

She jerked her head around, realizing that Swann was speaking to her. "Yes, Swann?"

She could see the concern in his eyes. "I'm going to follow you two to the hotel. Then you order room service and stay put. Okay?"

She nodded, trying to swallow past a dry throat. It would have been too much to ask whether someone could get past that discreet staff and invisible army that surrounded them. She couldn't consider it.

"I'll think of something to keep him occupied." She grinned shakily.

Swann laughed and gave Michael a punch on the arm. "Let me know when you get tired of the good life, Viviano. I'll bring by the burgers and beer."

Invoking the privilege every policeman assumes, Swann and then Michael executed U-turns on Clark and headed south. Abbie watched the passing stores and brownstones and thought that it would be really good when she could get out and walk her neighborhood again. It would be her first order of business when this was all over. Well, she thought with a surreptitious look over to where Michael scanned the same streets with measured eyes, the second order of business.

She found herself smiling, the light in her eyes a little sad. "Now I know how Lon Chaney feels when the moon comes up."

Startled at the words, Michael looked over to see a quiet understanding in Abbie's eyes as they tracked the passing scenery. The streetlights flickered through her hair and sparkled in her eyes, like distant stars in the sky.

"What's that supposed to mean?" he asked, turning his attention back to the street.

Her smile broadened ruefully as she considered him. "Your professional demeanor interests me."

"Abbie..."

"When you caught the scent tonight, you reminded me of a big cat out on the plains. There was...oh, a hunting look in your eyes."

He looked over briefly before allowing a certain surprise to lighten his features. Not at the observation; she was right. Maria had commented on it more than once. But Maria had never spoken about it in such a dispassionate voice. Abbie was more interested than outraged.

"Does that bother you?" he asked.

She shook her head. "Oh, no. I'm fascinated. I think I must look something like that when I walk into a trauma patient, or a cardiac arrest. You're walking the line then, so you have to be on all cylinders. I'm just not so...ferocious."

Michael chuckled. "Don't bet on it. You didn't see your face when you walked in after talking to Hector's parents."

She looked over at him, encouraged by the tone of his voice. "What happens if you meet up with Marlow?"

"You mean, do I exact revenge?"

She nodded.

Michael considered the question a moment as he drove. Abbie could see a progression of emotions skim his eyes, the memory of what Marlow meant and what Michael was all about. When he finally shook his head, Abbie knew he was being sincere.

"I'll take great pleasure in nailing him to the wall," he said. "And if he fights, I'll damn well fight back. But I'm not the kind of cop who gets in his licks before anybody else does."

When Michael turned to see Abbie's reaction, he was surprised to see her smiling. He was even more surprised to realize that he hadn't decided on that answer until this minute. For the first time in twelve years, he entertained a kernel of doubt that the way he'd always handled the job had been the right way. The beautiful, bright woman next to him just might have the capacity to absorb the worst and build something from it.

"Doesn't the hit scare you?" she asked when the smile faded.

He watched the street, automatically checking the cars that pulled alongside, noting the ones that had followed for a while and the faces that might be familiar. Then, not sure why it should make him feel better, he nodded.

"It scares the hell out of me."

They turned onto Goethe to see the hotel two blocks up. The neighborhood was quiet, softly lit by the gumball streetlights that flanked the Ambassador canopy where the doorman, an older man in a green uniform, was bent over a dark sedan in the process of giving directions. Michael pulled past the car, Swann behind.

Abbie turned just as they passed to see that two men were quizzing the patient doorman. She was turning back to prepare to get out when the faces struck a chord. She gasped, whipping around in her seat.

"Michael, my God!"

Michael yanked the wheel over, sliding the car to a stop as he turned to Abbie. "What's the matter?"

"It's them." She craned around for a better look, fear constricting her chest. There couldn't be any mistake. The same heavy, dark features, the same eyes. She could see them pretty well in the streetlight, but by now they could see her. The driver was poking his friend and reaching for the keys. "Michael, it's the Travelenos!"

In one fluid movement, Michael checked Abbie's observation and then reached over for her door. The car behind them was squealing from the curb. "Get out," he commanded.

"No—" she turned on him, understanding his intentions. "Michael, you can't."

"Get out, Abbie. Now. Fred!"

The doorman scuttled over, his hand already on Abbie's arm. She didn't have a chance. Before she could get out another word, she was on the sidewalk, and Michael was whipping back out in pursuit of the sedan.

"Michael, no!" she cried, a hand out as if it would stop him.

Swann was already on his tail, their lights disappearing down the street, Swann's portable light flashing from his roof. Fred held tightly to Abbie's arm, not really sure that she wouldn't try to follow.

She couldn't have. She was paralyzed, the sudden action leaving her devastated. Michael was running after the men who wanted him dead. He was hunting, and she was terrified.

Come back to me, her mind screamed. Come back to our safe room where the world was defined in soft pastels and comfortably familiar furniture. God, Michael, don't die.

Don't die.

"Come on, Dr. Fitzgerald," Fred was saying, his voice soothing, "let me take you inside. It might not be safe for you out here."

"No...I have to wait for Michael." She couldn't even turn from the now empty street, the crickets once again audible in the warm night air.

"You can wait inside. Come in and have something to drink."

Abbie finally let herself be guided away, up the lovely green stairs and into the lobby where the light from the chandeliers danced across the marble and sank into the velvet on the furniture. The flowers that filled the lobby gave off a fresh spring scent, and the concierge sat at her desk as she did every day and night. It was only Abbie who saw that the world was disintegrating.

Someone guided her to a suite of offices on the second floor where she sat on the sales manager's couch and sipped at something with Scotch in it. She hated Scotch. She hated the silence of this room, so insulated and private. She wanted to be with Michael.

"Is there something I can do for you, Doctor?" Fred asked from his corner.

Abbie brought her pacing to a halt by the window. The view of the neighborhood was closer than from the suite. Across the street a middle-aged woman was letting herself into the lovely gray stone house with arches for doors and turrets for bedrooms. "Do you have any ice cream?"

Fred looked a bit puzzled. "Ice cream?"

"Chocolate chocolate-chip." She couldn't do this. She just couldn't live through it every time Michael left her. Already she'd conjured up a thousand different disasters to befall him, each worse than the one before. She felt his absence like a knife wound, and couldn't imagine such an anguish that never healed. Every fear she'd ever courted returned to torment her. She couldn't think how she'd been foolish enough to think she could court this madness in the first place.

Abbie checked the street again, but it had grown empty, the woman once again safely enclosed in her home. She wondered if the crickets could still be heard beneath the canopy. No news, no action, no Michael. She checked her watch. God, he'd only been gone fifteen minutes. It already seemed like a year.

The door behind her opened, and a bellhop edged through with her bag. Abbie turned to Fred for explanation.

He smiled a bit thinly. "You won't be returning to your suite."

"What's the matter?" she asked, close to that nervous giggle that tended to get her into so much trouble. "Did the real Mr. and Mrs. Smith show up?"

His answering smile was uncertain. "You've been spotted here. It simply wouldn't be safe for you to stay anymore."

Abbie wanted to argue with him. That room was suddenly the last bit of sanctuary left in the world. She couldn't possibly be set adrift again. She couldn't leave the gently colored rooms where she and Michael had made love. Trying to camouflage the tears that threatened again, she turned back on the still-empty window.

"I'm not going to another safe house, thanks. I've had enough of those." Abbie leaned forward, her forehead against the cool glass, and closed her eyes. Maybe they wouldn't mind just dropping her off at work. There she could keep her mind off what Michael was facing.

"I'm sure we'll just stay here until we get some word," Fred assured her, still keeping a cautious distance. "Then I imagine they'll want you back at the station."

Abbie couldn't stifle a heartfelt groan. "Fred," she sighed, "you've just made my day."

Twenty minutes. Time was really flying. Well, if she'd managed to get through this five minutes, maybe she could get through the next. She'd try it that way. Like an alcoholic craving that bottle, fighting his demon one minute at a time.

Abbie turned a sympathetic smile on the little man. She knew just how volatile she must look, how little equipped Fred must be for handling out-of-control females.

"Would you mind if I listened to some music?"

Reassured by the far saner tone of voice, Fred nodded with some relief and faded back into his corner as Abbie pulled out her earphones.

Five minutes, she kept repeating to herself. Five minutes. That's all I have to wait. The promise became a plea, the plea a litany, chanted to the insistent beat of the music, lulling her in its own way. Abbie took up a chair and dragged it to the window facing Goethe, and sat down to watch for Swann's car to return. And after a while, Fred even found her some ice cream.

She was concentrating on Van Halen and pralines and cream, her eyes resolutely out on the unchanging street, when the door opened behind her. At first she just thought that it was another of those carefully placed people coming to check on her sanity and the condition of the room. But then she heard the chuckle.

"And here I thought you'd be worried about me."

Michael walked up and took the carton of ice cream from Abbie's numb hands. Then, pulling her to her feet, he contributed to a hug that threatened the condition of his rib cage.

Abbie couldn't manage a word. She squeezed against Michael's chest, listening to the reassuring drumbeat of his heart, soaking in the fierce joy of his touch. He was safe. Alive. Again. He was safe and she was falling apart.

But she'd made it through more easily this time. The wait had taken two hours, and she'd worked her way from being nearly hysterical to merely frantic. Abbie smiled to herself within the folds of Michael's embrace and took a long, shaky breath. Maybe she could find out some way to work out this waiting stuff after all.

"You know better than to run out on me like that," she accused, not even aware that two tears had escaped and trailed down her cheeks. "Poor Fred didn't know what to do with me."

"Well, at least you didn't faint on him."

Michael survived Abbie's well-placed smack with another chuckle, then pulled her back to arm's length for bright-eyed consideration. "I had some pressing business to attend to."

She saw the elation. The victory in his eyes. He never even needed to tell her.

"You got 'em?"

He nodded. "We got 'em. They fell right into the old squeeze play between Swann and me and a neat little roadblock on Lake Shore Drive."

Abbie shared his accomplishment, her eyes praising him. It was unnecessary for her to tell him that there were always more Travelenos to overcome.

"Nothing like a cop with a sense of accomplishment." She grinned.

Michael swept her tears aside with gentle hands and grinned back. "You're damn right," he agreed with enthusiasm. "I'm tired of sitting on the sidelines while everybody else does the job. These guys were mine!"

Abbie felt new vigor surge through his body and realized just what the forced passivity had cost him. "Back in the game, huh, champ?"

He flashed her a grin. "All the way."

Michael bent to gather Abbie back to him, suddenly needing the praise of her embrace. Oblivious to any audience they might have, Abbie brought her own arms up to him, her greeting prolonged and emphatic. Michael couldn't seem to get his fill of her. She tasted so soft and sweet, the remnants of pralines and cream spicing her lips. He savored her mouth, her lips deliciously sticky, and eased those lips open for a lazy exploration that shot him through with a sharp chill. When she threaded her hands up under his shirt, he all but lost his concentration, a soft moan rising between them.

It was Abbie who managed to pull upright first. "This is all very nice," she managed a bit breathlessly, a smile in her voice, "but I don't think your cousin meant to extend his hospitality as far as having you ravage me in his office."

Michael nuzzled her hair with his mouth, lost in its wild curls. "Aw, if he can't take a joke, the hell with him."

The shudder of Abbie's laughter against him drove the ache deeper.

"Michael..." She was doing her best to recover her decorum when Michael had just discovered the very sensitive skin just below her earlobe with his lips. She did manage to see that Fred had retreated, leaving them alone in the closed office. For a moment, her resolve wavered.

"We've been kicked out again."

"Well," he murmured, slowly giving up. "We weren't blown up this time. We're making progress."

She giggled. "So where do we try next, the Salvation Army?"

He returned to the depths of her fragrant hair. It had never occurred to him before how provocative the smell of freshly washed hair was. "Do you think they'd mind if I ravaged you in their office?"

"I thought we had to go back to the station."

"We do."

They settled into an easy embrace, each resting within the comfort of the other's presence.

"No fun being ravaged there, I suppose."

Now Michael chuckled. "Doubtful."

She nodded against the crisp cotton of his shirt and steady throb of his heart. "Well then, we're going to have to make an agenda. What else are we slated for until the grand finale at Midway?"

That brought Michael's head up and his hands to her arms. "You're not slated for anything." He held on to her as if expecting her to run right out now.

Abbie shook her head with certainty. "You can expect me at Midway. I refuse to sit that one out." The smile she gave him was her most encouraging. "Midway's a big place. You'll never know I'm there."

"There isn't a place big enough for that," he argued. "And there's no reason for you to be there. No reason at all."

Abbie's grin was deliberately mischievous as she pulled a little farther away to prevent Michael feeling the acceleration of her heart rate. "Why do you suddenly sound like you're going to say, 'Abbie, you wouldn't want me to help you put in chest tubes, don't help me do my job?'" Before he could answer in the affirmative, she continued. "I told you, I'm not going to do anything. I'm just going to be with you, like we agreed. I'll even sit and hold Magnusson's hand if you want, just so he doesn't get into trouble."

Michael scowled. "Magnusson doesn't know about it yet."

Abbie's first impulse was to protest. Michael held up a cautioning finger. "I'm not dragging everybody out there if it's going to be a lame bust. It's going to be Swann and me and a couple of narcotics guys until we ID that bag. From that point, I back out and Magnusson can take over to his heart's content."

Abbie couldn't help needling him a little. "Besides, you don't want Magnusson scaring the bad guys off too soon?"

Michael's grin was telling. "He does have a strike-force mentality."

"Your motives, sir," she said, giggling "are suspicious."

His eyebrows rose. "And yours aren't?"

Abbie challenged him with her best little girl's eyes. Michael tried his best to stand his ground. He was going to be running a delicate-enough balancing act with that drug deal as it was. What he didn't need was to have to worry about putting Abbie in more danger than she already was by giving in to her.

When she slid neatly back into his embrace, he had no choice but to kiss her again, long and lovingly, his resolve crumbling. She'd given him so much. And he could keep her out of the way so that she didn't have to face an empty four walls again.

"I'll think about it," he finally said with a scowl.

Abbie smiled and stretched up for another, even longer kiss. Michael's arms tightened involuntarily around her, and his hands roamed her back. When he heard the soft mewling sounds his touch drew from her, he knew that he was probably going to let her have her way again.

After a long, satisfying few minutes, Michael lifted his face to look down into Abbie's eyes where tears of relief still glittered over the deep, sky blue. She was smiling, and he saw the steel, the frailty and the strength that had first drawn him to her. Taking his finger, he drew a gentle line down her cheek.

"Was it hard to wait?" he asked.

Her widening smile held its own measure of triumph. "I made it, didn't I?"

Michael saw, then, just what it had cost her to be there for him. And what it had given him. He nodded slowly, never taking his eyes from hers, their light a brightening reflection of the risks both of them were taking, and the rewards the risks requited. "You tell me about your two hours," he said, "and I'll tell you about mine."

"Sarge. Doc."

The young officer nodded to the passing couple without blinking an eye. It reflected just how much Abbie and Michael had become a matched set at the station.

Abbie barely noticed. She was coming to the end of the "caper" as she kept calling it, and the tension was finally getting the better of her. The run to the airport was scheduled for any time now, and she couldn't decide whether that made her more relieved or more crazed.

She'd spent the past twenty-four hours playing solitaire and watching Michael pace and think and consult with Swann as he waited out the inactivity. He had been able to share a little more of the frustration he felt, but most of his energy was concentrated on the job at hand—which Abbie didn't mind in the least, since his life depended on it.

She hadn't dealt with the imprisonment as well as Michael, however. Stuck in a single bedroom with a TV full of daytime fare she wasn't used to watching, all she found herself longing for was her jogging shoes and Lincoln Park.

She'd become a jogger out of necessity four years ago, and had faithfully fulfilled the obligation every day. Each day she'd set out cursing the discomfort, the car exhaust and the bad weather. It took something like pacing a twelve-by-twelve room to impress on her how much the jogging had become a vital part of her physical and mental welfare. Once out, she kept promising, she'd never gripe about jogging again. Once out, she knew, she'd forget that promise the minute she crossed Lincoln Park West in a sweat suit.

"What are you doing here, Viviano?"

Lt. Capshaw caught them at the coffeepot, his eyes nailed to Michael's tan and blue pullover and white painter's slacks as if to say that someone out of uniform was inappropriate in a station. For Abbie he managed a quick smile of appreciation for the khaki jumpsuit that covered her long-legged figure.

"Checking in with Swann," Michael said, turning to his boss with an agreeable smile. Capshaw had not been able to make the early-morning party for the Travelenos the night before.

Capshaw nodded with that all-purpose scowl he so enjoyed bestowing on Michael. "They give anything away?"

Michael shook his head, sipping at the steaming liquid in his cup. "I didn't really expect them to."

Another scowl, probably for the Travelenos this time. "If you're up with Swann so much, why don't you just put in for that damn transfer and be done with it?"

Michael moved to take hold of Abbie's elbow and guide her on by the lieutenant as he answered with a placid smile. "The papers are on your desk, Lieutenant."

Abbie whipped around on Michael, her coffee almost ending up all over his arm again. "What do you mean, the papers are on his desk?" she demanded.

Michael shrugged, that self-pleased light still lingering in his eyes. "Like Swann says, it's time I got a suit."

"But I thought you liked working the streets."

"I do. But the more time I spend on this case, the more I realize that it's time I moved up. I like unraveling puzzles. I'm tired of losing kids like Hector every day. Besides, Swann and I would make a good team again."

Abbie nodded, still stunned by his offhand news. "Yeah, you would."

They almost made it to Swann's cubbyhole before she turned to him with her own scowl. "You're not doing this for me, are you?"

He grinned over at her. "If I were doing it for you, I'd become an accountant."

This time she believed him.

"Michael," she said a few minutes later as they waited for Swann to return from some errand. "Do you realize that since we met, we've been through one crisis after another?"

Michael looked over at her with a surprised grin. He'd just been thinking the same thing. Reviewing the course of events through this case, he'd been thinking that now that they were about to put an end to it, it would be a relief to not have to worry about Abbie anymore. He wouldn't have to steel himself against the fear of finding her missing or hurt again.

But he'd also been thinking about how much you learn about yourself and the person you love when you're thrown together into the crucible of peril. You fall in love faster and harder because of it.

Watching the quick, precise way Abbie punctuated her words with her hands, or how she threw off her most challenging statements with bright open eyes and a fearless grit in her voice, Michael found that he couldn't imagine his life without her in it. She'd become a part of its very fabric.

"Yeah." He nodded with a mischievous grin, restraining himself to reach out to her even now. "I have been wondering if you're the one who's been bringing me bad luck."

"You?" Her eyes were sharply amused. "Who had to replace the door to her apartment and try to pay bills without benefit of a paycheck because the police pulled her out of work? I checked, ya know, and protective custody does not make me eligible for sick leave."

Michael's eyes sparkled. "Oh, but just think of the invaluable experience you've gained . . . ."

Abbie's snort was self-righteous. "I can spot a safe house a mile away and make coffee in any police station in the city."

" . . . the excitement . . . ."

"Playing solitaire in a Howard Johnson's all day and dining on burgers and beer."

" . . . the romance . . . ."

A slow smile played over her lips. "Well, now," she admitted softly, "there you have me."

She wondered whether Michael could understand that as much as she wanted this whole nightmare to be over, she still wanted to drag her feet a little. There was a closeness you achieved with someone when you were thrown together as they had been. A dependency that set you apart and made you more special to the other person.

It had taken less than a month for Michael to become the most important person in Abbie's life. She just didn't want to take the chance that instead of continuing to grow closer, they would begin to drift apart.

Michael saw the fleeting doubt surface in Abbie's eyes and reached out to her. In the middle of the frantic chaos of that room where twenty people raced by in pursuit of station business, Michael did something he'd never done at the station before. Never done at work, since work was always meant to be kept apart from the rest of his life.

He bent to Abbie, his hand to her face in a gesture so intimate that it caught her breath, and offered her his soul.

"I love you," he said simply and almost brought tears to her eyes.

Her return smile was a little giddy, but just as tender. "I love you, too."

"About damn time," somebody muttered under his breath across the room, struggling to keep a straight face.

"Amen," a colleague at the next desk nodded and thought that Viviano sure as hell had good taste. The Doc was a drop-dead knockout in an offbeat way, all natural and bright and with legs that never quit. But that was okay. Viviano deserved a decent break in that department for a change.

"Hey, Viviano."

The lieutenant was back. Michael started, leaving Abbie one last look of private affection before turning to his boss. Abbie let him surreptitiously take her hand for a final squeeze before she turned her attention discreetly back to her coffee.

"Yes, sir?"

Capshaw didn't comment on the capricious humor in Michael's eyes. "What can you tell me about the DeRosa inquiries?"

It took Michael a moment to recognize the name. A lot had gone down since he'd made that request.

"Oh, him..." He nodded easily. "It's no big thing, Lieutenant." Even after the disclaimer, he dropped his voice for the rest of the statement. "Abbie spotted him a couple of times, thought he was Marlow. I just thought I'd be thorough and check him out."

Capshaw shot Abbie and then Michael a quizzical look over the glasses he rarely wore. "You know who he is?"

"I do now."

"You really think it's necessary?"

Michael shrugged, sipping from his cup as he moved to lean against the grimy wall. "Swann was doing it for me. No harm, really, just making sure. I told him to say I was the one asking, so Abbie'd stay out of it."

Capshaw wasn't encouraged. No one noticed Abbie stiffening at the words.

"I've been hearing unhappy rumblings from the chief's office about it," the lieutenant was saying. "DeRosa's a little insulted by all the attention."

Michael refrained from saying what he wanted to about self-important people. "It's mostly to reassure Abbie," he placated. "DeRosa really spooked her. Spooked me, too, when I saw him the first time. He's almost a dead ringer for our friend."

Capshaw shot Abbie another analyzing glance. "She recognized the Travelenos, didn't she?"

Abbie straightened enough to answer for Michael with a nod. "She did." Although how she did, she'd be the last one to figure.

The lieutenant nodded reflectively and pushed his glasses more firmly in place. "Well, don't beat it to death, Viviano. You're not a detective yet."

"You're doing it again," Abbie accused after the lieutenant had once more gone on his way.

Michael gave her an impassive smile as he took a long sip of coffee, his lean frame relaxed against the wall, one foot up on Swann's chair. "Old habits die hard. I have this unnatural urge to protect you. Though God knows why."

"From what?" she protested with a dry grin. "An irate builder? What's he going to do if he really gets mad at me, take away my birthday?"

"To a cop, everybody's a potential bad guy."

Abbie's grin grew wicked. "Is that why you always insist on frisking me?"

Michael almost choked on his coffee.

"You loafin' again, Viviano?" Swann asked as he approached, jangling car keys in one hand. "Here we have to be out there fightin' rush-hour traffic on the Stevenson, and you're just standin' there eyein' the pretty ladies. After the ID we got from the Doc last night, I should get Capshaw to partner me with *her*."

Both Michael and Abbie greeted the tirade with grins.

"We set?" Michael asked, draining his cup.

Swann swept Michael's foot off his chair. "All signed up and checked out. All I need is one hot-dog uniform sergeant and his sidekick."

Abbie grinned as she, too, straightened and set down her cup. "Let's go."

The plan was a simple one. The three of them would drive to Midway where Abbie would sit inconspicuously in the waiting room. Swann would watch for Doyle, and Michael would watch for the bag. The minute they were ID'd and on their way out of the airport, the two narcotics guys would follow in the two taxis they'd commandeered. It would be up to them to notify Magnusson and let him in on the party.

The way the airport was set up, Gate A-Seven was situated along the backside of the concourse, opening onto a narrow kind of blind alley by the bordering fence. At the closed end of the alley sat the garage where the baggage carts waited and returned after off-loading the planes. The whole setup was easy to visualize from any of the floor-to-ceiling windows that lined the walls.

"Houston gave me a description on this guy Doyle," Swann was saying as the three of them dodged the dinner-hour traffic in the Midway terminal. "Older-minister type, they said. He came in from Guadalajara." They showed their badges to the security guards and were ushered past the X-ray machine. Abbie followed without a word, her eyes sweeping the people she passed much as Swann's and Michael's were. No one looked familiar, but she was beginning to think that everybody looked suspicious.

"Thick white hair, horn-rims, ruddy features," Swann was continuing. Michael nodded throughout. "British accent."

Michael laughed. Now he knew where the name had originated.

They walked by the gates that advertised localities. Bloomington. Normal. Springfield. Small lines for small planes, businessmen waiting at the end of the day to go home. Abbie wished she were one of them, stepping up to the smiling agent and handing her a ticket to some innocuous place where life walked on at a sane pace.

She shook her head, her heart climbing a little higher in her chest, and thought that she deserved all this. She'd been the one to insist on it. She sure hadn't insisted on getting involved in the first place, though.

Gate seven. Abbie automatically checked the digital clock that hung from the ceiling. Seven-seventeen. The computer promised the plane would arrive on time. A varied mixture of people already congregated over the plastic molded seats in the waiting area, some to receive passengers, some to become them. Abbie flashed Michael a last grin and joined them.

Michael took up a position across the hall, leaning against the railing at gate six and crossing his arms in an age-old stance of waiting. Swann walked on down the hall, a waiting passenger pacing his time away. Nobody really paid attention to the tall black man who periodically leaned against the whitewashed cedar-block wall and peered out the windows.

Abbie leaned over to check the clock for the eighth time in half that many minutes when she saw Swann motion to Michael. Her stomach dropped. That was definitely not in the game plan. They weren't going to make any contact unless there was something wrong.

Michael strolled over to peer out the window next to Swann, his forehead slightly puckered. Seated in the first row next to the smiling agent's desk, Abbie could just see the quiet conversation. She was too far away to hear.

"It's not Jaime," Swann was saying.

Michael looked out after him and cursed under his breath. The baggage cart was just pulling up to gate seven to meet the incoming plane. The plane in question was just pulling around the far corner of the building. Something had gone wrong. Jaime was supposed to be the one manning that cart, and he wasn't on it.

That meant that all bets might be off. They might have scotched the deal completely. They might have found Jaime and taken him out. The deal might even be going down right here for some reason. It had all just gone very wrong, and they didn't have any time for contingencies.

"What about the kid?" Swann asked, his eyes on the trim 737 that had just eased to a stop at the gate.

Michael's attention was focused in the same direction. "Not much we can do about him right now. We have to follow that suitcase and see if somebody meets Doyle. When they go, I'll head back in."

That was when Abbie spotted the man—across the concourse, leaning much as Michael had, waiting for a passenger from a plane to arrive. Abbie's mouth went dry. It was the same man who had broken into her apartment.

She turned to find Swann and Michael. Did the man know them? Had he seen her? How could she warn them before one of them stumbled over him?

The two men were staring out the window, watching as the ground crew began to swarm. Abbie looked around for help, for some kind of inspiration. Perched on the next seat over was a prepubescent delinquent type with a huge radio, a Motley Crue T-shirt, and a "What are you going to do for me?" attitude. Abbie thanked all the gods of chance and leaned over to whisper in his ear.

The door of the plane had just opened. Michael prepared to turn back to the waiting room to pick up Mr. Doyle. Swann kept his eyes on the luggage rolling off the conveyor belt from the plane's luggage bay. No brown plaid bag yet.

Suddenly there was shouting across the wide, tiled hallway.

Heads turned to see a young punk run from a well-groomed man. The man, somewhere in his mid-twenties and dressed in the latest linen and brushed-cotton look, was cursing fluently about the loss of a wallet. Michael would have been amused, except that something about the man struck him. He'd just about been able to put a finger on it, when he felt a nudge at his arm.

"My late-night visitor," Abbie said, sidling past. "I wasn't sure whether he'd recognize you or not."

"Damn." Michael quickly checked the deplaning passengers. No minister types yet. "Who's the kid?"

Abbie shrugged with a grin. "I don't know, but he's ten dollars richer. Plus anything he finds in the wallet."

Michael wanted to kiss her.

"There it is," Swann snapped. A large brown plaid suitcase rolled out of the airplane. At the same moment, an elderly gentleman stepped into the doorway of the plane, his full white hair glowing softly in the oblique evening sunlight. Both Michael and Swann cursed.

Swann scowled. "It's goin' down."

Michael concurred with another bitten oath. "Right here, I think. Damn. Damn!" Abruptly he turned on Abbie, his hands clamping an iron grip on her arms. "Abbie, get us some backup. They're gonna make the deal here. We need to get ahold of Capshaw. Now."

Abbie stared at him. "How?" she managed. "Where?"

"You have to do it for us. Get out to cab A435. That's one of the narcs. Tell him that it looks like the deal's going down right here. He'll know what to do." Letting go, he turned to the detective, whose eyes were still on the approaching minister. "Swann, chances are better Abbie's friend doesn't have a make on you. You take him and Doyle. I'll get the case."

Swann nodded and moved. Abbie looked around her as if she were drowning.

"Now, Abbie," Michael urged. "Tell them to get to the luggage bays."

Michael slipped out a gate door. Suddenly, Abbie was alone.

Chapter 13

Wheeling around on her heel, Abbie headed back up the hallway. She saw that her assailant had returned his attention to the line of disembarking passengers. Swann took up a protective position, keeping Abbie out of view as she sprinted past.

A435. Abbie turned the corner from Concourse A and passed the little square of tables where croissants and cellophane-wrapped sandwiches were served. She swung around by the ticket counters and out the front door, her heart again in her throat.

A rather dismal line of taxis waited along the curved drive. Abbie came to a stop, her lungs heaving, as she tried to make out numbers, faces behind the windshields. The first cab in line automatically began to roll up. She didn't recognize him. Second, third. She walked on down the line.

There he was, leaning over toward the passenger door for her, a red bandanna around his too-long hair. Abbie ran for him.

"Get Capshaw," she panted, leaning in the window. "Michael says the buy's going down here. Something's wrong..."

"Damn. Okay. Stay here."

He did some quick talking into his microphone while Abbie pranced anxiously outside, her eyes straying toward the doors as if expecting Michael to appear. Something had gone bad. Something more than that man showing up. It scared her, because it meant Michael was right back in danger. And here she was, waiting. Again.

"Come on!" she urged impatiently. The officer tumbled from his cab and signaled to his partner in the vehicle behind.

"You wait here," he instructed Abbie, taking her by the arm to make his point.

She straightened as if she'd been shot. "No way!"

Michael, take care, she begged silently, her eyes stark. *Please.* She kept expecting to hear shots or screams from inside.

"Listen, Doc." The man had all-business eyes. "I told the lieutenant to meet you here. You tell him where we are. I figure it'll be the luggage bays." He shook her a little as her eyes wandered back toward the door. "You with me, Doc?"

Abbie turned back on him. "I'll tell him. Now get going!"

As Abbie stood by the front drive, the people around her began to thin out. The last long-distance flight had taken off for the evening, and airline desks were beginning to close down. Soon the taxis would begin to give up and move on. Abbie paced, waiting for the cavalry, the fear savage in her, her eyes stinging from the tears that choked her. What was going on in there? Why was there no commotion? Could they have given up? Couldn't they have been mistaken? Could they have been discovered too soon and killed? Damn, why didn't somebody come? Why didn't something happen?

They came as she stood there in the drive, four cars with a riot of flashing lights, Magnusson thunderous in the front seat of the first car.

"What the hell are those two up to?" he demanded as he joined the other ten or twelve cops piling out of cars behind him.

"That drug deal," Abbie said, leading the way back through the automatic doors. "Michael got a tip on the shipment coming in, but he thinks they're making the deal here.... Didn't that guy tell you any of this?"

They stormed through the near-empty terminal where cleaning people looked up in vague surprise. Strike-force mentality, Abbie thought with brief disparagement.

"Where are they?" was all Magnusson would say.

"I don't know." She wanted to give into the tears. It was just too much. "They were at Gate Seven. But a bag was coming in. Michael and the narcotics guy said they think the luggage bay."

Magnusson sent some men to check the luggage carousel. He went with the rest toward Gate Seven even though Abbie could see there was no one there. Then they slipped through the same door Michael had, and stormed the luggage bay.

Silence. Ten police wandered around in an empty garage with a herd of unused luggage carriers. They were alone.

Abbie stood by the door watching the search, her heart in her throat. Where were they? She'd been standing by the front door less than fifteen minutes, and yet everyone had disappeared as if they'd never even been there. For a brief, irrational moment, Abbie wondered if she'd really seen her assailant; if Michael had really sent her off to get help.

"Let's check back at the carousel," Magnusson barked, his great, long .357 drawn and threatening.

"No," Abbie protested instinctively. "They're here somewhere."

"What are you doing still here?" he demanded. "Somebody get her back in the terminal where she'll be safe."

Abbie turned to challenge Magnusson and his overkill weaponry when three quick cracks stopped everyone dead in their tracks. The closest cop to Abbie threw her to the ground.

The rest of them hadn't even begun to move when they heard a yell, and then two more flat pops, like a whip cracking. Abbie's head came up. The blood drained from her face as the police began to spill from the empty garage. She'd recognized the voice. Swann. He'd been calling to Michael, just before the second salvo of shots had been fired.

Someone probably should have been left behind to keep an eye on the civilian. But when a cop hears shots and knows that another cop is involved, he doesn't wait for an invitation. The man who'd protected Abbie took off at a dead run behind his companions, and Abbie was left to get up on her own.

She scrambled to her feet to see the entire force filter through a small, jury-rigged gate that had been cut through the fence into the parking lot, Magnusson in the lead like John Wayne. Without another thought but of the last time she'd heard that kind of commotion, Abbie followed right on their heels.

The assault turned out to be unnecessary. By the time everybody stormed through onto the half-empty lot, Swann and Michael were standing calmly over one penitent-looking minister type and a duded-up intruder. The two narcotics guys were bent over a large suitcase and a medium-size briefcase. A few feet away a very still form lay on the asphalt in a dark pool.

Abbie made it through the gate and came to a shuddering stop. The sight of Michael standing there trying to be patient as Magnusson grilled him took the stuffing right out of her knees. Damn him for looking so unconcerned. For laughing over at Swann in answer to Magnusson's indignation. Abbie closed her eyes against the terrible pain of relief that swept her. Giving up, she leaned against the warm metal of the fence.

She didn't see the unhappy surprise in Michael's eyes when he discovered her there.

Slipping his gun back under his pullover, Michael said something final to Swann and headed back for the fence, ignoring Magnusson's impatient warnings.

Abbie felt Michael's hand on her arm and slumped even farther, barely able to get her eyes open or focused. Tears burned along her cheeks.

"Just about had your fill of crises?" he asked, his smile gentle enough to lie down in.

Abbie managed a faint grin in return. "If only you didn't look like you were having so damn much fun."

He slipped her into his embrace, his arms strong and re-assuring around her. "I think this is your last caper, Doc. It's back to the quiet world of emergency rooms for you."

Abbie pulled her head back to challenge him, the realiza-tion of his safety still too tenuous to believe him. "You mean it?"

Ignoring all the increasing bustle around him, the disap-proving scowl of his superior and the smug grin of his friend, Michael bent to kiss his doctor. He couldn't imag-ine having been lucky enough to find someone like Abbie, so bright and sensitive and strong. He'd never hesitated in asking her to help, even though his life could very well have depended on it. And she'd come through, just as he knew she would. It was only now, once it was over, that she again betrayed what it had cost her.

He cushioned her trembling body, thinking that he'd never tasted lips so sweet or held a woman so beautiful. Her hair swept against his fingertips and curled against his cheek. Her arms circled his neck where long, elegant fin-gers closed against his skin with the fiercest possession.

"I can drop you off right at your front door," he prom-ised, the soft taste of her lips lingering on him. "Right af-ter we..."

"Stop by the station," she finished for him, the disquiet in her eyes tempered by a silly smile of relief. "Is it really over?"

He shrugged, motioning to the activity behind him. "You have your Mr. Doyle, the seller. You have Mr. Robbins, the buyer. You have a suitcase full of heroin and a briefcase full of money. And, for an added bonus—" now he pointed to the still form at Swann's feet "—the go-between, Mr. Marlow."

Abbie straightened at that, and looked over, her eyes on what she supposed were Marlow's feet. An unidentified tension rose in her chest. The man after Michael. After her. If he were really dead, it would be over.

"I bet Magnusson's a little put off with you," she said to Michael as she eased back out of his arms.

Michael wasn't terribly concerned. "He has no sense of humor. Especially since it was his fault that the buy went down wrong. He sent his men in early without telling us, and blew not only his man's cover, but the warehouse where the buy was going to go down. The whole deal was changed so that Mr. Doyle could sneak right back out on a commuter flight when the sale was made."

As Abbie listened, she began to edge her way toward the growing crowd of police, her eyes on the ground by their feet.

Michael reached out, his hand just missing her shoulder. "Abbie...?"

She looked up only long enough to exchange dispassionate glances with Mr. Robbins, the man who had so silently tried to kill her, as they led him past, handcuffed and surrounded. Then she stooped down to the body on the ground.

A couple of the police nearby automatically moved to stop her, their instincts wanting to protect her from the unpleasantness that was their job. It was Michael who motioned them away.

Abbie couldn't say what she felt. Confusion, relief, an oddly dispassionate interest. What she should have felt was finality, and she couldn't find that quite yet.

It was over. Tomorrow she would go back to her life, build a relationship with Michael in a more traditional way, and try to get used to a renewed feeling of security. No one would be banging on her door or following her home from work. The only time she'd visit the station would be to surprise Michael when he finally got his suit and overcrowded desk next to Swann's. She tried to convince herself of that as she crouched among the suddenly silent police who watched her with a mixture of interest and respect.

"What do you think?" Michael asked, his hand finally reaching her shoulder.

She looked up at him with a helpless little shrug and got to her feet. "I wish I could have seen him before."

He slid an arm around her waist and guided her away.

"Magnusson's satisfied?" she asked, not bothering to look back.

Michael nodded. "He's had an eye on Robbins since he broke into your place. Thought he worked for Marlow at first. Turns out Marlow worked for him. Robbins supplies just about every dealer on the South Side." Michael wished he could feel as smug as Magnusson about the whole thing. He had such a nagging suspicion that the DEA man had left a loose end somewhere. He just couldn't figure out what it was.

They walked back through the terminal, their slow steps echoing across the nearly empty space, Abbie leaning against the solid support of Michael's body as she walked. The life had drained out of her when she'd seen him safe. She was putting one foot in front of the other, content to let Michael provide navigation and pace. So nice to lean on, she thought with an absent smile.

"You want to go home?" Michael asked, dropping a kiss onto the top of her head, the sudden weariness in her posture tearing at him. All he wanted to do right now was gather her into his arms and hold her as she slept, keeping her safe and warm against him.

Abbie felt the edges of his shoulder holster with the hand that she'd wrapped around his back and realized that just the feel of it didn't repulse her as it once had. Its mere ex-

istence didn't terrify her. It was part of Michael, a tool of a
job he loved and excelled at.

"What about the station?" she asked, the exhaustion
finding its way into her voice.

Michael shrugged. "I don't see what good you'll do there.
I'll just drop you off on the way in."

Abbie just nodded. Michael reached the car and bent to
open the door for Abbie. He missed the slow smile that rose
in her eyes as she settled into her seat and reached for the
seat belt.

This time, she thought with a much wider smile as she
looked around the familiar room, we're going to do it right.
The bellhop set down her bag and went about checking to
see that all was ready. He wasn't little Martin, the man
who'd seen them in the last time, but everything else was the
same. Abbie had called the minute she'd reached her apartment to find their little suite once again available and then
had called on Swann to engage his help.

She walked through the rooms thinking how very different it seemed to stand in them now that she wasn't confined
to them. An adventure, an assignation with her lover in a
beautiful old hotel. Just that thought, so alien only a short
time before, set her pulse racing and put a sharp glitter in her
eyes. When the bellhop left, Abbie walked in to unpack her
negligee.

Swann had figured it almost to the minute: 5 a.m., he'd
said—just as the sun was getting ready to come up—was
when they'd be getting finished. Abbie napped alone in the
big four-poster until five and then took up her station by the
window overlooking Goethe.

Today the quiet life along this small street pleased her.
Streetlights melted light into fading little pools of white
along the sidewalks, and cars passed at a sedate pace.
Someone was up in the middle-aged woman's stone castle.
Somewhere over the lake, the sun was beginning to rise,
spreading a soft peach over the sky that matched the comforter on the bed. Warm, alive, promising. Abbie found

herself smiling even before Swann's battered old car pulled up before the canopy twelve floors below.

When Michael stepped out of the car, he stood where he was for a moment. Then Swann pulled away, and Michael looked up, trying to discern one window on the twelfth floor. There was a light on where he thought it would be, and a softly-shaped silhouette. The contour of a head full of sleep-tossed curls. He smiled to himself, shaking his head at the subterfuge she'd used to get him here, and walked in.

"Mr. Smith?" the clerk asked.

He smiled back. "I assume Dr. Smith is already here?"

She never bothered to mention a room number. "Go right up, sir."

Michael found his way to the elevator, still empty in the early-morning hours, and punched the button marked twelve. The doors slid silently closed on his brightening grin of anticipation.

It had been a long night. Magnusson had wanted his pound of flesh, and Michael had damn near been it. But then the extent of Magnusson's mistake had come out, and Magnusson was the one to find himself in trouble.

Just about the same time the shipment had been arriving from Mexico, Magnusson had taken his task force to storm a warehouse on the West Side where he'd been informed Marlow was about to meet his boss Robbins. He had netted no more than two mid-level workers and a stash of equipment when the call came in from the airport. Evidently Robbins had heard about the warehouse raid and completely changed the drug deal. The good news had been that Jaime had simply been left out of it at the last minute. The bad news was that if Michael and Swann hadn't gone out on their own, the deal would have gone down without interference.

Even more, they would have lost Robbins, who turned out to be one of the bigger czars in the Chicago drug business. Connected with quite a few crime families, he supplied just about every dealer in the West Side. They figured that he had also been the one to put the finger on Michael and Abbie, not wanting to take the chance that they would present problems. They had spotted Marlow, who could lead them to him.

There were still a few things that didn't jibe for Michael. Like just how the no-talent junkie Marlow was tied in with the oily-smooth Robbins, and just how they'd had enough time to change the deal to prevent capture at the warehouse.

Oh well, he thought as the doors opened up onto the soft gray and white corridor, not something he needed to worry about anymore. It was Swann's baby now, and narcotics' and the press's. He was out of it and on his way to two days off with the notorious Dr. Smith.

She opened the door before he even knocked. Michael saw the sleepy mischief in Abbie's eyes and the soft mauve silk and lace negligee that outlined her lithe figure. A swift fire seared his belly, and his hands itched to be against her. He stepped into the soft womb of the suite and gathered her into his arms.

Abbie never noticed Michael kick the door shut. The minute he'd seen her, the weariness in his eyes had vanished and delight appeared. He felt an arousal so ferocious that he crushed her against him. She raised her face to him, but he buried his own face in her throat, the freshly washed scent of her hair tormenting him, the smooth skin below her ear inflaming him. He threaded a hand into her glossy curls and another around the silk at her waist.

Abbie brought her own hands up to the tight, strong muscles of his shoulders. His hands incited keen chills that raced down her limbs. His lips nibbled at her neck and sapped the strength from her knees. A molten glow was swelling throughout her, its hot core settling deep where only Michael could find it. She stirred against the hard strength of him, instinctively moving to sweeten the fire.

"I thought you were home asleep," he accused, trailing kisses along the filmy material that outlined her shoulder.

"I had a better idea." She smiled, then gasped as Michael's hand slipped down to cup her bottom. She arched, her pelvis seeking the sharper angles of his. Heat seeking heat. "I thought I'd see how this place was without the castle guards."

Michael nodded against her, his beard chafing the tender skin at her throat and igniting fresh chills. Fresh shivers of anticipation. She could hardly stand upright anymore.

"And how is it?"

She closed her eyes as the soft morning light spread across the room and warmed her bare feet nestled in the plush carpeting. A new day had begun.

"Oh, I think it's going to be just fine."

Michael lifted her easily into his arms, his mouth finally settling over hers. Abbie slipped her own fingers around his head and into his hair, the thick texture of it enticing. Welcoming the insistent probe of his tongue, she never felt him carry her across into the bedroom where the four-poster waited for them with its warm polished wood and marshmallow-soft comforter.

Michael set Abbie on her feet next to the bed and drew his arms away. He let his eyes feast on the tantalizing light in Abbie's eyes, the desire-softened smile on her features, the wild tangle of her soft curls. Then he lifted his hands to her shoulders to slide the silk and lace confection away.

Abbie blushed again, the softest hue of pink high on her cheeks in shy pleasure at Michael's frank admiration. He hoped she'd never lose that touch of innocence, that endearing surprise at Michael's pleasure in her. His eyes lifted from their slow perusal and captured hers with a lazy smile. "I hope you have the next two days booked, Doctor. I don't think I'm going to let you out of my sight."

Abbie matched his smile, stepping up to rest her hands against the waist of his slacks. "Depends, Sergeant," she demurred, dropping her head to observe her work. "I have to get you in my sight first."

He laughed, restraining the urge to just rip his clothes off and get Abbie onto that bed. The flutter of her fingers against his belly was maddening as she worked snap and zipper. Then she took her hands to his hips to slide the slacks over, and the sharp ache flared in him, drawing a low groan that measured the cost of his control. Her scent was in his nostrils, frail and wild like a meadow of flowers open to the night. Her hair brushed against his arms as she straightened to help lift his pullover off.

Michael's breath caught when Abbie discovered the holster—strapped tight across his chest beneath the loose shirt, slung low so he could get to the weapon it held with a minimum of fuss. He hadn't known Swann had sabotaged his car so he'd have to beg a ride and end up at the hotel. And to be honest, once the surprise had been pulled, he'd forgotten all about the damn gun.

Abbie paused before him, her eyes raking the leather straps Michael no longer even noticed and coming to rest on the dull shine of the snub handle below his left arm. Michael's first impulse was to apologize to her. After what she'd been through—not just this past couple of weeks, but sixteen years ago—she didn't need this constantly thrown in her face.

Abbie must have seen the intent in his eyes. She gave him a reassuring smile.

"It's okay, Michael," she said, a hand out to test the substance of it. "I'm just trying to get used to it. I can't keep letting it surprise me anymore, can I? I mean, it's as much a part of your job as a stethoscope is mine."

She nodded to herself: a decision made, a crossroad reached. Then she lifted her eyes back to his, the impish gleam intentionally making light of her past traumas. "Actually, it's quite rakish. Makes you look . . . dangerous."

When she removed the holster, her fingers shook with the effort at constraint, but it was an act of sharing rather than rejection.

Michael took her face in his hands and sought the glitter of unshed tears. He felt the trembling in her as she fought to overcome her fears. "Know what?" He smiled, dropping his lips to hers for a fleeting kiss that prevented answer. "You're a pretty gutsy lady, Doc."

Abbie's grin was tremulous at best, but she couldn't look away from the intense emerald eyes that had first captured her trust. "Not me," she retorted more easily. "I just know a good deal when I see it. And you," she murmured, stretching to return the kiss, her breasts brushing up over Michael's bare chest, "are a very good deal."

The words even more than the action robbed Michael of his patience. Wrapping his arms around her, he lifted Abbie onto the bed. Her eyelids lowered as she pulled him down with her, her body moving to fit more snugly against his. The light from the window fell obliquely across her face, striking sparks in the blue of her eyes and warming the soft hollows of her throat. Michael buried himself within the solace of her embrace and refreshed himself on the music of her sighs.

He'd wondered whether some of the fire would fade from their lovemaking once they lost the spice of danger; once the world rushed back in and invaded the insularity of their special relationship.

He needn't have worried. Let loose from Magnusson's watchful eye and the oppressive fear for Abbie's life, his desire flared even hotter. She tasted sweeter, more dangerous and delicious, moved more provocatively beneath his hands. He found that now that he was able to concentrate more on pleasing her, his own excitement intensified. He explored her body with his hands, his mouth—stroking, suckling, nipping at the tender skin that shuddered exquisitely beneath his ministrations.

"Your beard," she gasped, her fingernails raking his shoulders.

Michael lifted his head from where he'd been nuzzling her belly, the gentle mound that met her thighs enticing him. "I'm sorry..."

"No." She giggled, her hips lifting to meet him. "I want more..."

He gave her more. She groaned, her hands to his head.

"I have this thing for sandpaper, ya know..."

Michael tested his arousal against her. "How do you feel about hot steel?" He grinned.

"That's cold steel," she managed with a giggle. "And hot lead. What kind of cop can't even...ahhh...tell your guns from your ammo?"

He pulled her against him. "Maybe you'd better show me."

When Michael found himself laughing with her, he realized that he had begun to treasure the playfulness so integral to their lovemaking. That same impish whimsy he'd fallen in love with colored Abbie's sensuality.

Finally Michael couldn't wait anymore. Abbie was warm and moist against his hungry fingers, her body writhing beneath him. He moved back up to find her eyes open and alight, her lips parted in a new moan as his hand slid along her thigh to prepare his way. When he eased his weight over her, she brought her hands around to his hips, ready, anxious for the release he promised. She fixed her eyes on his and cherished him when he lowered his mouth to hers.

Once again he absorbed her startled little gasps, mingled her name with the moans he uttered. He plundered her mouth and savored her skin, the dark, deep pleasures of her body igniting him like fireworks. Her hands clutched at him, pulling him to her. Her fingernails dug into his skin. Michael drove into her, the world around him disintegrating in her throaty cry and undulating body.

For a long while Abbie remained still, content to lie where she was, the still, cool air in the room bathing her damp skin. Michael lay against her, his weight pleasantly heavy. He rested an arm over her belly and his head by her neck so that she could feel the companionable warmth of his breath. If she pulled the comforter up, she knew it would nestle them both in its shelter.

Just that seemed to her the height of luxury. To fall asleep slowly, intertwined with the man you love, and then to wake with him again, waiting to do whatever you wanted. She smiled to herself, a hand unconsciously touching Michael's hair.

"So, what are you going to do today?" he asked, his voice sleepy and content. She laughed, the sound an alluring one. "I mean, besides that." He grinned into her shoulder. A languid heat seemed to encourage them both, a lazy savoring of companionship and pleasure.

"I'm going to sleep here with you," she assured him, finally pulling the cover all the way up and smiling anew at its rich comfort. How very decadent, she thought. How very wonderful.

"Then what?" he persisted. "What have you been aching to do?"

She laughed again, and it sounded the same.

So did he. "*Besides* that."

Abbie didn't have to do much thinking. "Walk. I have to admit that I really miss getting out and prowling the city. I want to walk to the lake, and say hi to the polar bear at the zoo, and get to Michigan Avenue and do some expensive window shopping."

She was warming to her subject now, the ideas tumbling around like entries in a lottery drawing. "Then there's Wrigley Field. I haven't been to the bleachers in weeks. And Chinese restaurants. And the seventh floor of Marshall Field's at the Water Tower."

Michael had some trouble following the last. "The seventh floor?"

Abbie found herself grinning again. "Gourmet foods. I'm dying for some Frango mints."

The mere thought of food set off other cravings like chain lightning. Other foods she'd missed. There was only one she knew Michael would instinctively object to.

"I want to go to the Donut Hole."

Predictably, he scowled. "Swann would love to take you."

Abbie turned a little so that Michael nestled more closely against her. He was yawning, the languor overtaking him. He hadn't really been to sleep in over twenty-four hours, and Abbie couldn't think of anything she'd rather do right now than ease him to sleep next to her. She wanted to see the residual tension drain away and the little boy reappear in her arms. That old maternal instinct again.

"What?" Michael's voice was drowsy.

Abbie hadn't realized that she'd voiced her last thoughts. With a soft smile, she ran a gentling hand down his cheek, her eyes inches from the sleepy peace of his. "Oh, nothing," she murmured. "I was just thinking about how I should follow my instincts more often."

Michael yawned again and pulled her closer, the hardness of his body eased around hers so that it seemed the only way Abbie had ever been able to fall asleep.

"Remind me when I'm awake to ask what you just said."

Abbie waited until Michael was sound asleep, his breathing deep and even against her, the sunlight gleaming white off his tumbled hair and sliding along the angle of his jaw. The sight of him, the feel of him so relaxed in her arms, filled her with an unspeakable poignancy. She had never known the simple pleasure of sharing her sleep with anyone. A basic need, but one so primal that when you discovered it, you knew that an empty bed is the coldest place on earth.

Abbie reached out tentatively and chased the sunlight in Michael's hair, soaking in the crisp wood-fire scent that still lingered between them and savoring the intimacy of his body alongside hers. He was making the first tentative steps to sharing with her, bringing her his triumphs and a few of his frustrations. Maybe now that the danger was past, he'd feel more comfortable coming to her with the other parts of himself: the tensions, the worries, the pain. And maybe, just maybe, Abbie would be able to deal with her own pain. If she tried hard enough, the sight of Michael's gun might not instinctively terrify her anymore.

She turned to see it now, set carefully on the small table by the window where it would be safely out of the way. And wishing she had that courage now, she closed her eyes to shut it out again.

Abbie didn't wake again until late afternoon. She stretched a little, turning an eye over to see whether Michael was still asleep. He had turned onto his stomach, an arm flung over the side of the bed, his head turned to her. Exhausted, she thought with a protective smile. Slipping carefully beyond his grasp, she eased out into the climate-controlled chill of the room and headed over to shower.

No, she thought, stepping into the marble and pastel bathroom, not a shower. A bath. A long, hot soak in a limitless hot-water tank with a book. It had been a long time since she'd had the opportunity to luxuriate in a bathtub. Another small decadence that an up-and-struggling emergency-room physician hadn't had the time for.

She bent to test the water and then thought of an even better idea: coffee. She'd order room service and sit in the water reading her book and drinking coffee. Maybe she'd get some finger food, too. She hadn't really thought of how hungry she was, but now that she was moving around, her stomach had begun to gnaw rather insistently at her. Why not kill more than one bird with a particularly self-indulgent stone?

She headed back out of the bathroom with a wicked grin on her face. It occurred to her that Michael had gone a long way toward creating a monster.

Michael turned in the bed a little later and threw his arm over to where Abbie slept. His hand found empty sheet, not even her body heat left. He opened his eyes to verify it.

The sky outside their window was fading back into soft pastels, the gold of a soon-setting sun gilding the uppermost leaves of the trees. Evening birds and car motors provided distant music, and the hotel room was silent. The place beside him was empty, the thick comforter thrown back and left, the pillow still crumpled up against his. He flipped over onto his back and struggled up, the sleep taking a while to clear. Funny how he hadn't been sleeping with Abbie that long, yet his first instinct on waking was to reach for her. Raking a hand through his hair and giving way to a jaw-splitting yawn, he looked around for her.

The clue came while he bent to slip into his slacks. Water. He heard a small lapping sound that emanated from behind the bathroom door. Michael grinned to himself. Thinking how very much he was beginning to like that porcelain tub, he padded across to the half-open door.

Abbie didn't hear the door open beside her. She certainly heard the sudden burst of laughter. A grape halfway to her mouth, she turned to see Michael standing there bare chested and half-awake, his eyes on the wineglass she held in one hand and the grapes she nibbled from the other.

She stopped, a decidedly unrepentant grin on her face.

"Now, this—" Michael laughed, leaning against the door with arms crossed "—is what I expect from a doctor."

She couldn't help a wine-fed giggle. "Really decadent, isn't it?"

"Outrageous on a cop's salary."

She nodded happily. "Mine, too. It started out to be a shower. Then a bath. Then I thought why not soak a while with a book and cup of coffee. When I talked to room service, though—" she grinned, taking sip of the cool, crisp Mosel wine "—it became 'What the hell.' Like some?"

"Just fruit and wine?"

She motioned to the tray set up at the corner of the tub. "And cheese. I'm watching my weight, you know."

Michael's eyes lit with arousal as he assessed Abbie's water-buoyed curves. "Looks fine to me."

Abbie threw a grape at him, which he deftly caught and popped in his mouth. "What about those Frango mints?" he asked, easing his tight tush onto the tub rim.

Abbie made a face. "Exactly why I'm being good now. I passed up pâté, and bisque for dessert."

Michael reached over and ran his fingertip along her breast where it rose glistening from the water. "You can always exercise it off."

Abbie gave him a lazy grin, her toes stretching out the sweet agony his touch ignited. "I thought we were going to walk Michigan and see the polar bear at the zoo."

He bent even farther, his hand sliding along beneath the water as his tongue plumbed the depths of her mouth for the last traces of wine. "Tomorrow."

Abbie moaned, pressing against his touch. "And tonight?"

Michael chuckled against her, his body almost horizontal to the floor. "Oh, we'll think of something."

Abbie knew she was a little drunk. She'd made it through a third of a bottle of wine before Michael had shown up. Even so, his touch ignited a fever in her that the cooling water couldn't quench. She brought a free hand to his chest, her fingers splayed against the delicious spread of hair. Her own tongue parried with Michael's, mingling tastes and textures—sleepy musk, and wine, and the tart sweetness of grapes.

"Don't you ever wear out?" she finally demanded, a breathless few minutes later.

Michael chuckled, his fingers caught in the soft tendrils that clung to her neck. "If that's the way you feel about it," he retorted, "maybe we should say hi to the polar bear now. Probably warmer there anyway..."

He never completed his complaint. Taking advantage of his poor balance, Abbie took hold of his shoulders and flipped him into the tub.

Michael howled. The tray clattered to the floor where grapes and plums rolled merrily across the white marble floor. About a third of the water volume landed right behind them with a resounding splash.

Calmly surveying Michael's ungainly position and the submerged state of his slacks, Abbie took another sip of her wine and flashed him a smug grin. "Guess it's gonna have to be tomorrow after all."

The next day was, after all, spent in a tourist's tour of the town. They didn't get to the Lincoln Zoo, but taking advantage of a Canadian cold front that dropped the temperatures into the upper seventies and evaporated the humidity, Michael and Abbie strolled the surrounding neighborhood down to the wind-whipped lake and then wandered along Michigan Avenue. Abbie made her pilgrimage to Marshall Field's and peered in the shops that stretched along the broad boulevard. She and Michael crossed the Chicago River bridge and then ate at an open-air café at One Illinois Plaza.

They sat along the open side of the square where they could see the river and the city stretch away from them in sleek geometrics. A brightly colored umbrella shaded them from the sun, and a band played for the lunchtime crowd around the corner. Abbie pulled her sunglasses up to her head and stretched her gaze upward to the buildings that rose to the sky. She felt so deliciously alive today. So free and full of promise. The sunlight full on her made her want to stretch, to take off her shoes and dance across the deliciously hot pavement. She wanted to live forever on a day like today. But most of all, she wanted to share it all with Michael.

"God, it's good to be back among the living." She laughed, her voice striking rich music against the buildings.

Michael scowled, his beer temporarily forgotten in his enjoyment of Abbie's enthusiasm. "Are you trying to tell me something about my company?"

She grinned. "I'm trying to tell you something about Magnusson's company. He could take over the cold-fish industry. Him and those damn mug books!" The derisive shake of her head was tempered by the mischief on her face.

"The mug books were ours," Michael patiently reminded her.

Abbie made a face. "Sure made me appreciate Gray's *Anatomy* again. The pictures are a lot better."

"Now wait a minute," he objected, having trouble with his stern expression. "Some of those mugs are our best customers."

She laughed, conceding. "Well, all I know is that I'm never going to be able to look at another 'white male subject' without comparing eye size and nasal hair."

She moved to pick up her iced tea, content with the cool afternoon and Michael's smile, when her stomach suddenly fell away. She dropped the glass back on the table, almost spilling the contents. Her eyes had strayed past Michael.

"Abbie," he said, immediately sensing her distress, "what's wrong?"

Abbie couldn't answer, couldn't take her eyes from the two businessmen passing just behind Michael. It was just an instant, a sudden panic when she saw the familiar face. She knew she was being absurd. They'd already sorted it out. Marlow was dead, the threat was gone. The man she saw was a businessman. An innocent man with a killer's face. But when she'd spotted him, he was angry, his eyes flashing cold black at his companion. And that look alone had kicked in Abbie's instinct to fall and roll.

It was Michael's turning that drew Mr. DeRosa's attention. He looked in time to see the two people watching him, one with assessment, one with blank terror. Abbie felt his dispassionate gaze brush her and shuddered. She could have sworn he recognized her. Then he moved his eyes to Michael. Without even a nod of acknowledgment, he turned back to his companion and went on his way.

Michael turned back to see that Abbie had gone suddenly ashen. She followed the back of DeRosa's head for a moment before returning her attention to Michael and her tea.

"The human mind is a wonderful thing." She laughed uneasily, throwing one more parting glance at the retreating figure. "After all the pertinent facts have been fed in and an answer arrived at, it still prefers to come up with its own completely arbitrary conclusions."

Michael took hold of her hand as if to save her from falling, his smile understanding. "He still scares you."

"Who, me? Nah, this has always been my favorite shade of stark white. The shaking and sweating is just a rank play for sympathy."

His smile broadened into that crooked grin that snatched her heart so quickly. "You have *my* sympathy," he assured her. "And anything else you'd like."

Abbie found herself laughing, the joy bubbling back up from where DeRosa's unexpected appearance had chased it. "Well, we've already established what I like."

Michael gaped. "Again?"

Abbie flashed him a lazy smile, her eyes alight in the age-old way of the seductress. "I'm just a greedy little girl."

Michael ingested the life in her eyes like sweet wine, the sudden sensuality in her posture surprising just as traditional a reaction from him. "You're no little girl, lady."

That evening, their last before each took up their lives again, was spent at Michael's apartment. Abbie learned even more about him there. Walking to the four rooms he inhabited in an older section of the city close to where his father lived, she felt immediately comfortable.

Michael had good taste that ran toward clean lines and minimalist decoration, all spread over a budget still recovering from divorce. The pictures of his father sat on the shelves with the opera records, and softball trophies occupied his den alongside French and Italian literature and art. His furniture was overstuffed and inviting, his bed a queen-size functional with the spread pulled up in the haphazard way men make beds. Abbie laughed at herself when she realized how much more she loved him for this place.

"Comfort and security," she said, coming upon him in a kitchen that rivaled hers for lack of size.

He looked up from his pasta, her assessment surprising him. He'd never really thought about it when he'd thrown the place together in the days after Maria had departed.

Abbie slid up and eased her arms around his waist, oblivious to the spatula and skillet he had in his hands. "I like you, Viviano."

He grinned, dropping a kiss on her upturned nose. "I like you, too, Doc. You have good taste."

"I'm a pack rat," she warned without much passion.

"That's okay. I'm good at throwing things out."

"Think you could make a little room on those hallowed shelves for Van Halen?"

His grin broadened as spatula and skillet crept around Abbie's waist. "Actually, I was wondering where I could stow Mozart at your place. If you don't mind settling for a policeman's salary, that is."

Abbie's grin was complacent. "Can you afford Häagen-Dasz?"

Michael's answer was a not-very-complacent kiss.

Finally Abbie straightened, her eyes bright with suppressed humor. "Viviano," she said, "I think we need to talk."

"Doc," he murmured, his lips brushing the tender expanse of hers. "I can't think of anything I'd rather do."

Abbie giggled, pressing closer and undulating, just a little.

Michael nodded his acquiescence with a bright smile. "Except that."

Abbie nodded back. "Except that," she agreed.

And that night as they lay together on Michael's big functional bed, they talked. Abbie told Michael about the years she'd sacrificed to be a doctor, and Michael told Abbie about Maria and the cold ashes of his marriage. He talked about his decision to leave the streets for a desk and a suit, and the relationship between the police force and a cop whose father had been a cop, and his father before him. And later, when the city noises dimmed a little and a slivered moon crested the buildings downtown, Michael told Abbie about Hector.

That same night, Swann came across the report. Oblivious to the chaos around him, he sat at his desk and stared at it.

Nothing earth-shattering, just a little inconsistency. A gap in history that wouldn't have troubled anybody but Swann. He read over the sparse words again and shook his head. Michael was due back on duty tomorrow. Swann couldn't make up his mind whether this was something to bother him with quite yet. After all, it was still only a gut feeling. An instinct. Michael respected Swann's instincts, but Swann had been wrong before, and he didn't feel like ruining Viviano's time off till he had it chased down.

Making a few quick, scribbled notes on the carefully worded report, he slid it into his "Things that have to be done myself to get them right and in on time" pile, and then went back to the rest of his workload.

Chapter 14

Abbie snipped the last stitch on the forehead of a squirming three-year-old and stripped off her gloves. Another night at the old zoo, she thought to herself with satisfaction. By her second night back, she'd handled two trauma patients, one cardiac arrest and at least forty-two head lacerations just like this one. The temperature had gone up again and summer was back in full swing in the emergency room. Abbie wouldn't have been anyplace else.

"Do you have a minute to see a man with back pain?" Phoebe asked, leaning in the door. A week overdue now, Phoebe had taken up a permanent station at the triage desk where she would do a minimum of carrying and bending.

Abbie nodded and turned to finish reassuring the anxious parents that their firstborn son would not only survive this trip to the E.R., but would undoubtedly be back for more before long. They were not terribly encouraged.

"How long has this guy been hurting?" Abbie asked as she turned the hot water and Betadine soap on her hands a moment later, the family safely on their way.

Phoebe leaned against the wall and grinned. "Ever since the police picked him up on a stolen goods charge."

Abbie had to laugh. Another day in the life of Chicago. "Tell the arresting officer that I'll cure his charge as quickly as I can."

"Tell him yourself." Phoebe grinned. "He asked for you by name."

Abbie looked up, a self-conscious blush spreading up from her neck. At thirty, she was suddenly acting more like a fifteen-year-old than she had when she was fifteen. "Michael?"

"One and the same." Phoebe's smile grew almost possessively happy. "You two sure were cute on the news the other night."

Abbie scowled. "The Fred and Ginger of law enforcement." The news crews had come down on the drug bust like ants on a Labor Day picnic. When they had come upon the unexpected plum of the heroic lady doctor helping her heroic sergeant, they'd milked it for everything but a prime-time soap. Abbie's family had been ragging her unmercifully about it—especially the kiss on the station steps, which Michael had finally been obliged to repeat.

Phoebe laughed at Abbie's discomfort. "Well, all I know is, I hope you don't mind my being personal, but it's sure nice to see Michael smiling again."

"You're not being personal," Abbie assured her with a like smile. "In fact, the first time something goes wrong, you're going to be the one called into service. Your advice is too good to pass up."

Phoebe refused to take the compliment lightly. "You doing better with that?"

Abbie nodded. "Better. Not perfect. I still make him hide his gun when he comes over, and every time the radio goes off around here, I brace myself until I know for sure we're not answering an officer shot call."

Phoebe's nod was empathetic. "I know. It's a hard reflex to overcome."

Abbie's eyes grew distant as she looked beyond her friend. "It's just suddenly so important for me to be able to grow old with him."

"One step at a time, Ab," Phoebe advised, a hand to her arm. "One day at a time."

Abbie looked over, surprised that Phoebe should echo the very philosophy she'd taken. She realized then that by falling in love with Michael she had joined a special confraternity of men and women. It gave her an unexpected feeling of companionship, of support.

"Let's go lay hands," she offered with a smile, "and let Sgt. Viviano get on with his paperwork so he's not late for his date tonight."

Phoebe laughed and preceded Abbie back out into the bustling hallway.

"Well, well," Abbie spoke up when she spotted the trim figure in crisp blue standing a little farther down the hall. "If it isn't the notorious Sgt. Viviano. Who's lining up to shoot you this week, Sergeant?"

Michael's smile lit his features like a sunrise. Neither he nor Abbie seemed to notice that all her co-workers turned to them with corresponding smiles.

"A certain lady doctor I'm supposed to be taking out tonight after work," he told her. "I had the bad luck to catch a bad guy half an hour before end of shift, and that means two hours of paperwork."

"Tsk, tsk," she admonished, walking over. She was going to miss him in his uniform, all lean lines and military buttons. And that cap, set so precisely over the clean angle of his jaw. No wonder women kept falling for men in uniforms. "If I were she, I'd probably demand some kind of apology."

"Who from?" he asked with a mischievous grin. "Me or the perp?"

"I don't know," she said, very close to him now, her voice low and her eyes suggestive. "Does he apologize anything like you do?"

Michael bent his head to her, locking everyone else out. "Nobody apologizes like I do."

Abbie's surprised laughter drew more glances. "In that case," she decided. "My place, Sergeant. Say, three?"

"I have some wine and cheese at my place," he countered, his eyes soft and beguiling. "Which I know you have a weakness for, Doctor. Say, two?"

She nodded. "You, Sergeant, have a deal."

When she turned to go into the room where Michael's charge waited, she did a little sashay past him, brushing her hips ever so lightly across his very susceptible groin. Michael turned into the room with her rather than have to stay in the hall and be found out.

Abbie got off late that night herself, getting caught in with a bad patient at the last minute. By the time she made it to her apartment, it was already close to one. She was going to have to shower and change and then catch a cab on over to Michael's. Much as she hated to admit it, if this relationship continued, she was going to have to lease a car. Getting back and forth on their schedules was beginning to present a prohibitive taxi bill.

She checked her watch as she stepped off the elevator and calculated just how much time it would take to make it back over to Michael's. There should be plenty of time. She could just slip in with the key he'd given her, and then, armed with strawberries and a hot-red teddy she'd bought at Lord & Taylor that morning, she'd greet him at the door and begin to work out the details of his apology. The smile on her face was wickedly anticipatory as she slid the key into the lock of her new front door.

By the time Michael reached his apartment, he was beat. Two-thirty. He hoped Abbie wouldn't hold it against him. Oh well, she was probably going to be late her share of nights, too. It was just something the two of them made allowance for. He slipped his key in the door, half expecting it to be yanked open at the scrape of metal, and Abbie to be standing on the threshold. She wasn't.

The living room was dark, only a small glow from the kitchen lighting his way. He looked around for signs of Abbie's presence. Maybe she'd ended up having a bad night, too, and had just gone to bed.

He walked into the bedroom to find it just as empty.

"Abbie?" he called, already knowing it was useless. "Are you here?"

He didn't think she'd come and gone already. There would have been at least a note. Abbie wasn't the type to get angry and then sulk away without at least one well-directed barb being launched. Besides, it was only two-thirty, not four or five. She obviously hadn't made it over yet.

He placed his first call to her apartment. No answer. Maybe she'd been held up at work and unable to reach him. He placed the next call to the E.R.

Yes, the secretary remembered, Dr. Fitzgerald had gotten off pretty late. She couldn't say just when, though. They'd been unbelievably busy since. Michael hung up feeling a little better. He had a cop's imagination, and couldn't help picturing Abbie accosted on her way over to his apartment that late at night. There were lots of bad guys out there. She'd probably just been stuck late at work, and then stopped by her place to change. He'd give her another half hour or so before he started worrying.

Michael was in decanting the wine when the phone rang. Grinning to himself, he set the bottle down and walked into the living room to answer it. Probably Abbie apologizing for not getting there in time for her apology.

"Viviano?"

That wasn't the voice he wanted to hear.

"It's after your bedtime, Swann."

"I need to come over and talk to you."

Michael sighed, his eyes searching the ceiling for patience. "Wouldn't you rather be talking to your wife? I'm waiting for a date."

"I'd rather be sleeping with my wife," the detective assured him without humor. "But something came up that I finally tracked down tonight, and it's time you heard all about it.''

"In the morning," Michael bargained.

"Now."

Michael checked his watch, his eyes drifting expectantly toward the door. "I can't leave. I'm waiting for Abbie to show up."

"That's okay. I'm next door. I'd like to come up before I die of bleach fumes."

Next door was an all-night Laundromat. Michael stifled a chuckle.

"Well, in that case," he acquiesced gracefully, "come on up. I'd hate to have your death on my conscience."

Taking a few minutes to put on an album of *Turandot*, Michael walked back into the kitchen to finish preparing the hors d'oeuvres. The apartment filled with the rich music of Puccini. Once more picking up the wine, Michael began humming the minor refrain.

Turandot had been the first production his father had taken him to at the Lyric—all lush Oriental costumes and minor keys, the story of a prince who wins out, for a change, and not only gets the girl but gets to live. The haunting melodies of it always resurrected feelings of discovery and delight in him. He couldn't ever remember the emotions filling him so thoroughly, though. The music seemed to speak to him tonight, a heady elixir of anticipation.

The door and phone rang simultaneously. Michael was just coming into the living room with a tray of cheese and a decanter of wine. Cursing at the bad timing, Michael set them on the coffee table. One wouldn't have thought his life would be so busy at three in the morning.

Pulling the door open on Swann, he swung around to make a grab for the phone. "Make yourself at home, but don't eat the food—Hello?"

Swann stepped in and closed the door behind him, a slim folder in his hand, a dearth of humor in his flat, black eyes. Even though Michael motioned for him to take a seat, he stayed by the door. The bearer of bad news, but Michael didn't see it. His attention was immediately taken by the caller.

"Abbie? Where are you? The..."

"Michael, you're finally home," she gushed, overriding him. "I've been trying to get you. Did you get off work late tonight?"

"Abbie, you know..."

"I got off late, too. I've been sitting over here thinking of you, and I had the most wonderful idea."

Even though Abbie sounded perfectly fine, something icy slipped into Michael's gut. "What's that, hon?"

She giggled, an oddly off-key sound that grated. "Well, since you're up this late anyway, I thought you might like to come over and visit. After all, you're the one with the car. Wanna make the most of a sleepless night together?"

"I don't know, Ab..." He didn't realize that he'd taken a tighter hold of the phone, all of his instincts on warning mode. His gut was twisting with it.

Then she clinched it.

"Oh, come on," she coaxed. "I even went out and got a bribe."

"What's that?"

"Crullers." She sounded positively delighted. "I got a big box of 'em, so you couldn't possibly say no. I know how much you love 'em."

Swann saw Michael's eyes grow stark.

"Well, if you put it that way," he was saying easily. "You have a deal. But I just got in. Okay if I take a shower first?"

"Well... make it a quick one. I'd hate for the doughnuts to be all gone before you got here."

Briefly Michael closed his eyes. "I'm on my way, Doc."

He replaced the phone carefully, his stomach churning. Something was terribly wrong, and he had no idea what. One thing was certain, though. Abbie was in trouble. Her coded message had come across too clearly. He stood a moment staring at the phone, rubbing his hand over his jaw.

"What's up?" Swann asked carefully.

Michael looked up at him, his eyes startled, as if he'd forgotten Swann was there. "Abbie. She was supposed to be over here." His eyes crept back toward the phone, then met Swann's. "That was her. Inviting me over for doughnuts."

Swann's eyes widened at the information. "Did she sound okay?"

"No," Michael mused, the foreboding taking hold where he'd sworn it never would again. "She was giggling." Giggling. Why did that strike such a dreadful memory in him?

Then, with a chill of prescience, he had it. "Some people cry. I giggle." He remembered Abbie saying it when she'd been afraid during the robbery. Just before everything had gone bad.

"Michael."

He returned his eyes to Swann's and immediately felt worse. The expression on that dark face told him he was about to find out more, and that he wasn't going to like it.

"I have something to show you," Swann said, fingering the folder.

"I have to get to Abbie's, Swann..."

Swann nodded. "After you read what I went to all the trouble of getting for you at eleven tonight." He held out the folder. "Go on."

Michael looked from his friend's taut features to the folder and back. Then he took it. Swann stood up and walked over to the phone, affording Michael a semblance of privacy as he read.

"Oh, God," Michael breathed in disbelief a moment later. "Marlow. His name is really Marlow."

"I can't prove it," Swann cautioned. "Not yet."

Michael turned to challenge him, and Swann saw a terror in the policeman's eyes he'd never seen in the twelve years he'd known him.

"What do you want to do, man?"

Michael never hesitated. "Get over to Abbie's."

When Abbie set the receiver back on its cradle, her hand was shaking. Not just trembling. Shaking so badly it took a concerted effort for her to get the phone back on target. She had thought the fear would be over. They'd told her that it was time to get on with her life, that her part in the whole operation was gratefully appreciated and applauded. And over.

They'd been wrong.

Sinking carefully back onto the couch, Abbie returned her attention to the man who sat in her other chair, her expression deliberately calm. The same expression she'd pulled on the night of the robbery, the second time in her life she'd had a gun pulled on her. Who'd have thought the third would be so soon?

Try as she might, she couldn't dredge up any humor this time.

"He's coming over."

"I know," the man answered with a satisfied nod. "We'll just wait."

He'd been there when she'd walked in the door. Passively sitting in the dark as Abbie had clocked in her overtime on a little old man with heart disease, while she'd sat on the bus laughing with her friends and planning her surprise for Michael, as she'd ridden up the elevator and unlocked the door. He was patient, like a spider setting his trap. And she was to be the bait.

What terrified her was that Michael was to be the prey. Michael, who had put himself right back in jeopardy by signing his name to those inquiries born of Abbie's uncertainty. He had once again endangered himself to protect her, and she was truly afraid that he wouldn't survive this time.

Abbie took a slow, deep breath to quell the renewed urge to giggle. Her stomach heaved. Her lungs were on fire from holding her breath. She ran a tongue over dry lips. God, please let Michael have understood the warnings she'd tried to send.

She couldn't think of any other way to tip him off that something was wrong than that stupid Nancy Drew ploy. Would he pick up on it and not come over, sending a SWAT team instead, or would he walk in oblivious to the danger awaiting him, figuring that Abbie was just tired and confused? Would he carry his gun with him, snug against his chest where it would be impotent to save him?

Across from her, the hunter sat easily in her mauve-flowered tulip chair, looking absolutely comfortable in his St. Laurent suit and Italian loafers. There was no anger in his eyes tonight. No emotion of any kind to be found in their undistinguished brown except the satisfaction of a plan well laid. Abbie had the feeling that he saw the whole episode as a business transaction. The idea made her angry.

"Then it was you I saw?" she asked.

Crossing his long legs, Albert DeRosa instinctively pulled the crease back into its razor-sharp line and smoothed the lint from his suit. He was completely at ease, shrugging away her observation. The gun he aimed at her head never so much as wavered.

"A fair assumption," he conceded.

"What about Marlow?" Abbie asked. "I thought he was the person I saw."

"You might have seen us both. I went to the hospital to pull them both off that stupid little action. They had no patience."

"And Robbins? The man who tried to kill me? The other man who tried to kill me," she amended without much humor. The list was beginning to grow. "Did he work for you, too?"

All she got for that effort was a noncommittal shrug. Mr. DeRosa was evidently much better at waiting than she was. He shifted his gaze to just beyond her and resumed his silence.

Abbie was sweating now. She could feel little rivulets of it slide down her shoulder blades and pool beneath her arms. Could it really be that hot, or was it just the effort it took to remain still? Michael, please come get me out of this. No! she amended with a fierce shake of her head. Don't come! Send the cavalry. Don't risk your life for me this time, because this man will take it from you without even blinking.

Moving very carefully under Mr. DeRosa's watchful eye, she reached up with a finger to wipe a moist forehead.

"Lousy air conditioning," she apologized, and stifled another giggle. This man would definitely not appreciate giggles.

He shrugged again, his own crisp linen shirt suspiciously dry. It must be nerve-racking to deal with a businessman who never worried enough to get rumpled. "It shouldn't take your policeman friend much longer to arrive."

He had an accent. Not foreign, but not Chicago. East Coast someplace, different vowels broadened, different consonants clipped. Abbie tried to concentrate on it rather than the minutes that crawled by even more slowly than the two hours she'd waited at the Ambassador. Tried to concentrate on the increasingly complex pattern of this whole setup.

First it had been Marlow she had to be afraid of. He was the bad guy who wanted her dead. Then it was Robbins, appearing out of nowhere. Now, apparently, Marlow's boss. He'd wanted her dead, they decided. Now Mr. DeRosa sat across from her with a gun in his hand, and it was a dead cinch he wasn't here to get his stitches out. Was he the boss now? Was he the one she should have feared all along, sending Marlow and Robbins out on their little jobs? Hiring the Travelenos and giving them Michael's name?

Twenty minutes of nerve-shattering silence later, the buzzer sounded. Abbie jumped a foot, desperately wanting it to be someone else. Anyone else. Avon, the Hare Krishnas selling flowers. Just don't let it be Michael walking blithely into this trap. She knew better and buzzed him up.

Leaving the gun pointed in the exact proximity of Abbie's left temple, DeRosa walked over to the window and pulled back the curtains. When he turned slightly to survey the wide street and the park beyond, he never thought to warn Abbie about moving. Abbie never thought to move, knowing he'd strike like a cobra if she did.

She held her breath, not sure what she wanted to happen. If it were quiet out there, she'd be safe. If the street were alive with lights again, Michael would be safe. Pray for lights, Abbie. A whole streetful of them.

The night outside remained dark. Only a distant street-lamp reflected from DeRosa's even features. Abbie hadn't known she could feel worse. She did.

The elevator rose in its emphysemic way and jerked to a stop. Abbie heard the door scrape open, then slam shut. DeRosa motioned for her to get her door. She nodded blindly, her chest so tight she couldn't breathe, her stomach on fire. She grabbed the arms of the couch and tried to heave herself to her feet. Please, God, let it be Swann or Capshaw. Let it be Magnusson with his .357 Magnum. Just don't let them send Michael to his death.

The bell rang, an absurdly jaunty sound that grated on her already taut nerves. DeRosa took up a position just beyond the door and urged her to hurry. Abbie did her best. Her knees weren't working very well. She wanted to cry, to faint. She wanted to do anything but deliver Michael up to this monster.

Acutely aware of the gun barrel just at the edge of her field of vision, Abbie reached for the door. Opened it. Held her breath.

"All right—" Michael grinned brightly, pushing his way through "—where are those doughnuts you promised me?"

Chapter 15

You may close the door now, Dr. Fitzgerald."

When Michael walked into the room, he came to a frozen stop. The gun DeRosa brought to bear on him was inches away. Abbie stood alongside, her hand still on the door, her stark eyes on Michael. DeRosa showed no emotion at all. The eager cheeriness on Michael's features died, giving way to blank surprise and then harsh anger.

"You," Michael growled, his eyes on DeRosa. Those beautiful soft eyes Abbie loved were unrecognizable. "Abbie was right, after all."

Abbie didn't move. DeRosa turned briefly to her and repeated his request, his voice still level and unconcerned.

"I said to close the door, Dr. Fitzgerald. Please do it."

She did it. Michael turned on her, his eyes sweeping her. No bruises, no pain in her eyes. All he saw were the effects of waiting, the torment of not knowing. Michael knew her well enough by this time to recognize the fragile control she managed to stretch over the terror. She was sweating, and the look in her eyes was brittle.

God, he wanted to hold her. To tell her everything was okay. Only it wasn't. Not yet. But at least DeRosa hadn't hurt her.

"Are you all right, Abbie?" he demanded, a hand tight to her arm. "Did he hurt you?"

Her skin was ice-cold and clammy, but she nodded with an encouraging smile. "No. I'm okay. A little tired of surprises, that's all."

Michael nodded for her, and she found herself once again relying on the control in those eyes. The strength. He'd greeted her with her own lie. Surely that meant he'd understood. But he'd come alone, breezing in here as if on an everyday date. There was no backup, no Swann standing alongside him. He was alone, and that frightened her even more. She was terrified that he'd put himself further out on that limb for her.

"Your gun please, Sergeant," DeRosa said, hand out. "Left-handed."

Leaving Abbie with one last look of encouragement, Michael complied. Lifting up the corner of his University of Chicago sweatshirt, he pulled the gun from its holster and passed it over, butt first. Abbie saw an expanse of bare torso that seemed to encourage DeRosa somewhat.

"Any other surprises?" he asked conversationally.

Michael shook his head. "One gun's usually enough to handle Abbie on a date."

"You won't mind if I check."

Shrugging his acquiescence, Michael lifted his arms away from his sides. DeRosa expertly ran a hand down his sides and along the expanse of Michael's jeans, then straightened, satisfied.

"Sit down," he said, motioning with the gun.

"Why?" Michael asked. "The investigation's going through, DeRosa. Doing something stupid tonight'll just make everybody more interested."

DeRosa's answering smile was in absolute control. "I never do anything stupid." He motioned again with the gun. "Now, sit."

Michael led Abbie over to the camelback couch and sat her down, easing down next to her. She thought he squeezed her arm, as if in reassurance. A message? Maybe he was trying to say that everything was okay. Maybe he just hoped it would be. She couldn't be sure. Everything was finally beginning to overwhelm her, throwing her system into autopilot. Pay attention, she thought desperately. It might make a difference. Not a snowball's chance in hell, she argued right back as DeRosa took his seat. There isn't a damn thing I can do to help this situation. Either Michael has his own surprise waiting in the wings, or we end up a business deduction in Mr. DeRosa's unofficial ledgers.

"I would think you'd be more surprised," DeRosa said to Michael.

Michael shrugged, his jaw still steel tight with anger. "Abbie just reacted too strongly to you. If anybody showed up around a corner with a gun pointed at my head, I'd be least surprised for it to be you."

That seemed to make sense to the man. "Who else knows?"

"Knows what? That I suspect that you were at that robbery?" He shrugged again. "Abbie and I. I sent the requests through in reference to another case."

Michael was lying through his teeth, and Abbie sensed that DeRosa knew that. But as she'd realized before, DeRosa was a patient man. Crossing and settling once more, he considered Michael with calm eyes. Abbie wondered whether Michael was frightened. He couldn't possibly be as unconcerned with his own well-being as he seemed.

Michael moved and spoke very carefully. He didn't want to rush DeRosa at all. His life depended on it. More important, Abbie's life depended on it. He prayed she could hold together until he could get what he needed. Until he could get the cavalry in. Casting a brief look over at the stark set of her eyes and the shine of perspiration on her face, he prayed that the cavalry would get there at all. So much could go wrong. Hang in there, my lovely Doctor. Just hang in a few more minutes.

"Then you and Marlow were both at the robbery," Michael said, turning back to consider DeRosa. "Why?"

DeRosa gave no hint that he'd answered the question once already. "That robbery was Marlow's job. An independent action. I realized that it might jeopardize something we were...involved in, so I went to try and dissuade him. I arrived in time to pull Marlow out."

Then she *had* seen DeRosa. And Michael had seen Marlow. Abbie had thought that they had seen the same person, first to get the car and then to discover the cops. But DeRosa had been the one to come back, checking on the "stupid little action." Cleaning up Marlow's mess. Only Michael hadn't seen him. Abbie had, and had set this all in motion when she'd recognized him again.

"I don't understand," Michael was saying. "Why waste your time with Marlow? You certainly have better-qualified people to work your operations. Like Robbins. I assume you're the one who sent him after Abbie." DeRosa didn't see fit to answer. "If you have somebody who's as slick as Robbins, why depend on a nothin' like Marlow? The guy's a two-bit junkie."

For the first time, DeRosa showed a reaction. Abbie saw him set his jaw. A sharp crease appeared across his forehead. He sat very still for a moment, trying to reclaim his composure before answering. Michael didn't seem to want to give him the chance.

"He blew the entire drug operation," he persisted. "An amateur. I can't figure on a pro like you settling for him."

"You don't settle for family!" the man snapped.

Michael's eyes widened. Abbie gaped. "Family?" she instinctively asked.

"It was his chance to prove himself again." There was a real anguish in the chocolate-brown eyes. A real grief. It seemed that even evil men felt the pain of loss.

"Family how?" Michael asked.

DeRosa leveled a hard stare at him, the muscles of his jaw working more rapidly. "DeRosa was my mother's name," he finally said. "My father is John Marlow. You killed my brother."

Both Michael and Abbie found reason to stare at that. Abbie, because she'd had no warning. Michael, because he had verified the connection Swann had suspected. The family connections Alberto had mentioned...the family Robbins had been connected to...a Philadelphia branch, very heavily into drugs and prostitution, evidently making their move into the Midwest. Good Lord, he thought, his mouth suddenly dry. The fish in this pond were bigger than they'd thought.

"The drug deal was a family operation?" he asked.

"It was my operation..." With a snap, DeRosa reclaimed his composure. "I want to know, Sgt. Viviano. Who else knows about your investigation? Who do I have to worry about?" There was an impending smile on his lips, as if he'd almost forgotten to anticipate getting what he'd come here for.

"You have to worry about me, DeRosa," Michael told him evenly, his eyes suddenly cold as glacier ice.

"Not for long, Sergeant. Now, make this easy and tell me what I want to know."

"Let Abbie go first."

DeRosa actually smiled. Abbie had a passing thought of two people enjoying a haggle over merchandise at a bazaar. "I don't think so. The two of you have cost me quite a lot of time and peace of mind. Now, I'd like to find out just what you've spread around before I take care of you."

Take care of you. Abbie shuddered at the melodramatic words delivered with such dispassionate pragmatism. He wasn't threatening. He was simply informing. Abbie wondered just what the hell the three of them were doing sitting around her living room as if they were passing a civilized summer-afternoon visit. This guy had a gun aimed at them. He meant to kill them. Shouldn't at least one of them be outraged about it?

Michael cast a quick look over at Abbie and tried to gauge how much longer she could last. He shouldn't have to put her through this.

"Who, Viviano?"

Michael offered his own slow smile. "Meet my demands, I'll be more inclined to meet yours."

DeRosa shook his head. "I don't think I'd like to bargain." Without another word, he swung the gun just a little to the left until it was pointing dead square at Abbie again. "Did you notice that I have a silencer, Sergeant?"

So that's what that ugly little thing is, Abbie thought, her throat closing off. She could see down the barrel.

"I noticed." Michael didn't seem quite as concerned. She desperately hoped that that meant something more than that he was a brave man.

"I don't have to kill her," DeRosa continued. "I could...incapacitate her."

The gun lowered slightly. "A doctor isn't much use without her hands."

Michael leaned forward to concede. He saw the trembling set in along Abbie's arms and knew that it had gone too far. Nothing was worth this torture. He'd have to call an end to it now.

Control, Viviano. The key word is control. He let his breath out in a slow stream, trying to keep DeRosa from seeing the new fear that had ignited in his belly.

"All right." He held up a conciliatory hand. "Don't hurt her."

Stupid statement, Abbie wanted to say. He means to kill me. What do the semantics matter? She was so terrified she could hardly feel her limbs anymore. She only knew that Michael's hand was still on her arm because she saw it there. Maybe if she concentrated on the flat metallic sheen of the lake at sunset, the smooth harmonies of the Moody Blues, she could shut some of this out. Maybe then she could think straight. She could see her own fear reflected deep in Michael's eyes, and became more afraid.

"I brought your name up to Magnusson at the DEA," Michael said. "He didn't seem interested. Said he had everybody he needed."

DeRosa shook his head. "Don't lie to me. You never spoke to him."

Michael had been set to call in the reinforcements. DeRosa's statement stopped him cold. Never letting go of Abbie, he leaned forward a little, the sudden light in his eyes predatory. "How the hell do you know that?"

DeRosa just leaned back a little, his smile one of satisfaction. Abbie found herself staring again. Michael leaned farther forward, recognizing that smug look of superiority.

"How do you know?"

DeRosa enjoyed the moment of control. "Do you really think I would leave a blind spot in an operation that size?"

Something in DeRosa's eyes sparked a reaction in Michael. A hunch he knew was right before he even asked. "Magnusson's on your payroll, isn't he?"

He got no answer but a shrug.

It had to be. The ineffective raid on the warehouse, the convenient loss of the Travelenos. The attempt at Abbie's life at a DEA safe house. Only Magnusson controlled that. Only Magnusson knew everything that was going on and told no one.

Letting go of Abbie, Michael launched to his feet, fury driving him, a sick astonishment of discovery. "Tell me, damn it! Was Magnusson working for you?"

DeRosa came close to smirking. "If it hadn't been for you and your persistent little friend here, this whole operation would have been under control. Mr. Magnusson is an expert at showing all sound and fury that signifies nothing..."

DeRosa stalled when he saw the gleam rise in Michael's eyes. Lurching to his feet, he brought his gun up. His eyes had gone just as feral, narrow and suspicious. He looked wary, predatory. Just like Michael. Only this man had no scruples. He was the hunter and the hunted. Abbie watched them square off in silence and felt a sick dread.

"Get over here, Sergeant," DeRosa ordered, the first stirrings of anger in his voice. Abbie shuddered. She'd seen him angry before. There was no mercy in those eyes.

Michael arched a wry eyebrow. "Why? Wanna dance?"

DeRosa didn't answer. He just swung the gun back over toward Abbie again. Michael moved without another word.

His movements as graceful as a panther, DeRosa grabbed Michael and whirled him around.

"Get the shirt off."

Abbie stared up at them. She couldn't follow. Bile rose hot in her throat. She couldn't keep her hands still. They shook uncontrollably as she wiped them down her pant leg. She found herself watching DeRosa as if he were a snake, mesmerized by the terrible malevolence in his eyes, the cold anger he directed at Michael.

Michael never took his eyes from DeRosa. Without a word, he took hold of the bottom of his sweatshirt and began to lift. When it got to his arms, Abbie saw the small box taped to his back. About the size of her tape player, the kind she wore with the earphones when she jogged. A wire ran up over his shoulder and around to his chest. She stopped breathing completely.

DeRosa saw it and shrieked. "Wired! You're wired! You're a dead man!"

The gun came up and Michael fell.

"Drop!"

Abbie hit the floor next to Michael. DeRosa's gun went off twice, tiny popping sounds. He stopped to aim again. The door next to him splintered, shuddered again beneath the assault of a set of feet.

Abbie instinctively curled up into a ball. When the gun went off, she rolled under a table, hands up over her head. When the door began to break, she began to weep.

Michael rolled as DeRosa swung the gun around toward the door, then toward Abbie. He hit DeRosa at the knees and brought him down. The gun went flying. As police poured into the shattered door, Michael caught DeRosa by the throat.

His quarry wasn't about to give in. Kicking and clawing, DeRosa fought like a cornered animal, his howl of rage directed only at Michael. Michael struggled, ducked, punched his way out of the battering DeRosa tried to give him. The fury of the attack brought the police to a dead stop and Abbie back up again.

She saw a matching fury ignite in Michael's eyes. DeRosa hadn't counted on Michael. His street fighting was even dirtier than DeRosa's. Within moments he had the upper hand and sent DeRosa crashing against the bookcase. Abbie's silver service flew. Books rained down. DeRosa caught Michael and pulled him over. Within seconds, Michael had him in a headlock, ducking DeRosa's renewed fury.

More policemen poured in the door, many in riot gear. Swann brought up the rear, his face tight and anxious. When he got to the knot of people at the door, he came to a halt.

"Well, give him a hand," he snapped.

Four men in the front turned a bit hesitantly. Then they waded into the fray. It took all four of them to pull Michael and DeRosa apart.

DeRosa came up hissing and yelling, the cool demeanor shattered. Abbie could do no more than watch open-mouthed, the fact of their rescue not yet sinking in. She saw Michael slowly rise to a crouch, rubbing at his jaw, and scooted over to him.

Swann beat her to him. Holding out a hand, he helped Michael to his feet. "Man, you look like you've been in a cat fight."

Michael looked down at his arms to see scratches and a bite at his wrist. He shook his head. "That man takes his family responsibilities seriously. Did you get it?"

Swann smiled without humor. "Every fascinating word. Aren't you glad we hated the bastard Magnusson all along? Saves us from that last-minute rush."

"Michael?" Abbie stood before him, the trembling once again setting in. She knew damn well she looked like a wet poodle, but there wasn't a darn thing she could do about it.

Tears streamed down her face, and her voice sounded as if she were a lost ten-year-old.

Michael took her by the arms, his eyes raking her hungrily. "Are you okay?"

She giggled, a real giggle of relief. "If we keep this up, we're going to need our own TV show. God, I was so scared for you."

"Me?" He encircled her in his arms. He was trembling, too. It had gotten a little too close. "I'm the one who's trained for this, remember? You keep getting drug into it."

She grinned into the soft wool of his shirt. "No pun intended." She was at eye level with the word Chicago, spread out across Michael's chest. She slid a hand across it in search of comfort and found it. "I wasn't sure you got my warning."

"I got it." He kissed the top of her head, drinking in the feel of her in his arms. Was it finally over? Now, would he finally be able to leave her without worrying? He felt her trembling increase and held on more tightly.

"You gonna faint?" he asked gently.

Abbie peeked out from her shelter to see at least twenty police, every one of them turned her way expectantly. "I don't know," she demurred with a new grin. "I *do* have a reputation to uphold."

"Tell you what," he bargained. "After all the worrying I did about you tonight, I think I might faint. Then you can take care of me again."

"Sarge?"

They turned to find one of the SWAT team waiting with DeRosa in cuffs. Swann had disappeared for the moment.

"I have Lt. Capshaw on the horn. He wants to talk to you. They have Magnusson there at the station."

Michael nodded and led Abbie back to the couch.

"Magnusson?" she demanded, the full realization of what had been revealed finally sinking in. "Did DeRosa say he was involved?"

DeRosa wasn't saying. Michael had already picked up the phone. Abbie sat back down on her couch with a dispirited sigh and considered the magnitude of what had gone on here tonight. Magnusson. Good Lord, he'd known all along what was going on. He'd let Michael be set up time and again. Maybe he'd intentionally lost the Travelenos that day so Michael would be killed.

When Swann appeared, he was carrying a couple of glasses of wine. He handed one to Michael, who nodded from his conversation, and one to Abbie. Then he took up a seat on the chair DeRosa had so recently vacated. The SWAT team was beginning to clear out, taking a now sullen DeRosa with them.

Abbie asked Swann, "Did DeRosa really say that Magnusson was involved?"

Swann nodded.

Abbie shook her head as she sipped the cool, clean liquid. "Did you know it?"

"No. That one was a complete surprise to us." He allowed a brief smile. "A bonus, you might say. The only thing we knew when Michael came over was that DeRosa's name was really Marlow, and that he was probably related to a crime family in Philadelphia."

"Philadelphia," Abbie breathed. "Where the Travelenos were from."

Swann nodded. "Isn't it nice how everything falls so neatly into place?"

She took another sip of wine. "So then Marlow worked for Robbins who worked for DeRosa, and Magnusson was finking for all of them. Right?"

"Something like that."

"Yeah, that's what I thought." She tilted her head, considering her room. "I'm going to have to buy another door. Damn. I liked this one."

Swann took a brief look over at shattered wood and sleepy neighbors once again in the hall. "Your neighbors are gonna expect a show every night."

Abbie snorted. "Afraid not. My crime fighting days are over, thanks." For a moment her eyes lost their humor. When she looked over at Swann, it was with uncertainty.

"They are, aren't they?" The terror that lingered in her small voice belied the ease of her words.

Her answer came with a kiss on the neck. "Absolutely," Michael assured her.

"You've told me that before," she reminded him as he settled into the couch next to her.

"But this time I mean it." Taking a long sip of wine, Michael took a moment to stretch the tension from his neck. "They had no more snatched Magnusson than he was screaming state's witness. You're a hero again, Doc."

Abbie snorted, exhibiting the front of her shirt where most of her wine had landed on the way to her mouth. "I'm afraid I'm just not the hero type, my Sergeant."

"I'm afraid that's not quite true."

The three of them looked up to see their friend the reporter stepping gingerly through the debris. Abbie motioned toward it with a grand sweep of the glass.

"You'll excuse the place—" she grinned a bit giddily "—you know how parties get out of hand."

The man grinned right back and came to a stop near them. "I came across the most interesting information a little while ago."

They waited, none of them able to gather the energy to ask.

"It seems," the man went on, referring to his little notebook, "that our doctor here has a history of this kind of thing. She was involved in a hostage situation when she was fourteen."

"She was?" Abbie asked in mock surprise. "And to think she never told us."

Michael looked over at her in real surprise. This had been something she'd dreaded.

"Wanna talk about it, Doc?"

"I swear—" she sighed, finishing her wine "—hanging around this crowd I feel like one of the seven dwarfs."

"That's not what I was hoping for."

She smiled coyly. "I know."

"Well," Swann said, getting to his feet, "I have to make the party at the station. See you all later?"

"I'm sure." Michael waved him on. Abbie scowled.

"Anything else I can do for you...Abbie?" Swann asked.

She grinned. "Yes." Taking another quick look at the reporter, she waved him over.

When Swann bent to hear her whispered request, Michael saw a fleeting grin on his features. He bent to answer, and Abbie nodded. Michael saw Swann's lips move and recognized the word Llewelyn.

"Thanks, Swann," Abbie smiled.

Then, with the biggest smile Michael had ever seen Swann bestow anyone in the line of duty, the big policeman bent over and gave Abbie a kiss goodbye.

"Here's a surprise. Abbie at the police station."

Abbie looked up at Michael with some disdain, her fourth cup of coffee in hand and the sun coming back up over the city. No matter how much she liked the night, she was beginning to feel like a vampire. And there was still the press to face sometime before breakfast.

"It'll only be a while longer, Ab," he promised. "Then we'll head home." Raking his hand through his hair, he bent once more to the report he was trying to finish.

"Home where?" she asked. "Yours, mine, or the Ambassador?"

He grinned over at her. "Oh, I'm saving the Ambassador for something special. I called the concierge while you were in lineup with DeRosa..."

Abbie flashed him a scowl. "Another fun sight-seeing spot in beautiful downtown Chicago. Do you know that that room has roaches?"

Michael checked his watch. "Yeah, it is just about six, isn't it, Anastasia?"

Abbie couldn't help but grin. "As in 'the Hun'? Well, get used to it, pal. I'll become pleasant in the morning just about the time you give up that gun."

Michael finally gave up on the report and got up to join her on the hardback chairs along the wall by Swann's desk. Both of them looked wrung out from the night they'd just put in. Michael sat next to Abbie and brushed her hair back from her face with a gesture of sweet familiarity. Abbie found herself smiling at it.

"I think I can put up with it," Michael assured her. "The suite is ours on our wedding night. You pick the date."

"And another thing. You're usually just about as pleasant as I am in the morning, so I don't want to hear anything about my moods ... Wedding night?" Her voice died into a surprised little gasp.

Michael bent to kiss her. "I'm tired of worrying about you getting over to my place late at night. You should be there already."

Abbie lost the rest of the station bustle in the peace of Michael's eyes. She grinned at him. "Well, now. If that isn't a declaration of love, I don't know what is."

"I'm a cop—" he scowled playfully. "—not Shakespeare."

"You're not even Raymond Chandler. But that's okay. You're cute."

"Will you say yes?"

She wasn't sure if she was about to or not when Swann showed up. And not alone. He was guiding Magnusson past, the DEA man looking disheveled and unhappy. What he wasn't, was handcuffed.

Both Abbie and Michael whipped around. It was the first time they'd seen him.

"Where are you going?" Michael demanded of Swann, his eyes suddenly darkening. This was the guy who had cost two good cops their lives. The guy who had damn near had him killed, who'd set up Abbie.

Swann shrugged uncomfortably. "Front door. They dealt."

Michael stared, first at Swann and then Magnusson.

"He's on bail, man," Swann said simply. "He'll be back."

Michael stood before the man, his stance tense and ready, his jaw like steel. Abbie came slowly to her feet beside him.

"So," Michael breathed, a white-hot anger damn near blinding him. "You're walkin'."

Magnusson offered a superior little smile. "Everyone has their price, Sergeant. Even the federal prosecutors."

Michael didn't answer him. He just hit him.

The dull crack could be heard across the station. Magnusson flew back against the wall and landed on his back. Swann didn't seem to notice that the DEA man had suddenly disappeared from next to him and was now on the floor rubbing at his jaw.

"Well." Michael smiled with quite a feeling of relief. "That's my price, I guess."

"Mine, too." Swann nodded, finally taking in the scene. "I had a bet you wouldn't deck him until it was all over. Thanks."

Michael grinned his concession. Turning back to Abbie, he ignored the protests Magnusson was beginning to formulate as he got to his feet.

"I thought you weren't that kind of cop." Abbie couldn't help but grin at him.

"I'm not," Michael assured her. "This was a special case."

She nodded reflectively. "Made me feel better."

"I'm gonna sue you, you sonofabitch!" Magnusson was yelling.

"You going to marry me?" Michael asked Abbie. Swann waited for her answer before going on.

Abbie wrapped her arms around Michael and smiled up at him. "I guess I'll have to," she said. "Somebody's got to keep you out of trouble."

"Did you hear me?" Magnusson demanded.

Michael looked over at him and then back at Abbie. "It seems you'd be taking a risk, ya know."

Abbie never saw Swann usher Magnusson past. She didn't even hear the applause that broke out around her at her answer. "But it would be worth it, my handsome Sergeant," she assured Michael, with laughing eyes. When he bent to kiss her, she knew that she meant what she said. So she told him again: "Worth any risk at all."

Take 4 Silhouette Special Edition novels
FREE

and preview future books in your home for 15 days!

When you take advantage of this offer, you get 4 Silhouette Special Edition® novels FREE and without obligation. Then you'll also have the opportunity to preview 6 brand-new books —delivered right to your door for a FREE 15-day examination period—as soon as they are published.

When you decide to keep them, you pay just $1.95 each ($2.50 each in Canada) *with no shipping, handling, or other charges of any kind!*

Romance *is* alive, well and flourishing in the moving love stories of Silhouette Special Edition novels. They'll awaken your desires, enliven your senses, and leave you tingling all over with excitement...and the first 4 novels are yours to keep. You can cancel at any time.

As an added bonus, you'll also receive a FREE subscription to the Silhouette Books Newsletter as long as you remain a member. Each issue is filled with news on upcoming books, interviews with your favorite authors, even your favorite recipes.

To get your 4 FREE books, fill out and mail the coupon today!

Silhouette Special Edition®

Silhouette Books, 120 Brighton Rd., P.O. Box 5084, Clifton, NJ 07015-5084

Clip and mail to: Silhouette Books,
120 Brighton Road, P.O. Box 5084, Clifton, NJ 07015-5084 •

YES. Please send me 4 FREE Silhouette Special Edition novels. Unless you hear from me after I receive them, send me 6 new Silhouette Special Edition novels to preview each month. I understand you will bill me just $1.95 each, a total of $11.70 (in Canada, $2.50 each, a total of $15.00), with no shipping, handling, or other charges of any kind. There is no minimum number of books that I must buy, and I can cancel at any time. The first 4 books are mine to keep.

B1SS87

Name _____ (please print) _____

Address _____ Apt. # _____

City _____ State/Prov. _____ Zip/Postal Code _____

* In Canada, mail to: Silhouette Canadian Book Club, 320 Steelcase Rd., E., Markham, Ontario, L3R 2M1, Canada
Terms and prices subject to change.
SILHOUETTE SPECIAL EDITION is a service mark and registered trademark.

SE-SUB-1A

Silhouette Intimate Moments

COMING NEXT MONTH

#193 KISS OF THE DRAGON—Barbara Faith

Her dying father's request brought Bethany Adams to Hong Kong. There, Tiger Malone swept Bethany up in a hunt through China, where they risked their lives to find a golden dragon and discovered a greater treasure—love.

#194 LEGACY—Maura Seger

Gwen Llywelyn came to Wales to see her ancestral home, but she found much more: mysterious tremors and power failures—and Owen Garrett. Owen wasn't exactly who he said he was, but Gwen quickly decided he was all she'd ever wanted.

#195 THE GENUINE ARTICLE—
Katheryn Brett

A. J. McMichaels expected life in her small hometown to be uneventful, not sizzling with rumors of political corruption. She didn't expect to find herself feuding with the mayor, Rich Beckman, either—and she certainly didn't expect to fall in love with him.

#196 GYPSY DANCER—Kathleen Creighton

For Lily Fazekas, going to Hungary was a romantic quest for the family she had never known. Joseph Varga's assignment was to stay with her until the search was over, but long before that time arrived, he knew he wanted to stay with her—forever.

AVAILABLE THIS MONTH:

#189 WANTED WOMAN
Parris Afton Bonds

#190 AFTERGLOW
Catherine Coulter

#191 WORTH ANY RISK
Kathleen Korbel

#192 BRIDE OF THE TIGER
Heather Graham Pozzessere

ATTRACTIVE, SPACE SAVING BOOK RACK

Display your most prized novels on this handsome and sturdy book rack. The hand-rubbed walnut finish will blend into your library decor with quiet elegance, providing a practical organizer for your favorite hard-or soft-covered books.

Only $9.95

Approximately 16" x 8" when assembled

Assembles in seconds!

To order, rush your name, address and zip code, along with a check or money order for $10.70* ($9.95 plus 75¢ postage and handling) payable to *Silhouette Books.*

Silhouette Books
Book Rack Offer
901 Fuhrmann Blvd.
P.O. Box 1325
Buffalo, NY 14269-1325

Offer not available in Canada.

*New York residents add appropriate sales tax.

BKR-2R

GILLIAN HALL

The magnificent novel of a woman fighting for her greatest passion— and for a love to fulfill her deepest desires.

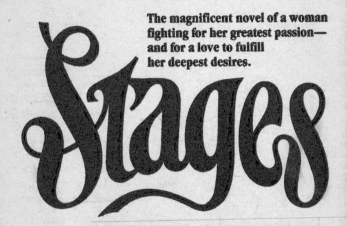

The desire to break from an unbearable past takes prima ballerina Anna Duras to Broadway, in search of the happiness she once knew. The tumultuous changes that follow lead her to the triumph of new success . . . and the promise of her greatest love.

Available in MAY or reserve your copy for April shipping by sending your name, address, zip or postal code along with a check or money order for $4.70 (includes 75 cents for postage and handling) payable to Worldwide Library to:

In the U.S.	In Canada
Worldwide Library	Worldwide Library
901 Fuhrmann Blvd.	P.O. Box 609
Box 1325	Fort Erie, Ontario
Buffalo, NY 14269-1325	L2A 5X3

Please specify book title with your order.

 WORLDWIDE LIBRARY

STA-1